THE LOGANS
IN FLOOD BROOK

A novel by

J. Carol Goodman

First published by Dog Ear Publishing
4010 W. 86th Street, Ste H
Indianapolis, IN 46268
www.dogearpublishing.net

dog ear
PUBLISHING

ISBN: 978-1-4575-2194-2

This book is printed on acid-free paper.

This book is a work of fiction. Places, events, and situations in this book are purely fictional and any resemblance to actual persons, living or dead, is coincidental.

Printed in the United States of America

Dedicated to my children and grandchildren who also helped me.

THE LOGANS
IN FLOOD BROOK

Chapter **1**

*F*ierce hysterical crying came from far up the orchard. Florence Logan yanked on her coat and bolted out the kitchen door, slugged across the scummy yard toward the yelping beyond the steep woods where none of them had ever been. Her small feet sank in the muck of corn snow and over her city rubbers as the biting air swirled up inside her tweed skirt, chilling her legs into peg-stiffness.

Yelping, yelping. City dogs, tethered dogs. She shouldn't have let them out. What was that? A gun blast. Somebody shooting their dogs? Out of breath. Out of shape. No spring chicken and everything in her life was also muck deep. Pull your weight up and sink into a hole. Depressing as hell. What am I doing in this wilderness?

The mud petered out as she reached a narrow deer path lit yellow by afternoon light. The yelping seemed no closer.   Bristly evergreens scratched her face and laden boughs dumped snow on her head. Must get to them. Her sister hadn't offered, and Papa called out, -Better not. Could be tangling with a bear.-

Her sinuses stabbed her. She pulled her hat tighter over her plucked eyebrows as she met the scribble-scrabble of last year's blackberry bushes that clung to her sable coat. Did they really think the three of them would be happy here?

Another explosion. She lifted her hands to her throat and crouched, afraid to call out to her pets. Should she go ahead, run back? Couldn't be a hunter. March, not hunting season. That much she knew about Vermont. She crawled toward the dogs' echoing cries. But it was sudden how she came upon them, under a huge sugar maple, as they spun and careened up against her. Except for Borie, the old dog. And then Babcock, the maverick, turned and raced on up the field after him.

Dark clothes, plaid hat and gun on his shoulder, someone slipping into the forest. Florence was too frightened to call out to Babcock. Would the shooter turn and blast her brains out? Weren't there always lunatics in the back woods? But the figure didn't stop, didn't turn and Babcock kept racing after him. Oh God, please come back Babcock.

-Shush. Hush, Tanya, Jessica.-

The hunter had disappeared.

Babcock crashed back from the underbrush, skittered toward her and leaped into her arms, knocking her flat. Must race them out of here. Was the gunman watching from behind trees? But Borie. Where was old Borie? Her eyes scanned the cluster of human footprints around the huge maple tree. There was a snowy mound. No, white fur. Borie. Just scared or exhausted, lying there, tongue hanging out, panting for breath and his body twitching as he struggled to rise. She tried to help him up when she felt a warm seeping from underneath quickly dyeing her hands red.

-Borie,- Florence lifted him in her arms gently. His head dropped back and his chest rose and fell, gasping, gasping as she ran down the path, hardly able to hold his weight, the other three dogs madly bumbling against her legs.

-Borie, Borie, - she whispered. With his dusky eyes, questioned her, questioned her and died.

With his blood running down her fur coat and sopping her skirt she shouted at the kitchen door, -Help.-

Noncie screamed.

-Maybe he's okay.- Florence wished. She laid Borie on the floor blanket where the dogs slept. The other dogs whined and sniffed him. Florence told what she had heard and seen...the third blast of a gun, that was the one that killed Borie. Then the back of a man in a plaid coat and hat, not even running, just walking away like he'd done nothing wrong.

Noncie covered the large wound on Borie's side with a fresh towel.

The other dogs' nails on the wood floor set all their nerves wild.

Noncie touched Borie's nose with her finger. -Poor thing, old love, poor darling. Why did you let them out?- She yelled at Florence. -You're always doing things like that.-

Florence flung her coat on the rack. -Why didn't you go with me?-

-Stop it,- the old man said. -We have a...who would shoot an old dog, and on our property?-

-I'm glad you went up there and saved the others,- Noncie said, feeling guilty for not going with her sister.

-And with a shotgun,- Papa went on. -So terrible.- They didn't want them here.

-We'll have to bury him.- Florence said, as if just coming to the realization.

-How do we bury him with the ground frozen?- Noncie asked.

-You're right,- Papa said.

-And it's not cold enough to keep him in the woodshed until we can dig.- Florence's tears swam.

Noncie tried to keep any weaknesses in check, tried to be the strong one, tried to be brave, and to believe the future was in her own hands but her voice quivered and her eyes misted against the back of her hands. -I couldn't stand to… just dump…-

-We'll think of some…,- the old man said. They looked up to him once in a while, the tall, straight father, Coleridge I. Logan, the initial meaning nothing, a tradition in the south. Yet he thought I was the I of himself, the secret self, never given to his dead wife or even completely to the daughters he loved.

Florence had turned thirty-eight, the day they moved to Vermont from Chicago two weeks ago. Wispy dark wavy hair, cupid lips and black optimistic eyes. Obsessive and unpredictable Florence. Ran off years ago and married a scoundrel. Nonetheless, he admired her for her whiff of strength, like a field of deceptively fragile cattails swaying as if to break but holding fast against high winds. She was here to reform. He had faith she would. As a child when they still lived in Kentucky, she ran to the river mud, to slide down the embankment with the Colored kids. Disgraceful, people told him. They had even heard her swearing. She hated to be told what to do and often played sick so she wouldn't have to go to school.

Noncie was forty-three, elegant and ravishing, with sharp ocean-blue eyes, a taut high forehead above which blossomed coiled whorls of pure white hair. But Noncie was sadly unhappy, though she didn't talk about feelings. Private and stoic she thought of herself. They had all come to this beautiful place, the green mountains, the meadows of golden rod, wild blueberries and the colonial village to snatch Florence from her depraved life. Yes, start over with new vigor, where contentment and perhaps even happiness would be theirs, and don't forget, cheaper to live with the Depression still on.

It was Florence's idea, though they rarely listened to her. Noncie eased the bright yellow touring car from the barn and Papa, with sorrowful rheumy eyes, held Borie. Seventeen years he'd been theirs. Did someone kill him to drive them away? Had they come to a lawless village that abhorred strangers?

What emotional endurance did he have left in his rugged Scottish being? Holding the stiffened terrier wrapped in one of their company-come-to-dinner tablecloths, his skinny legs felt chilled through his tweed trousers. The only sound in the car came from Papa clearing his throat of post-nasal drip, as if about to make a speech.

Noncie drove in her sable coat and cloche, purchased when they heard Vermont winters were more brutal than even Chicago. Florence, since her fur coat was ruined from Borie, held them up rummaging through a box for her cashmere and took forever powdering her nose and carefully applying lipstick.

-Stop that, it's the dead of night.- Noncie scolded.

-Better not, or-... Papa disliked finishing sentences as if there was always something too unsettling, or his mind drifted vaguely in the wrong direction, so he often stopped midstream and let the thought flow by.

-Besides, some is smeared on your teeth.- Noncie said. Maybe they shouldn't have come here to live. She had long had the suspicion that the back woods hid twisted secrets, hidden violence.

The treacherous icy night made Noncie creep down their lane and the long hill, a mile to the village. Yet Papa still let her drive, in spite of her eyes. Near the bottom, on the side of the hill they passed some kind of dilapidated mansion...that is, mansion for that village. Then came a boarded-up railroad station where trains had once gone to Brattleboro, thirty miles away and the long narrow grain store, one of three buildings standing on the bank after the hurricane of l927, three years before.

-Hope nobody hears us,- Papa said as the car klump-klumped over the shaking covered bridge.

-This bridge will collapse under us someday, Noncie said.- Her fore-sight, which could have brought her panic, helped her be prepared. *Face up to things* was her motto.

On the other side of the river sat a small white building with the words, U.S. Post Office, Flood Brook, Vermont. Across the street among the fifteen or so houses was the tiniest grocery they had ever seen, where you could hardly buy bacon or a piece of beef. Never fish and only a few canned goods.

Before Noncie drove up the opposite hill they passed a ghost-building, remains of a burnt-out mill that had ended any hopes of prosperity as the Depression sank the small community. She turned into the steeply graded driveway, ah oh the Packard wouldn't make it. Yet she gunned it straight up to the parking lot, which was hidden by dense hemlocks almost as high as the Christopher Wren spire. She parked the car as close to the church door as she could.

-I hope it is unlocked,- she said.

Papa lifted the dog out of the car. Florence walked as if from a night-mare, her mind and body staggering. But after all she was used to feeling a little off her pins. She liked the unsteadiness, reminding her of the buf-feting blustering beach of Lake Michigan. She pushed away homesick longings, the alleyways, her prized, secret unmarked doors. Don't think about what had been.

Both sisters pulled at the warped oak doors until they surrendered. Noncie held the door for Papa and Borie.

-And who knows where the lights are?- Florence groped.

-Don't turn them on, - Papa whispered.

Florence leaned against the vestibule wall then jumped forward, the from the church walls too clammy. The moon emerged through the clear windows spreading spidery light from the empty tree branches, making the mystery deeper.

-We'll show whoever did this to Borie, one of God's sacred creatures, should not...- Papa started.

Florence rolled her eyes. Though she felt a vague sense of ghostly spirits, she didn't believe one bit in God. -This place is cold as the devil's snot.-

-Disgusting talk.-_Noncie shoved her.

-Cut it out. I can't carry him anymore.- Papa rushed forward.

Florence led them down the worn carpet, past the bare wooden pews, nearly toppling as her foot snagged on a torn spot. Papa laid the dog gently on the altar cloth and Florence sang loudly off tune from her bright lips a hymn when in her childhood they had attended church. – *In sadness and thoughts of grief I cried for his relief and did not cry in vain.-*

-Stop. The police and...-

Florence laughed. -In this Podunk?- She sang on. –*In sickness fear and pain I cried for His relief.... -*

-Stop, I mean it. We're doing something illegal. How did you remember that hymn?- Papa whispered.

Noncie stared at her. Why was Florence so...?   What good was her word? Yet, she mustn't always be suspicious. Must try to trust her. Be kind.

-Can't remember the rest.- Florence leaned against a pew.

-Let's get her out of here.- Noncie took her hand.

-Wait.- Papa pointed to the pump organ. -Dried up flowers.

-Darn.- Noncie realized. -They probably don't use the church much; funerals or weddings.-

-They won't find him until summer. We should take him back home,- Florence said loudly.

-Somebody must check on the church. I mean with the door unlocked. People maybe come to pray. He won't smell for a long time.- Papa said.

-Like you think someone will do right by him?- Noncie asked .

-A small mausoleum is right out back, - Florence answered.

-Like they'll bury a dog in the churchyard?- Noncie turned once more to see Borie in the eerie light. -Keep warm, old darling.-

Papa took each of his daughter's arms. -Out the door.- Borie a sacrifice, gift to God.

Occasionally he liked to be superstitious. Maybe now they would all be safe...from?

At the door Noncie stopped. -What if they burn him or throw him out to the wild animals to tear apart, or dump him in the river?-

-Keep going.- The villagers were harrying his brain.

Florence had one last look at Borie, his white face and black nose, his delicate ears that had once pivoted with the wind.

Noncie slammed the warped door behind them. The chill made Papa's sciatica cramp him into lightning pain as his steps rocked steps through the shadowy moonlight to his car. Parted with another pound of his own flesh .

When they thought of coming to Vermont, Papa had said, -Puritanism and strict moral standards still reign.- And you like adventure Flossy.- He called her Flossy with affection when he wanted to cozy up to her. -Besides houses are dirt cheap now.-

Being summer they hadn't known how cold and drafty their hundred-and sixty-year-old farmhouse would be. The real estate agent had glorified the place as authentic colonial and the day was bright and warm. The house was enchanting, stood on a slight rise...with a view. As they walked in the small center hall the agent pointed out, -Charming wavering air bubbles in the antique glass.- Florence liked the feeling.

-Lovely old bricks on the living room fireplace, That's the west wall, - The real estate woman went on. —See out the south window an outstanding look at Mount Equinox and north the orchard-

Everything about the simple rooms had possibilities, Noncie thought. She had an eye for beauty, though in some ways she had to admit Florence was the creative one, the daring one. She hoped there would not be fights.

-Glorious light,- the real estate woman chirped. The dining room on the opposite side of the hall was graced with windows facing south. Camel-Hump Mountain sat gray and rocky in the distance, intriguing in its perfect melon shape.

-Now the sick room. Every house had one for sick children or old folks.- She looked at Papa.

He grimaced back -That will be my study.-

She blushed. How he loved blushing women.

In the kitchen Noncie touched the stove.

-Oh yes.- the real estate woman kept her smile. -Yes, one of the best, made up in Burlington.- Her crisp hands waved. -Heats this whole end of the house.-

-Where is the stove to cook on?- Noncie asked.

-This is it.. Keep the stove going.-

-All summer?- Florence asked

Then her smile turned smug, as if you dummies, didn't you know? - It never gets that hot here in Vermont.-

Papa realized nobody else had asked where to buy groceries.

She pursed her lips. -People raise their own chickens and beef and a pig now and then, and the vegetables from their garden they can for winter. They never sell any from their gardens. Don't yield enough. And then there is hunting.-

-Where's a meat market and big grocery?- Noncie asked.

-A pretty good one down in Brattleboro thirty miles away or up in Rutland thirty miles away. Oh and at the end of the village is a cheese factory.-

Worse, Papa realized, his girls didn't know a thing about cooking. Mysteriously sumptuous food had appeared on the table, back in their lavish apartment, from their wonderful cook. They had arrived with staples and cartons of canned goods. Campers meals is what they ate morning noon and night heating them on the stove, which repeatedly died out. Nobody remembered to feed it wood.

Deadly meals, Florence thought, that no one was in charge of. On the other hand she didn't want to get involved. Papa gave Noncie credit. She sort of tried to plan: a green, (canned spinach}a starch, (canned spaghetti)—and breakfast oatmeal, which she had read, keeps you from getting arthritis.

Florence asked every morning to annoy, -What is this, sister?-

Noncie clamped her narrow lips.

-What are the bumpty-bumps?- Florence went on. Papa hid his smile with his napkin.

-Okay you make the damned oatmeal.- Noncie slammed the spoon back in the pot.

Papa shook his finger at her. One more swear word like that and he'd punish her, make her stay in her room, wash her mouth out with soap, beat her with a willow switch…all methods he had never used while raising them. The truth, he had always reminded himself of how utterly moral and kind he was.

7

At night he dreamed of his ancient cook, her lips closing on her wooden spoon and the slurping tasting of her creations. He dreamed of her baked Alaska, her soufflés and little meringues. But most of all he missed her roly-poly, the sensuous faintable pleasure of citron, the crunch of almonds and the caress of sweetness. Oh, what a sweet tooth he had, getting worse and no place to satisfy it. When they moved they put her in a retirement home. She did not relinquish her precious spoon. Carried it against her bosom. They should have brought her with them. She was all alone in the world. Broke his heart.

During their meals now they would hardly talk as they scooped up and waded through the over-cooked, or under-cooked dishes. –How am I supposed to regulate a wood stove?- Noncie moaned.

-I know, honey, but…- Papa conceded.

He tried to think up conversations. Difficult, since they no longer had a newspaper or gossip about friends, concerts to attend or current books to read. Papa had loved to discuss these, mostly with Florence, but they now seemed irrelevant, even his beloved William James. The radio was a disaster with static that could break your eardrums. Florence hummed through the meal bits from her Caruso records, but way off tune, until one of them sharply rebuked her. She stopped...for a while, then continued out of absent-mindedness or revolt. Who could ever tell with her? The meal often ended up with one of them talking about Borie. Not only mourning the loss but with increasing fear about the villagers. Was Borie a warning shot? He nightmared about murder, murderers breaking in, killing them and burning their house down.

The next day Noncie dressed for her secret search. She looked around to see where Florence might be, certainly didn't want to be caught, even by Papa. She heard him catarrhing and smelled his aromatic pipe. Florence wouldn't be out of her bathrobe and sheepskin slippers until noon.

Drove her nuts the way the two of them lazed around. Was she supposed to be mother to both of them? That word, mother, when it slipped into her thoughts, accordioned her diaphragm against her ribs, squeezing out an awful sigh. Mother. She was almost too old at forty-three, now, even if she knew where to find a man, which seemed hopeless among the village yokels. Although she would always hope. She had to, otherwise she couldn't bear it.

-Hi,- she said to the two of them in a false voice as she peeked into the living room. Both looked up from their reading, he from the Flour Miller's Journal, received weekly by mail, she some very thin book of English poetry that she was reading aloud, not to him, into the air.

-What are you doing? - Florence asked her in a suspicious voice.

-I'm going up to my room to straighten up.-

Florence narrowed her eyes. -In jodhpurs?-

-I was chilly.- Noncie left quickly as her heart beat fast and waited in the hall to be sure neither came after her. She moused her way to the cellar door, listening as she lifted the wrought iron latch. The steps too narrow for her long feet she descended sideway. And she had to duck so she wouldn't hit the sloping ceiling. She had to step high across the dirt floor, boxes of silverware, Spode and Lenox china, Belgian table linens and the crewelwork draperies they hadn't yet hung. Even though she could hardly see she must keep her eye on the purpose, after all they had sacrificed everything to live here. Yet didn't a search degrade her? And being caught by Florence was scary, even though what her sister might be doing was illegal. She had an explosive temper.

Must be methodical. Florence was careful and cunning. She had wrapped tissue paper around each item, placing a note naming it. Of course she wouldn't name the unnamable. Noncie squinted to force her eyes to adjust. She discovered, draped over a box, Borie's leash. She lifted it to her nose for remnants of him. Why? Borie never would have attacked. Gentle sweet thing. She had so loved his mangy eczema-ridden body. Slept on her bed, though she had to lift him up recently, now unable to jump. Sometimes she pretended he was a man warming up against her.

She often had whispered to him about her problems. She was beset with disappointment over men and only partially aware that some came from her own making. Borie's eyes had searched hers as if he understood. Who could she whisper to now?

One box seemed heavy. She quickly tore it open but found Florence's collection of kitsch Bavarian figurines. Really bad taste unlike her usual taste. Her clothes were elegant, though too garish for Noncie. They hung on her dumpy figure with lovely grace. She took even more time than Noncie to fuss over her body, her scrappy hair and her face...layering her makeup as thick as a streetwalker's.

She would try to see that she didn't display the figurines. One already dominated the kitchen table, a silly ceramic cow creamer, the tail twisted into a handle, the mouth a spout. And Papa always irritatingly bellowed, -Moo, moo, - when he poured cream in his coffee.

As she peered with trouble seeing into each crate she worried what the church would do with Borie. And when people found out would something worse happen to them? They shouldn't have laid him on the sacred altar.

She opened Florence's trunk of party clothes she would never wear again. Here there would be no fancy party to go to. Florence loved silk,

Noncie wool crepes which gave her substance on her slender hipbones. She pulled out flowing slips, a two-toned red dress cut on the bias, a needlepoint belt, a white lace dress with blue pongee silk slip beneath, showing through lace like secret eyes. She drew a painful breath remembering Florence wearing that when she was sixteen, more than twenty-two years ago. A bouncing flirt, flitting as in air, a spirit like milkweed buffeted in the wind, her voice swept with laughter. *He* saw all that also, Irving, her horrible ex-husband…how incorrigible, how ripe and plump and ready to pick she was. Now she hated men. Hadn't dated in years.

Her waist had thickened, unlike Noncie's but Papa often said, -Comparisons are odious.- Nevertheless she compared. Her own hair was abundant. Florence's hair was so delicate that even a gentle breeze roughed it into a mess.

In the darkest corner of the cellar Noncie had to feel in the boxes. Her eyes couldn't adapt. Nothing. She set her lips. There had to be some. The way she behaved in church. Noncie climbed the stairs sideways again and made her way outside and down the edge of the mud-sopped driveway and across the dirt road to the pigeon shed leaning toward collapse. Who would eat pigeons?

-Doves,- Papa had corrected her. That idea revolted her even more.

She pushed hard to open the crooked door. A sliver of light seeped through a window at one end. Oh my Lord, a pigeon do-do carpet. Walk in? Never. But she did spot a box, big enough to contain maybe six months supply. Noncie pressed her hands together. The discovery would make herself furious but also triumphant. She hoisted a fallen tree branch to pry open the box top. The rusted hinges gave way, letting the lid bang back to the floor. She leaned as far into the coop as she could without stepping onto do-do. She struggled to see. What? Just a tangled corroded mess of old tools. Maybe her sister was true-blue.

More places to search. Back across the road she slipped into the barn attached to the woodshed and the woodshed attached to the house, the way houses had been built in order not to walk through snow to the barn. She made out smashed flies graying the windowpanes. Webs hanging from the beams and she shivered to think, they might be weaving nets close to her face. She despised untidiness that she could do nothing about and moved gingerly over the caked dirt and grease that grouted the floorboards.

Up high she thought she saw a rifle balanced on two square-headed nails. ancient, nobody used square nails anymore. A hayrack, a bent snow shovel and a discarded truck tire lay at the end. Nothing to find here and no more places to hunt. She was glad . Yes very glad she could trust Florence. She stepped onto the stones of the woodshed. Oh my, down to a few sticks of wood. They would have to buy some right away. It was still very cold at night and of course for cooking. But must be easy to buy wood with all these forests.

She was counting how many pieces were left when she saw something, something gleaming in the sunlight, hidden only slightly behind a fat log. She pulled it out. Vodka . -VODKA.- she shouted. She raised the bottle to smash just as Florence bounded out the kitchen door, her bathrobe in flight, like a ground-bird flapping its wings in futile hopes of flying.

She tore at Noncie, accidentally knocking her down on the rough stone floor. The bottle flew and smashed between them. Noncie's tall frame rose up, wavering and stumbling with pain as Florence yanked her arm and swung her around. -My only bottle. This time I'm going to kill you!-

But as Florence lifted her fists, something held her, kicked her shin and pulled her away. Through her rage she glimpsed Papa who quickly pinned her arms behind her back. But the old man's joints couldn't take it. He had to let go. He was, however, satisfied he still had some power over them. He brushed his hands together and stood up straight as a soldier. -You two ridiculous clucking hens, I'm...-

Florence ran through the kitchen and upstairs. She locked them out of her room.

Noncie, long-legged raced up, two at a time, stopping at the top to calm herself. She knocked on the door. No answer. -Florence, darling, you promised to reform. Help us here. Where have you hidden the rest? You promised.-

-The promise is to myself. It's none of your business.-

-None of my business? None of my business?- Noncie screamed. –We're only here to save you.-

Florence didn't answer. She curled into a ball on her bed. She had no more bottles. How would she get more? No, no, no, She must, she wanted to stop. How could she be thinking this way—why was she a flawed, morally depraved person? She must be strong. She must over come.

Noncie called through the door, -You once were a wondrous girl. You could have taught the teachers. They called you a genius.-

-Shut up.-

-You read straight through most of Dickens when you were nine or ten and at fifteen you played Hamlet and the newspaper said you did the best acting they had seen in a school production, and you got the highest score in math they had ever seen and...-

Florence opened the door and shouted, -Get away.-

They faced each other for a moment and Noncie pleaded, -Please, sister.-

Florence shouted, -Leave me alone.-

Noncie turned to the stairs. She had no intention of leaving this up to Florence. She had thought many times that it was actually Florence's brains that had done her in. Her restless mind that moved quickly across continents of books and ideas that recklessly threw her onto the edge. More, more, more of everything. Her greedy mind, hoping, longing, scavenging. And Papa wouldn't let them go to college. -Evil seeps from the walls of academe as powerful as the college curriculum...drinking and gambling and corruption, shallowness. But worst of all rampant sex.-

Noncie hadn't cared about college but Florence told her many times how angry she was. Some of her friends had been allowed to go east to those girl's colleges, Wellesley and Smith, why not her? But Papa stuck his pipe in his mouth, lit it and that was that.

Later that night a man opened the heavy oak doors to clean the church. He walked up the aisle and discovered an object wrapped in a white linen tablecloth. What was this? With care he pulled the cloth back and saw a white terrier. He knew whose dog it was. Everyone knew the dogs around there. Those foreigners. He covered the dog again and lifted it up and carried it out of the church.

CHAPTER 2

*S*he would get revenge. Treating her like a child, a nobody, a crimi-nal. How dare, dare, dare she? She will get revenge.

When Noncie and Papa drove to the village to pick up the mail, Flo-rence sneaked into Noncie's room. She had the largest room and the most furniture, a chest and two bureaus and a large eighteenth century secre-tary. She would find the diary. She had once seen her sister writing in it. But she quickly shoved the book behind her back. Florence hadn't imag-ined her controlled careful sister revealing herself in a diary, knowing someone might find it.

She would taunt her with exposing her secrets to Papa. Even if she didn't expose her she would have had her revenge by just telling her she had read it. She unfolded and folded back underwear, nightgowns and stockings. Lifted the lid of the jewelry box. The three dogs followed her around, wagging their tails, but she was too consumed to pet them. When she reached on the shelf above Noncie's clothes a hatbox fell, spilling not a hat... but ha, ha, the diary.

Florence had burned all memorabilia from Irving, not that there was much, two notes, the clothes she wore when she left him. He never bought her an engagement ring but a huge emerald broach surrounded by black and pink pearls, that she sold immediately and spent the money immediately. Blood money, in more ways then one.

The dogs were bothering her, with their click, clicking on the floor. She shut them in her bedroom, then stood by the window in order to see the car coming and opened the diary.

She read:

The men I cannot possibly marry or be a father of my child.

1. Toddy...weasel-sneak.

2. Richard...endlessly clears throat, like Papa.
3. Stanley... silly hopeful nature. "Of course the Depression isn't that bad."
4. Leonard...motor mouth.
5. Charles...disagreed with most ideas of mine and pawed at me and when I said stop, then he'd say, why?
6. Forrest...almost could have married.

Forrest

I might have given in to Forrest's touch if he had just done it, instead of the foolishly asking -May I touch your breasts. Is that okay?- For god-sake what else was a decent girl to say but NO. Why didn't he just take charge the way a man should? I pondered how he might have said it while touching..., *the beauty of your breasts overwhelms me with desire*...for instance. What had amazed me most was that I could be so in love and yet in just one moment, in a few seconds, love could be massacred. Love was the most gossamer, illusive passion. The face I adored the instant before grew distorted, narrow-eyed, narrow-lipped, mushy soft. The words he uttered were like stones coated in marshmallows. I glimpsed Forrest months later with another woman, of all things at the opera in a box across from me. He had fallen asleep. I couldn't imagine that I had loved him, FALLING ASLEEP AT CARMEN. I wonder if I should have over-looked his faults, but Florence's experience with horrible Irving affected me deeply. Be careful.

Brim

Brim was the courtliest. He laced my arm through his, just to cross a room. We rode horses in the park. He wanted me to ride sidesaddle, because he liked to see both my legs in tight boots hugging my calves. And what I liked was my legs swung over the saddle on both sides with that pounding sensation on that certain spot. I am now frantic. What is wrong with me that I should be so picky? And I want a baby so badly?

But I had another fear now.

Luellen

That brings me to Luellen the ophthalmologist. On our first date we strolled into Drumming bookstore. He noticed me squinting, tilting my head to the side to the book more clearly.

When we walked out he said, 'Noncie I want to show you my office.' 'Sure,' I said. He sat me in the patient's chair and swung his chair close to my face. 'Let me look into your eyes?' I nodded as he shone his intense flashlight into my eyes he breathed into my face, his lips so near all I had to do was to lean slightly to touch his. I wanted to but I didn't. I felt the man must move first.

The beam of light penetrated so sharply I was almost blinded. I felt all hot, flustered and swept from myself. Luellen pulled away, shook his head. Took my hands in his and rubbed at the freckles on my fingers and said, 'Noncie, I am very sad telling you this, you have macular degeneration. Slowly your eyes will dim. But the good news is, you will never go totally blind.' He took me in his arms. 'I want to be your eyes for your whole life.'

He would be my eyes? How dare he say such a thing? I got up, stumbled out of his office. 'Please," He called.

When I arrived home I walked for hours with the dogs. I cried leaning against a tree so no one would see me. Couldn't tell my family for a long time. Of course I couldn't be with Luellen anymore, though he tried, sent me roses every day for a month, begging me to return to him. Never, I was ruined. I was a damaged woman, no matter what, no matter that he held me in his arms, that he said he wanted me. That seemed sick to me for him to want a ruined, damaged woman.

I was distressed, humiliated that he knew even more than me what my future would be. It was as if he had torn the clothes off me in public and I had no where to hide… knowing secrets about me that even I didn't know. I couldn't bear that.

Months later I began to wonder about me. Was all my falling out of love with men just me falling out of love with myself, the blemished human being that I am. My own lack of insight…and at last, lack of sight. I wish I could abandon myself.

Florence turned the last page.

Papa likes to lie in the tub, sometimes fall asleep there. And when I have to *go* I holler through the door at him. Once he had staggered out half awake, barely covered with a towel and I tried to see his privates but he quickly covered them. Couldn't I, just once in my whole life, glimpse a penis?

Florence stared at the words in shock. Her sister wanting to see a penis! She had never thought of her as sexy, or wanting sex, or that kind of daring. Florence read the diary again and stopped at where she wanted a baby. Noncie had never told her that, her secret longing. She closed the diary and put it back on the shelf. My poor Noncie. She would never tell her that she had read it.

CHAPTER 3

W hat? goddamed, son of a bitch, almost out of wood. Where could they buy some? The postmistress would no doubt know. She knew everything about everybody. Probably steamed open their letters. Probably the only reading she ever did. Her straight corn colored hair and raised chestnut eyebrows gave Papa the feeling she was in command.

He hustled up Noncie to go with him to the village, but he hadn't let on he was unsure of how to approach Miss chestnut eyebrows. As he turned the corner the white church spire came into view. Oh God, Borie. Real stupid, dangerous idea in retrospect. People would know damned well who he belonged to.

The postmistress gave a little jump as though rudely awakened from a consuming dream.

-We'd like to buy some firewood.-

She squinted.

-Firewood,- he repeated.

-The United States Post Office doesn't sell firewood, Mr. Logan.-

Was she teasing or assuming he was a dumbbell city person. Her unadorned natural mouth was wide open as if finishing a yawn.

-We mean do you know anybody who sells wood?- Noncie stepped in.

-I gather you think this is the information booth at Grand Central Station.-

He felt a sparkle from her light gray eyes.

-There's lots of wood stacked around the houses. Just thought you'd...-

She leaned over to pass mail to a woman behind them. -What about Edifice McHuron?-.

16

-What about him?- the postmistress said.

-I bet he'd come loose with some.-

The two women grinned at each other. Noncie took that in. Maybe he was retarded, unreliable, or a thief. But they had to have fuel immediately.

-How do we get in touch with him?- Papa asked.

The woman beckoned them to the door. She pointed to the deteriorating rambling mansion at the edge of the hill.

When Papa drove the Packard up the driveway Noncie discovered what her poor eyesight couldn't see from the street, damaged hay rakes, car parts, a discarded table and rug and God knows what other fantastic heaps and tangle of undefined junk on the porch.

Noncie stayed in the car, rubbing her chin against the softness of her sable coat to soften her worry and gazed at a tree that had grown through the porch roof and seemed to be its sole support, with spreading limbs like a skeletal structure of an umbrella.

Papa slipped his cold pipe in his mouth for a more official appearance.

The curled clapboards seemed ready for spontaneous combustion. Only touches of white, like freckles, were visible along the thinning boards. He channeled his way through the debris and up the porch steps to knock on a door that looked as if it hadn't been opened in centuries. No answer.

Waited. Then he headed to a back door. His knuckles smarted from knocking. Peering through the door with half glass into the kitchen he realized that instead of pots and pans hanging on the walls there were at least a dozen guns— rifles and shotguns.

A woman, skinny as a rail, with abundant breasts, a narrow face and a prominent chin that defined her blunt-cut, bark colored hair, came toward him. Yet what remained was a vestige of not a bad looking woman. She opened the door so wide and fast that he nearly fell backwards.

-What do you want?-

-My name is Coleridge I. Logan. We have just moved in and...-

-I know who you are.- Her teeth chopped at him.

Papa nodded deciding not to smile at her icy look. –Firewood. I heard that your

husband might sell us some.-

-Who told you that?-

-The postmistress.-

-Buzzing drone.-

He wanted to contradict her, but thought better of it and tried to think up something flattering to say, something to soften her up. Just couldn't. She waited also, raising her eyes fixing them above his head as though taking in the scenery, crossing her bony arms over her frontal largesse. -Doesn't know nothing, always thinking she does.-

He waited again and then said, -Well, would he? Your husband?-

Without taking her eyes off the outdoors, she coughed out a dry laugh. -I'll tell him.- As she slammed the door, the glass rattled in protest. He watched the back of her, her skinny ass. Who would have want to snuggle in bed with that one?

Two days they waited. Florence, who hated to be cold, ran in from the woodshed shouting,

-Only two pieces, that's it.- However she announced this with a thrill of the possibility. Back to the ringing, noisy, dashing conviviality of the city streets and the glorious elixir of life flowing behind hidden doors?

-He isn't going to bring us wood,- Noncie announced.

-People chop their own. So we should buy an ax,- Florence said, as the two of them looked at her as though she were crazy.

-Cut down a tree, the wood would be too green to burn,- Papa said. -You ever tried chopping with...-

-Well we have to take care of ourselves,- Florence went on.

-Money will buy anything,- Papa said.

-Not if they don't want money,- Florence said.

-Who ever heard of that?- Noncie grinned at her. That was as if they had come to a foreign country where the people looked like you and spoke your language but whose ways were a total mystery.

Papa wanted to get away from those two. Why hadn't he had boys? Boy affinity, boy strength. Yet had to admit his girls could be tender, intimate. They could reveal themselves, well not so much Noncie. And he disliked her female fussiness wanting everything annoyingly just so. Yet he appreciated how beautiful Noncie had made everything. Back in their old apartment, she filled little vases, big vases with fresh flowers from the market… even taking up space on his bureau where he liked to fold and unfold his money, lay out his pocket coins. And of all things she once floated rose petals when the maid drew his bath.

If Noncie's houseplants grew spindly or died she felt as despondent as a doctor losing a patient. At least out here she had no houseplants. But he knew her spirits would descend if the right color for, let's say, for their couch couldn't be found or a perfect color for the walls.

-But Papa- she once told him, -I wish I could quiet my eyes, not feel so beholden to them. Ironic, wasn't it, that his poor darling was slowly losing the very sight she was most beholden to. And her life, she once told him, sitting by the fire, those few intimate times deep in the night… that she didn't like that every day had new challenges. She longed for the static. And he had many times pondered over that, wanting his life to be so much less static.

She went on, -But I want to create a baby of my own, a creation of mine to care for, a creation of mine with promise.-

-It will happen,- he had told her…but how in this village?

Florence could be as obsessed, like that period she was crazy about basil. She wanted basil on everything. Caught her brushing her teeth with the mashed up leaves.

-Better than that god-awful soda and salt you use.-

-No using God's name in vain,- he scolded her.

-I'm using it in vain,- she sassed him back.

On the other hand her basil eccentricity amused him. But you couldn't find basil around here, you could bet that on a sow's ear… or her main addiction. She wouldn't find that here either, thank God.

He banged on the bathroom door.

-Please, I need to get in there.- The two sisters, even here, even when going nowhere, made themselves up every morning with powders and lipsticks and blush and eye stuff. It took both of them a good hour in the only bathroom. Maybe they were doing other stuff. Made his insides swerve. Not those two old maids…though he disliked thinking of them as old maids.

-Come on, please.- In Chicago they had two bathrooms. Well now, he chuckled to himself, if he had to go bad enough here he could run outside. He liked that idea, breezes on his jack-knife. Couldn't have that kind of fun in Chicago. He wondered, though, winter. Could the little guy get frostbitten or would the pee make a cycle shaped icicle? He yelled, -Come on, please.-

Noncie slowly appeared smiling nicely at him.

Will I ever have peace in my old age? He too had believed this quiet life would bring peace. Though he longed for other things, other than his mind spinning around in the past, like having something to do worth doing or just being content over sunrise and sunset. Back in Chicago he was sought after. People wanted his opinions and advice. He had friends.

He heard Florence calling at him through the closed door, -We need wood. It's all gone.- What was he supposed to do while sitting on the crapper? He didn't answer. Anyway he didn't want to be in charge even though he wanted to be in charge. It was enough that he was in charge of the money and hid his money from them. They had squandered it, gowns for endless   party-going and events, the latest tableware and new draperies, jewelry, necklaces of little fur animals, and animal fur down to their ankles. On the one hand he thought having money was vulgar but when they had entered those social events he felt proud he could adorn them. He sighed. Yes, back in Chicago he was somebody.

Noncie, Miss *noblesse oblige*, would go on buying sprees for the kids in the settlement houses. Bought them party dresses. Like they would be likely to go to parties? It was open your veins, Papa dear, and let it run. He suddenly woke up and got smart, smelled the wind and took his money out of the stock market and bank and kept it in cash long before the crash and here he had put all the greenbacks in six metal cigar boxes and buried them, placing small stones on top, like a miniature grave yard, near the stone wall where he thought of making a garden. He could keep his darlings in comfort, though it would be better if he were dead and they would get his insurance and better too if he didn't have to think about them, but what would he think about then? The past and all he missed, the love of his life who was the woman he didn't marry. And look at him, how inadequate, unable to find someone who would sell him wood. Maybe they would freeze to death. It was still getting down into the twenties at night.

That night the stove fire died completely. Florence shivered in her bed, rose and put on her fur coat, which still had Borie's dried blood. She called Jessica to sleep on her bed. The dog laid her head on Florence's belly and she stroked the dog's ears.

As a child her father had teased her for being so sensuous, fingering the velvet of a gladiola blossoms or running her lips up on a cool window glass and that time on the wintry school yard tasted the swing's chain and her tongue froze until a teacher ran to get hot water to free her. But the best sensation of all had been taken from her, forever.

As she fell asleep Jessica's fur suddenly reminded her of her ex's coarse hair that he slicked back with thick oil to hide the coarseness. Gave her such a shiver of horror she stopped petting the dog. Sometimes Irving's face sneaked in, even as she tried to slam her mind shut from him. Would he hunt her down? Kill her? Twenty-two years, she still feared.

-We got to go to the orchard and look for broken branches,- Papa said as they staggered to the kitchen at dawn. All three trudged up among the gnarled apple trees where lay a few slim broken branches, and came home with little. They filled the stove in the kitchen, and laid out some by the fireplace.

-Oh my, the water pipe from the spring might freeze. One of you run upstairs and drip it in the basin?- Papa turned on the kitchen faucet.

-What are we going to do?- Noncie asked as they sat in the sun in the kitchen, shivering.

-We should take a ride down to Brattleboro and see,- said Papa, knowing that would be hopeless. Who would bring wood to them from that far away?

-We should go home,- Florence said.

They looked at her.

-Can't we just start calling on farmers and begging, go back to the Post Office?- Noncie's voice faded into discouragement.

He wanted to swear but of course not in front of his daughters.

-We should go back to Chicago- Florence repeated.

—We heard that- He rubbed his forehead.

-Back to Chicago is the only answer.- Florence said loudly.

- Stick to the subject.- Noncie wagged a finger at her.

–There isn't even an inn around here.- Noncie said.

-We could start burning the furniture. I always hated that wash-stand in the hall,-

Florence said.

Noncie groaned and banged her hand on the table. -We have to go beg people.- But she abhorred seeming pathetic.

No one spoke. The sun silently lowered behind Bold Mountain.

-Okay, lets get in the car and turn the heater on and drive to New York City.- Papa said, wondering if he had enough gas, knowing stations closed at dusk.

-If we got stuck, or broke down at night we would freeze. Look, - Non-cie called out. She saw a truck come up the drive. The three dogs plunged toward the door, barking. The knock was tentative. Papa opened the door.

-Edifice McHuron, bringing you wood.-

-Come in...-Noncie glanced at his muddy boots.

Florence took one look and backed into the dining room, her heart pounding as if from a nightmare. He was dressed in blue jeans and a brown lumber jacket, thick as a rug, Wellington boots and plaid visor hat. She had rarely seen a beard. When he took off his hat out popped unruly blond hair. What was there that repulsed her so? Not his looks. Some-thing deeper. Something untrustworthy. She wondered if she had seen him in a dream or some clairvoyant moment. Her heartbeat distended up into her throat and into a burp.

Hiding, she watched out the window as he carried the wood from his salt-corroded truck to the woodshed. She called out to Noncie and Papa in the kitchen, -I don't like him.-

-So what,- Papa said. -It's wood he's bringing, not niceties, Flossy.-

Florence kept her eyes glued to the bearded man as he walked back and forth, carrying without gloves on his broad hands. The swaggering rhythm of his body as he hoisted himself awkwardly up onto the truck and leapt back down, somewhat off balance. She couldn't conceive of his frame in his bulky clothes. Was he fat or thin and what was his age? He didn't leap like an old man but his hesitations weren't like a young one either. When he was finished he leaned for a moment against the truck but not like relaxing, more like waiting tensely, gathering his strength. She thought of a stalking tiger, she thought of the murder of Borie. When the truck was empty he knocked at the kitchen door. She heard Papa open it. Heard a few words exchanged about the price, and Papa paid him and thanked him with a charm that Noncie echoed, hoping to keep him coming. Florence watched him climb clumsily into the driver's seat and speed away over the driveway gruel, splattering a mess onto the lawn.

In her eyes was the clue to examine later, the erratic rhythm of his stacking wood, the over-relaxed posture against the truck, and his slow climb into the truck. Her heart continued drumming her fear... whatever it was. She only hoped she would never see him again, but knowing in this small community she would.

CHAPTER 4

*H*e ran quickly looking back over his shoulder, stealthily moving into the copse of maples, down an impression and up the field through the thicket of ash trees, blending among yellow birch and over the crest where no one could see him. He breathed lightly as he always did at this spot. He assumed she had never found him out. Even without this he wanted her to know as little as possible about him...his wolverine crone of a wife.

Strange those new people. Why come to this small village? And who would come not planning enough wood? And they would see this place, not the way he did, awed by scrims of fog flitting across the valley, or hovering over the prickly coating of evergreens blanketing the mountains. Those city people no doubt saw the hills as hostile, and the village as a rutty, dreary hole.   Definitely weird. Didn't know if he could trust them...maybe snooping types.

The church paid him a pittance to see that the building remained standing and mice weren't making nests where woodpeckers bored into the wainscoting. The congregation couldn't afford to heat the church or pay a full time minister, only for a wedding or funeral or baptism.

Shocked to find what they had done with the dead dog, lay him in the church, he had carried the stiff body down the embankment and dropped it in the swollen river. He watched in the cold moonlight as it rode, buoyed up like a bobbing log, downstream to some other village or to be banked along the way where it would be eaten by marauding animals or hungry buzzards.

He sold those people the wood mostly out of curiosity even though he needed the money. Had they absorbed nothing about reality? Need wood at the last minute? He kept shaking his head. He had an eerie feeling none of them wanted to be here.

Maybe they were criminals hiding out. The tall one with her hair stark
white bubbling in curls. She ran the show maybe. The other, was she a
recluse, Emily Dickinson style? He had seen her hiding in the dining
room, probably a little tetched in the head. The one glimpse, she was
pretty in spite of her meadow-like hair. Her eyes struck him, round
hooded black, a sleepy look...a robbed look. The women were dressed to
the nines like going to a tea party. The old man shivered in a raccoon coat
and going to the office suit. Really a weird bunch.

Now before he came to his destination he crossed the field to find the
stone. The stone was flat, flat to the earth. He had trouble finding it, covered with shedding pine needles. He didn't want to, didn't want to think
about what lay beneath, and yet of course he did. He came less often
because seeing the stone hurt him more each time. In deep mossy letters
that his father had chiseled into the marble:

ELIZA BRANFORD McHURON
LOVE TOOK HER.

Edifice had begged to go with her that day. But she had said, -Not this
time,- and kissed him several long kisses on his cheek and forehead and
called his older sister from the parlor in order to kiss her also. His mother
carried her leather-bound sketchbook in a picnic basket. She sketched
every Sunday afternoon. Usually he accompanied her. But that day his
father took him to a baseball game in the next village and his sister
wanted to practice her piano.

He pictured his mother running up the hill, her blond curls like his,
flying in the sharp wind. May the eighteenth. Ten years old he was. On
his birthday three days before she had made a cake with whipped cream.
He sat on the stool and watched her turn the eggbeater so fast her slim
hands were blurred and seemed about to lift her up and out the kitchen
door and into the sky. The love that had taken her was the love of nature,
his father had told them.

His parents had met in Boston. After they were married they came to
Flood Brook and built the largest, most elegant house for miles around,
which was the house that he and his wife, Gerty lived in. His father had
settled in the village because he owned the railroad that had run from
Flood Brook to Brattleboro until the river rose one devastating spring and
took out the tracks along the edge. He didn't rebuild.

That was when Edifice was a teenager. After that his father did nothing much but putter about or read. He tried not to bring his children into
the path of his mourning. Tried to be cheerful for their sakes, engaging
them in conversation. But Edifice would see him trudging the hill to be

alone with his bride and his grief, sometimes carrying a little bouquet of meadow flowers to lay on the stone.

The Depression took all the money Edifice had inherited. But before that neither he nor his father took care of their house. Even then the gracious, distinguished place had started its downhill slump. They didn't paint it. The porch rotted. The once beautiful walk in herringboned bricks had buckled from frost heaves. The place would crumble to the ground some day.

Edifice never met his father's parents and met his mother's only once. His mother and father never ventured back to Boston, and his grandparents didn't come to Flood Brook. Only that one time his mother's parents came to hear the minister at their daughter's funeral invoke heaven to take the soul of Eliza McHuron.

Back at the house they stayed but a few hours. When they kissed Edifice and his sister goodbye his grandparents tried not to break down, kept their New England faces tightly wrapped against their prominent bones. He was sorry he had never asked his father more about them.

His father had been a generous man, and people called him the nicest man they knew. He stopped to listen to anybody's troubles, although sometimes Edifice thought he stood so patiently because he had gradually grown a little deaf. He helped folks when they fell into a financial hole. He would buy a cow or goat if theirs died. The irony was he saw to it their houses were painted while his began to peel.

When he was ten and the sun had slid behind the mountain and they had returned from the game his father said, -Where could she be for so long?-

The three rushed as darkness came. Calling and calling. Up the cow path tracing where they'd seen his mother go. The same land Edifice owned today. Not until the meadow did they move in separate ways, calling. He came to the copse of trees.

"Mommy," he had called and the echo came back from the hills and granite rocks. At first he thought she was answering, as if mocking and teasing him, "Mommy," rang back in echoes. He was the one who found her. Oh how often he wished he hadn't, as if then she would be alive today.

At first he assumed she was simply napping, leaning against a maple tree, her sketchbook resting on her breasts. -Mommy, Hi.-

But when he touched her face, the face that had been strong and warm was marble cold. The rest, the march home, his father carrying her in his arms and weeping, the funeral, the mystery of what she had died of, all seemed vague compared to the touch on her chilled face.

He sat down next to her grave now and thought how all these years he had looked for the same intense love he felt for her, a love to capture him, an innocent, fanciful all consuming love, that he could give back as his father to his mother. He had been too young to know all of her except what he felt in his soul. His father tried to tell him what his mother was like but each time he stopped to control his tears. So it was only bits here and there. Events that folks told him about, and her sketches with the inscriptions: *old maple near where the best blackberries grow.* Edifice loves to make jam with me. *Cobb Brook, a pool of tadpoles.* When they become frogs the kids will help me catch them. I'll fry up frog legs for supper. *The sky over Flood Brook.* My husband loves to look at the sky to predict the weather. This sketch is for him. The one for Edifice's sister, who loved music was, *a tree full of migrating birds.* The sketch that was open on her breasts was of a buttercup and underneath she had written: *how fragile.* That was her last entry.

The dedication in the front of the sketchbook: "to Priscilla and Edifice whom I hope will remain wild as the brook and may they go where the brook takes them."

Why had she written that? Did she write it that day? Did she know she was dying? Have a premonition? Did she kill herself, impossible, impossible to find the answer. "Where the brook took him?" Wouldn't she be disappointed where he had let the current carry him!

His father cut off a lock of her wild blond hair, the exact color of Edifice's, and kept it in the carved wooden box that Edifice now kept on his bureau top. His sister Priscilla moved west and didn't want to take a thing. She married a man she met on the bus to Rutland and they worked until they bought a ranch. She didn't come back to Vermont except when their father died but she and Edifice had long correspondences, about four times a year. He had always been fond of the written word. She wrote him cute stories about his three nieces and sent pictures. He was envious.

Later in the season, when he would walk barefoot, the scent of crushed ferns would fill him with such erotic tension that he exhaled loud sighs of despair. He had once wanted to bring his new bride here but soon realized he would never bring her to this sacred spot.

CHAPTER 5

*A*s he stood gazing at the familiar valley below and at the one-room schoolhouse he had attended. In fifth grade when their teacher, Miss Genette, went to the closet to get some books, he and three boys locked her in so they could stay out longer at recess. But Miss Genette was so good-natured she announced that from then on they could have ten more minutes recess, that is if they knuckled down. Edifice liked that it was kindness that had brought success. They received certificates for their better grades, crayoned by her, a cartoon of each face for the eleven children in the school.

His eyes followed the river where the flood of 1929 had taken Leland Howe's house. He built again on Scenic Hill. The Robert's house where the widow Dugan was boarding had been taken. They moved to Londonderry. Nothing but the foundation was left of the Grinwall cottage. It had been ripped by the flood and floated away with all five of the family inside. They were rescued when it stopped at the bridge in Rawsonville. The sweet-faced motherly Dee Buckston died of shock that day. And the population of the village began its harsh dwindling. Yet he would never move away.

As he left his mother's grave to go on to his final destination his eye, by mistake, caught the charred remains of the house where his wife had grown up. He didn't want to think of that place and the ongoing misery it brought him.

While walking on he felt the money in his pocket from those Logan people. Now he could buy sugar. In winter he snow-shoed up to the shack, but he tried to make enough supply in summer and fall to last him through snow season.

Inside he filled the stove with wood and lit it. He drew in a deep breath to take in the aroma. In the small space was a wooden chair with gold letters on the back, Harvard, where his father had gone; a table with an oil lamp and two shelves.

He had conducted plenty of experiments to come to this perfection. Along with buying some sugar there had been enough honey from his bee hives. Gerty thought his raising bees was for her. She liked to eat the cone and all, chewing with her mouth open just to annoy him, now and then swiping her lips with a handkerchief she kept in the bosom of her dress. For years he had not wanted to think of Gerty's breasts but thought about other women's breasts all the time, and glanced at just about every breast no matter what age.

High on the nails hung dried wildflowers to make his thin wart. Wondered if he had enough asters, feverfew and elderberry. Once he sneaked out at night and pilfered a few nasturtium blossoms from his neighbor's yard. He often wondered about other villagers. He was sure around here there was no operation like his. Maybe just letting cider go hard. But once he saw the postmistress collecting dandelion leaves in her yard. Startled, -I love them cooked up with vinegar don't you?- Oh yeah, she was making a bit of wine.

He had built the galvanized pot, the reflux tower packed with steel; saving every penny to buy some, but mostly he dug through the dump. He sealed the gasket with a rubber lid cut from an old tire and a metal band he found in his barn to screw it tight to the walls. Took a while adjusting the length of the tower, drilled in brass nuts and fit a suitable set of screws to tighten the band. That took a bit of doing. He groaned loudly, trying to pull the band tight enough.

Made the cooling tower tubes from metal he found at the dump, flaring one of the tubes so it wouldn't slip down the other one and then he roped the whole thing to the ceiling to keep it steady. He thought it was beautiful, like a fanciful sculpture.

His drinking had injured him a couple of times, once falling asleep next to the stove his hand fell on top, blistering his fingers. And once, spending a winter night, the fire went out. When he woke he had frozen his big toe. As he rubbed the blood back in the hurt was bad.

Although she never dared ask, she cared; Gerty cared that he spent the night out only because he was up first to light the stove. Otherwise she didn't care a hoot about him.

The villagers wouldn't tell the Prohibition authorities on him, but couldn't count on that 100 percent if Gerty found out. Vodka had no odor but she had seen him staggering straight to bed.

She could hang him for more than that if she wanted to. He pushed aside the thought that he stayed with her because she might blackmail him. No, he stayed with her out of decency, didn't he? He stayed with her

28

because of conscience, not guilt. He was not ashamed of what he'd done. And he pretended to himself he was afraid of nothing, jail or death…only afraid of loving anyone again. But there would be no chance of that.

He was getting excited while waiting for the vodka. There was nothing like that first smooth stinging liquid slithering down his esophagus. While he waited he read Hawthorne out loud, letting the sound of the words hum at his cheekbones, sometimes without worrying about their meaning. Took him on a journey, flattened out his bad thoughts, which, if let loose might score a ditch big enough to plummet him into.

CHAPTER **6**

*A*s Florence lay in bed picturing Edifice McHuron, his slumped restlessness and his uneven walk, memory slung her unwillingly backward. She wished she could forget. Never think of the hateful man.

She was sixteen. Her mother dead since she was eleven. They were living in Chicago and her father didn't care about discipline. She did pretty much what she wanted. Wandered into forbidden back alleys on her way home from Bristle Hill, a finishing school that almost finished her off. Such a bore. And angry with Papa for forbidding her going to college, removing her from all those wonderful temptations…too much knowledge and rampant sex.

Her school had only girls forced to wear all the same flat blue, like a chain gang. Every day she ran to the place she knew was a bar, long before Prohibition, excited to see bums, brawny men dressed like athletes in undershirts and old men in run down shoes. Muscle men swearing and brawling in the streets. She loved it all.

But one day an incongruous man appeared, dressed like Papa going to a funeral, a morning suit, a stripe down his trousers, but oddly, brown shoes with spats. His black hair was plastered down. His face was as beautiful as a Greek statue with its harmonious proportions.

She knew what she possessed, charming ways of outrageous flirting, even at her age. She tried it on uncles and cousins and even her father when she wanted her way. Had never tried it on a strange grown man, maybe even twenty-four or five. She knew perfectly well that was dangerous, she being sixteen.

He didn't give her more than a glance when he passed but she called out to him,

-Hey, what's your name?-

He paused, looked back for a second at her body curved out at him, legs apart, daring smile on her open lips. Her come-on eyes were turning blue-black in the late sunlight. He entered the bar and slammed the door.

The next day she was back waiting. He did not come. The day after that, no sign of him. He finally appeared, stepping out of a chauffeur-driven car and heading for the bar.

-Wanta give me a kiss?- She called.

His half smile gave away to shock. A schoolgirl. But she saw a glimmer that he liked her nerve.

-What's your name?- She called to him again. He ignored her. When he opened the door plums of smoke and loud jazz rushed at her and then he disappeared. She wanted to follow him into darkness and exciting noise. She paced the sidewalk waiting for him to come out, even though she was very late coming home from school. She was about to leave when he appeared.

She rushed to him. -I want to kiss you hard on the mouth.-

He frowned at her with disbelief. -Go suck your thumb.- The chauffeur-driven car he stepped into moved away.

The next day she ran to find him. But he wasn't there. She paced up and down the sidewalk. He didn't come. She couldn't look for him for two days because Noncie, who from the moment their mother had died, tried to mother her, told Papa she was two hours late coming home from school. But Papa didn't take notice thinking that Noncie loved to snitch on Florence.

Almost a week later she thought she saw him...Yes, there he was and she was a block away. She ran and just as he started to open the door she blocked him.

-Why won't you kiss me?-

He looked at her carefully. -Didn't I say go?-

-I'm not a kid. I'm twenty-one. I've had boy friends,- She lied.

-So what. Have you had a lover?- He tried to move to the side but she blocked him again, his jacket brushing her shoulder roughly. The spicy smell of his shaving lotion kneaded her brain into mush.

-I'd like to have a lover.-

-Out of my way.- She didn't move. Glanced at him full of meaning and slowly parted her

lips. - I'll fly away home and come another day.-

-You do that.-

She moved away, though she had wanted him to touch her, even if to shove her aside, feel his broad hand against her back. The door shut behind him. She waited many days after that but he never came into the alley again.

In June she graduated, barely. She thought about the man and did almost no school work,

instead reading dime novels, hiding them on her lap. The math or science book out on her desk.. She whispered to her classmates or passed them notes on toilet paper. She stacked up demerits that kept her in at recess. But she liked that because she could keep on reading.

Papa had long ago given up. Even as a five years old, though he forbade her, she kept on climbing the tall chestnut tree and fell, breaking her arm twice. A little older she disappeared into the colored section when they still lived in Kentucky and played kick-the-can down in the scrub lots, and neighbors, aghast, would come tell her parents, -She's playing with coloreds.-

Her mother, alive then, locked her in her room to miss a summer party, but she climbed out of her window onto the porch roof and to the ground and off on her bike to her colored friends.

-Let her play, what does it matter? - Papa said.

-You get away with murder,- her sister said.

After Florence graduated from high school the summer heat was unrelieved with only shreds of hanging clouds and not even a slurp of rain. The thin tendrils of her hair stuck to her temple. The July of nothing. Nothing to do. She was nothing.

She strung up a hammock in the bedroom and lay naked, reading Jane Austen. Her father knocked on the door and said, -Time to dress for the party.-

He liked parties. Men talk. She hated society parties with a capital H while her father and Noncie thrived on them. All that puffing themselves up, pretending not to brag, sugary talk. But at that time she began, with Noncie's instruction, to make herself up, to dress with finesse. And unexpectedly Florence was drawn into playing the game.

Lawn parties at their friends' summer places outside the city...diminutive parasols, mint juleps and long gloves. Everyone but them, it seemed, had a country place. But Papa had said, -Why should we? We get invited to theirs.-

Papa made them learn tennis so they would mix with boys in a proper setting, but she felt he was unfair. She was clumsy on the court. Everything was unfair. Three months since she had seen him. She would never see him again and she didn't know his name, the man with black hair.

She drew a broken heart in lipstick on the palm of her hand.

Papa called to her. -Florence we're going over to the Polvers for a supper party. Get ready.-

-No.-

Papa was too used to her antics to start recriminations. -I'm waiting.-
He stood outside the door.

What the hell. Just bored enough to obey him, she donned her most
becoming white dress but then spent a good twenty minutes trying to
apply the makeup she had taken from Noncie's drawer.

Noncie gave her the steel-skewer-eyeball look and grimaced when she
came out.

-Drop dead.- Florence said.

They arrived at the stately old house, ten miles north of the city, with
a useless turret on the top as though it were built next to the sea for the
grieving widow waiting for the fisherman to come home. The three
ambled across the lawn.

Her feet turned to jelly. Right there. There he was. His red face told her
he remembered too.

And she was being led to him. Mrs. Polver introduced them, -This is
Miss Florence Logan and Miss Noncie Logan and Mr. Logan, my grandson
Irving Polver.- Papa shook hands and then Noncie, but Florence rushed
away toward the lawn chairs. Mad for him and humiliated.

All afternoon she mingled away from him. Or did he stay away from
her? She could hardly think and hardly notice the sprinkles of rain.
Floating at her neck was a red silk scarf, which began to run on her white
dress. She rushed into the powder room and took the scarf off and threw
it in the wastebasket. Her washing the spots on her white dress merely
dimmed the red. Giving up she stepped out of the powder room into the
hall while the other guests coming in from the rain were milling into the
great library at the other end of the house. She froze. Irving Polver was
waiting for her in the hall.

They stared at each other. He moved toward her.

He took hold of her shoulders, pushed her against the wall and placed
his lips on hers with such force that her teeth came down on her lip. She
cried out.

He pulled back. -You better learn how to kiss before you chase a
grown man.-

The wall was holding her up.

He didn't move away.

-On the other hand I'll sacrifice myself and give you a lesson. Tomorrow at Linden Park near the west entrance, two p.m. Her hand covered
her lips as if the kiss had made them forever wordless.

CHAPTER 7

*F*uck it, where were those two? He told them to meet him in the barn. He figured, even though the driveway mud was about two feet deep from the rain and melted snow,

he would be able to race the Packard through.

Florence was getting worse about the makeup, taking it off with salad oil, beginning again. And what for? Papa would cool his heels like always. Sometimes he felt his life was nothing but waiting. Sometimes he was proud to remember he didn't wait, like the time he got so angry with one of his mill hands, who was punching out a colored man. Quivering with fear that he would be fired the colored man didn't defend himself. Papa grabbed the white man by the scruff of his neck threw him out onto the sidewalk.

-Never come back.-

The colored man bowed his head as if in a prayer. -You coulda got punched out bad, yourself, Sir.-

Papa patted him on his back. He thought, not a big deal. Many times he had rushed to separate gnashing growling dogs to save one of his dogs. Then he was ashamed

of how he had put it to himself, equating the colored man with a dog. Yet he knew how he felt about coloreds, raised by them, the garden tended by them. Fed by them. He could call how he felt as love. Made his heart burn. And here he was in pure white country that made him nervous as hell.

He started up the Packard, sat on the horn and backed it into the flat at the top of the driveway. The rain started again. He took a quick look at the steep driveway. God almighty, pure mud. Not waiting anymore. His girls would have to walk on the grass and meet him at the end of the driveway.

He gunned the car, moved three feet. Jammed. Moored. Gunned it again. Reversed, Shifted, gunned. The car moved a few inches, then stopped. The back wheels sank. High pitched sound of spinning. Rock. Rock, spin and spit. Splattered crap on his beautiful yellow car.

-Running shits.- Thick oily smoke poured out of the fuselage. He nixed the engine and stepped out. -What the god damned devil.- The mud was quickly above his mukluks. He held up his coat, looking, he knew, like a woman in a long dress, crossing a puddle. He tried to walk back up to the woodshed. The girls weren't in the yard yet. Tried to yank out one leg at a time... damned immobile. Son-of-a-bitch, trapped in mud. -Girls, girls.-

No sight of them. Called as loud as his pipe-smoke throat would allow.

Noncie peeked out. Though her eyes were clouded, nothing wrong with her ears. But Florence could switch off her ears and float in the trees like a goddamned leaf, Papa thought.

-Where were you?- He growled

-Papa?-

-Look at me. Look at me,- he hollered.

Florence came with a baffled expression. They were both dressed up, skirts and stockings for going to Rutland to shop.

-Is this one of your games?- Noncie accused him.

-Would you mind getting me out right now?-

-Why aren't you in the car?- Florence asked.

-Why do you think?-

-You got stuck,- Noncie said.

-Brilliant. Ever heard of Sir Walter Raleigh? Throw down your coats. Hike up your skirts. Pull me out.-

-Oh sure,- Florence answered, with a short giggle.

- Noncie reassured. –We'll go back to the house and find something to help.-

The sisters careened back in the house and laid their coats on a chair and took off their shoes, stockings and skirts and ran out in their silk bloomers. Neither one wanted to change into good riding boots and jodhpurs so they ran barefoot through the woodshed. Florence asked, -How are we supposed to get him out?-

Noncie ran toward the barn. -Let's find a board.-

She found only a slim piece of wood and laid it down to reach him. But when she stepped on the board to take his hand the board sank just enough to throw her off balance and roll her plunk into the muck.

Florence held her hand up to her face, hiding her smile over her dig-
nified sister wallowing in what looked like manure. Thank God she was
close enough to pull her sister to the grass.

-Crisis,- Papa shouted. –Go to town. Get help.-

Crisis, Florence thought, they have no notion, these two unworldly,
coddled...

-That's okay, I'll be dead by the time you get back.-

-I'll bring you hot coffee first,- Florence said.

-Just go, both of you.- *Takes two of them to make one nitwit.*

They dressed again, stayed over on the grass and moved carefully
to the edge of the road.   -Hurry up, hear me Flossy?- Papa called
sweetly. She was the slower one. He really wondered if they would be
back in time to rescue him before he died of the cold.

He felt ridiculous. Not just now but a lot of the time. Maybe you were
finally mature only when you were able to claim that image of yourself.

The postmistress said, -I'll pass the word along to see if somebody
would help.-

It seemed to Florence the customers were all smiling an I-knew-it
smile, when the postmistress said aloud,-You folks know, that yellow
Packard? Needs help pulling out.-

Forty minutes later the sisters came jogging up to where Papa had
been able to pull himself back into the car.

-Where's the help?- He called out.

Seeing how upset Papa was Florence wanted a taste, just to wet her
tongue. Just a sip to perish her anxiety. Papa moaned loudly from the car
as Noncie said, -The postmistress is trying to put the word out. Someone
will come.-

It crossed Florence's mind the old man might be hiding a bottle
or two. Maybe she should go on her own hunt, right now while he was
stuck. Then she slapped her mind and tried to dream of milk shakes.
Noncie stood at the bottom of the driveway in hopes someone would
come soon.

Papa yelled, -I'm going to die.-

Noncie said, -Know you aren't. Someone will come. I'm making you
coffee,- although she was not sure how she would get it to him

- The villagers hate us.-

Florence sat on the steps to the kitchen looking out through the arch
of the breezeway. At least an hour went by. Now she was really worried
about Papa. A sound. A familiar sound came along the road. That truck.
She rose and rushed to hide in the dining room to peer out the window.
Yes, that truck, that man with the reddish beard and oversized outfit

stepped out at the bottom of the driveway, greeting Noncie. She thanked him several times.

Florence's stomach turned. A strange fear. Tingling hairs at the nape of her neck. And she was certain that he had killed Borie.

-Well, we'll get you out Mr. Logan.-

He hauled thick boards from his truck and dropped them in the mud to make a path to the car and pulled him out and helped him into the house. Edifice attached a chain to the Packard and his truck. The truck tugged and the dirt spit wildly but the car didn't move. He tried again, this time slowly inched the car down the driveway.

Edifice McHuron seemed like a hulk more than most men, Florence thought. He seemed like a singular force, like a storm coming down before you can reach shelter.

Papa tried to give him money. Edifice shook his head and smiled, though it was difficult to see his lips with all that beard. Then, how awful. Papa invited him into the kitchen.

-Have a seat.- From her hideout in the dining room she heard him pull a chair out from the table for McHuron. Then she heard footsteps toward her. Oh God.

-Florence you come too? We're having coffee and...- Papa insisted.

God in heaven this was Papa's policy, be nice to the servants and workmen. She didn't have to be part of his...but she couldn't think fast enough to retreat into the front hall or run upstairs. She obeyed, saying to herself, I'm above it all. He's nothing to me. What am I afraid of? But she felt like calling the dogs to protect her.

She sat in the chair to the right of him and noticed he had taken off his boots and saw he had small feet. She too had small feet. Why she thought of that she couldn't say.

-Tea or Coffee?- Noncie asked.

-Coffee, thank you.- But he was looking at Florence, not Noncie when he answered. Florence rose quickly to get the cups.

-You lived here all your life?- Papa asked.

-Yep, born in the house I live in now. How did you folks happen to come here?-

-I'm retired and...- Papa paused as Florence sat and touched her father's arm in case he might spill the real reason.

-We were looking for the countryside, the beauty and-... Papa stopped.

-That's about it?- McHuron narrowed his eyes. -Not easy to find books, or the theater or museums...or dress shops here.-

-We did plenty of that in Chicago.- Noncie served him coffee.

-The beautiful countryside.- McHuron touched his beard.

-We came to feed our souls,- Florence said.

He smiled at her, showing uppers and lowers of the strong, slightly serrated edges of his teeth bringing to mind a rat. He said it back to her. -To feed your souls.-

Florence couldn't stand another minute. She started to get up.

Noncie quickly said, -Wait. We have some shortbread from England.-

Edifice thought again, law-dodgers.

They drank their coffee and tea and took their blessed time over eating the shortbread while Florence looked at her cup, not at him.

-Maple sap running yet?- Papa knew how to be whoever he was with. Was he even trying out a New England accent?

-Too much trouble for me. Maples on my place too spread out. Then there's all that hauling wood to keep the vats going to make the syrup. I do enough of that already and it isn't like you can live on drinking syrup.-

Inside of Florence a volcano was about to spew. So that was it. Hauling wood for something else. Calm down, he has to heat that huge house of his.

-But could you think of anybody else to help around our place?- Papa asked.

-Nope, even with the Depression, folks don't look for work. They got to keep their farms going and a lot of time the young people leave for the city. It won't be easy to find help around here.-

-How about you, couldn't you take on getting gravel for our driveway? Help us out now and then?- Papa tried.

-Sorry,- he said slowly, -I also have my own work.-

Thank God, Florence thought.

He stood, deciding the conversation was finished. –Thanks for the coffee.- He wiped his lips with his hand.

The hairs at the back of Florence's neck quivered when she noticed his third finger on his right hand was missing. That was a sign. A sign of what? Not sure. Something bad.

As he was leaving he turned. It was Florence's face he took in. Impish, playfully sad, frightened.

-But anytime you need wood, I might have some to sell.- He was halfway down the steps when he turned again and said,   -Yep if you need wood.-

*A*ll three of them were clustered at the post office counter. Though she smiled the postmistress was also irritated, Noncie thought. -Gravel,- The postmistress said, people don't have gravel around here. You wait until mud-season is gone by. Park your car at the corner.- She went on with a deadpan expression. -Or you could have marble delivered. The quarry is only fifty miles north and wouldn't a marble driveway be something nobody else had?-

Papa smiled at her. He liked that... the big blond mocking woman. But then Papa set his teeth, cemented his lips. He also was just not used to being made fun of.

As the three were leaving a sharp-chinned woman with a hoarse voice said, -Over in Dover is a boys' home, orphans. They like folks to take boys. You might find help around your place and also be giving one a home.-

-Really? Thank you very much,- Noncie said.

The woman extended her broad knobby hand. -I'm Doctor Peabody. You'll be needing me one time or other.- She grinned, showing all the gum above her upper teeth, like a grinning monkey. Her face was corrugated, her eyes lime-green. She was wearing a gray suit, that is with trousers, George Sand style. Florence took against her.

Noncie's excitement rose. A child. Maybe her prayers would be answered. And she was confident about raising children. She had been the sane one in this family, after all, and had been a mother to Florence more than their own mother, who had no clue what to do with her. Noncie was the one who had run after her when she disappeared into the empty lot to play ball or swim in the river before they moved from Kentucky. Later she listened to Florence's problems, (In the early years when Florence had confided in her). Sometimes she felt guilty that she had not understood her well enough. Although Noncie did not ponder over her own inner self. She walked too narrow a path, and her dimming eyes were tunneling her into herself even more.

Five miles away was the home for boys on an old farm at the end of a long road. They stepped up to the door. Papa knocked. A round woman answered, displaying the friendliness of a sales person who won't take no for an answer. Noncie thought she smelled heavenly, like cinnamon toast. Good sign.

Papa had gone along with this idea reluctantly, as far as getting the driveway done what help would a kid be? Yet he liked the idea of another male among the morass of women. Florence could take it or leave it. Her mind was full of tense distraction, increasing discomfort. But lets hope, he might be a diversion enough to keep her on the straight and narrow.

The round woman called out, -Hugh.-

A tall man with football shoulders came into the hall. His hair full and wavy flopped up and down in a jolly dance on his forehead. The way he walked, hard down on the floor, Noncie thought of as disdainful at first, but that soon disappeared with his easy demeanor. Although Noncie couldn't hear a sound he gave the feeling that he was humming, humming at them and inviting them to hum with him.

Very glad to meet you.- He looked at each of their faces with a gentle gaze. -Do have a seat.- His eyes were merry and sincere but slightly unfocused or distracted.

He pointed them to the living room sparsely furnished.

Five boys were crowded near him. He sent the boys outside, handing them a basket ball. Papa explained to him they would like to think about taking a boy into their home.

Noncie surveyed the dingy hall and the living room with a worn sofa, five wooden chairs and a long table spread with checkers. Some pictures done by the boys hung on the bleak wall and no curtains at the windows. Her heart thumped at the idea of rescuing a boy.

Hugh interviewed them, listened to them, cocking his head to one side as if he had one bad ear. He listened to how Noncie had loved children and that she had once been a social worker. She exaggerated that for him. She had filled in to help a friend social worker for a few weeks.

Hugh said, -I have someone in mind. You could even take him today if you wished, on a trial bases, and I'll come out and visit him soon. He's fourteen, not all that bright, but obedient and a hard worker. Most of all he wants badly to be part of a family. -

-How perfect,- Noncie said. When Hugh spoke his booming voice vibrated along her ribs, like sitting very close to a strumming harp. She put out her hand to shake his and when he took it he placed his thumb at her palm. Her heart rolled into her throat.

-I'll be coming by to check on him soon,- he repeated.

-How very nice,- Noncie said.

The kid was small for his age. He was tense and uncertain. On the way home Noncie sat in the back seat with him trying to make him feel welcomed. He smelled faintly of manure. He told her that this week his job was shoveling out the cow stalls. But she didn't mind. He reminded her of the stables where she had ridden in Chicago.

-You have blue eyes like me,- she said.

-Yep, but I don't have white hair.-

She grinned. -I like your name, Persons. It has a pretty sound.-

-It was some relative's name that I ain't ever seen. I get teasing from it.-

-In what way?- Florence asked from the front seat.

-They call me the opposite.-

-The opposite?-

-Animals. Hi, animals.-

-I'm sorry.- Florence thought a minute. -But we're all animals aren't we?-

He looked puzzled. -Anyways, sticks and stones will break my bones but names will never hurt me, that's what Hugh says. -

-Does he?- Noncie knew she shouldn't ask. -You like him?-

Persons smiled and shook himself as though he were a wet puppy. - He's the best man I ever knew. He lives with us full time since his wife didn't make it.-

-Didn't make it?- Noncie sat up straight.

-She was sick with something. Her belly all swelled up and by the time they got her over to Rutland hospital she was dead. Deader than a door nail. We never did hear exactly why. Hugh didn't like to talk about it. Somebody said it was something she et that scratched her 'till she bled out. Yep, she bled out.-

-Awful. How long ago was that?- Noncie asked

-A year last Christmas.-

-We're almost home,- Papa announced.

They were silent as they drove from the village. Noncie wondered, hoped Hugh was over his bereavement, although she was ashamed for thinking that.

-Well, here we are,- Papa announced as he parked the car at the bottom of the driveway for them to walk up on the grass. Persons' hands were covering his eyes. Noncie gently pulled them away.

-Now look.-

-A white house, boy oh boy.-

Inside the kitchen he didn't look around but asked, - Where do I sleep?-

-Your room is next to mine, over the woodshed. - Noncie pointed.. - We'll buy some paint for you to paint the walls.-

-You can choose the color,- Florence said, so that Noncie wouldn't take him over.

-I don't know painting.-

-That's okay.- Florence touched his arm . -We never painted either, never cleaned, never cooked, or washed up.-

-You live like the pigs?- His eyes fearful.

Florence laughed. When he reached the living room he exclaimed -I never seen a place like this. A white floor and bear rug. -

He wanted to stare. Noncie led him to her room where a door opened to his. But he hesitated at the door of her room. –Come on in,- she urged.

-I'm a scared of stepping on them apples. They might split open.-

Noncie held back a smile -They're painted on the floor. I painted them.-

Papa just behind them thought, God help us what kind of brains are we getting ourselves into here? He gave him a little pat on his back to send him in. Still he avoided every apple.

-We'll fix it all up.- Noncie showed him the attic room.

-I don't like apples on the floor,- he said.

-You don't come through my room. There are stairs from the wood-shed.-

-But I mean you won't paint them on my floor will you?-.

-I promise.-

When Persons saw Florence's room at the end of the hall all lavender and dark purple he wrinkled his nose. -This room gives me a stomach ache.-

-Don't you like the color?- Florence asked.

-No, girls like colors, boys don't.-

Now down the hall to Papa's room. They hadn't decided on the color for his room and he didn't care what color. The floorboards were worn and the walls were mustard yellow with age. Maybe they would never get around to painting it since he didn't mind. -It sort of suits what I am, yellow with age.- Made Florence sad that he was old. He was the only man she had stayed loving.

-I think I like it here.- Persons was petting the dogs. -But do you got hot cocoa?-

In the next two weeks they divided up Persons' usefulness. Florence took walks with him and the dogs to gather kindling. Papa had him weeding grass in his neophyte garden and Noncie gave him a few cooking lessons. But he began to spend more time with Florence. She was grateful that he kept her distracted from wanting what she shouldn't and she believed she might enlarge his mind.

Noncie wondered when Hugh would come while she thought of ways of praising Persons to Hugh . He wants badly to be helpful. He burns the garbage and clears the table. Last week he washed the windows. Very obedient.

At night Florence tried to teach him to read better. She was patient. She didn't know why she was patient since that was not her nature, but curiosity about his brain kept her going. She was becoming very fond of him, his red cheeks, ears that stuck out and his compact willing body. And she was the one who did most chores with him.

Noncie seeing Florence and Persons working in harmony realized the truth that she wasn't much interested in him because he wasn't a baby. She couldn't cuddle him, mold him from the beginning of his life, think of him as hers. She was disappointed in herself, wanting badly something seemingly impossible. But Hugh was not far from her thoughts.

But when the knock came at the door, Noncie was in her jodhpurs. Her boots were muddy and her wiry hair askew. No makeup. She had been out clipping the unruly lilacs. Without any phone call Hugh was at the door.

-I've come to take a look at how Persons is doing. Is he around?- She called out for him while escorting Hugh into the living room, trying to finger-comb her curls, and rubbing her cheeks to give them blush, kicking off her boots.

-Well I'll be.- He stared at the floor. -Never seen that before. White looks beautiful.- Thrilled, she showed him to the couch and then rushed to lock the jumping dogs in the study and run her fingers through her hair again and bite her lips into color.

-Nice old house,- Hugh said. -Light rooms. But more than that artistic. Is that you? Yes, it is you.- He smiled broadly. She smiled broadly. The boy ran to Hugh to hug him. Papa was napping and Florence was somewhere, who knows.

-I'd like to see your room,- Persons took Hugh through the breezeway up the back stairs. When Hugh discovered Noncie was following them, he turned, politely, but formally,

-I'm sorry, but I would like to speak to Persons alone.-

-Certainly.- She blushed. But she quickly tiptoed up to her own room from the front stairs and put her ear to the door that was locked on her side. But their conversation was too soft. As they were leaving she heard Hugh, -Anytime you don't like something you call me.-

Noncie rushed down stairs into the kitchen before them.

-Why don't you sit in the living room? I'll be right in. Coffee or tea?-
she asked.

-Both,- Persons said.

-Pick one,- Hugh said.

-Which one you pick.-

She put on the teakettle and opened the tin of Scottish shortbread and
placed them on a silver plate that she worried was a bit tarnished, took
down the tea pot decorated with strawberries and the few fancy sugar
cubes she had left, embedded with real violet blossoms. She had to hunt
for a cream pitcher that wasn't Florence's cow pour-out-the-mouth one.

Papa had wakened and was now settled in his wing chair and Florence
had come in from a walk and plopped on the love seat opposite Hugh
and Persons. Florence's hair was ruffled, though Noncie was glad her
makeup looked perfect.

Noncie sat in a straight chair beside the fireplace where the sun wasn't
shining into her dimming eyes. She hoped she'd made the tea strong
enough, since she had been in a hurry.

-Does spring ever arrive here?- Papa asked. -My garden is so slow.-

-Indeed it does, in a few weeks, about June.- Hugh laughed his big
laugh.

Papa lit his pipe. -Would you like a cigarette?-

-No thank you. How did you find this house?-

And why, Florence thought he meant.

Noncie quickly gave her stock answer, -We adore country life. It was
August and lovely, winsome really. We had never been to New England,
though we had been to Colorado.-

Florence noticed Noncie's skin was red not only in her face but down
her neck.

-I like it here,- Persons said.

Hugh squeezed the boy's shoulders. -I can see why, you have well, two
mothers and a father.-

-Grandfather,- Persons corrected.

Papa said, -I've always wanted a grandchild.-

His daughters glanced at him. They had never heard that. Papa's
coughing fit always came when he was fibbing.

Hugh set his teacup down and asked without a second thought, -You
haven't got well, something like TB have you?-

Papa stared at him in disbelief. -Now, where would I get that? I don't
exactly pal around with unfortunates.- Then he thought uh-oh I
shouldn't have said that.

-I didn't mean to offend. We are foremost in the business of protect-
ing our children.-

-Want another cookie?- Florence said quickly. Persons eyes had been glued to the plate.

-I'd like to tell you more about our home . We have been having a hard time raising money these days, the continuing slump. We are struggling.- He directed that comment to Papa with an I bet-you-have-money look.

-Us too. Very hard,- Papa lied. But said what he really had done, -We should have buried our money in the ground.-

-Too bad nobody did that.- He smiled at Papa, his large form slipping down comfortably on the couch. -At least it's a little cheaper up here, yes indeedy.-

Papa thought maybe sometime he *would* give a little.

Noncie followed every inch of Hugh, his white shirt and brown pants, his open legs, his hand resting on his inner thigh...the other hand propped against his chin. Wasn't he fetching, fetching her to come to him?

-Where do you get books around here?- Noncie asked. -Is there a library? I'd like to get some for Persons.-

The Persons part was put on as an after thought. She just wanted to know how educated Hugh was. Could she, maybe, finally come across a man in this godforsaken place that she could stamp with approval? And she would try not to be so fussy. Though his accent was thickly Vermont, his grammar was okay, so far. She thought of him as a work of bountiful art like an outsized sculpture of a hero in a town green. She let herself hope, well...provisionally. And she realized he was being provisional too, with all of them, even a little suspicious.

Right there serving him tea and taking in his face to catch the exact lines of his cheekbones, his wide mouth, his mild eyes, she wanted to make up her mind about him, settle it right now. She disliked ambiguity. She decided he was either very determined or very lenient, but nothing in between. She held the teapot with both her nervous hands to steady them and never remembering having to do that with any other man.

As he prepared to leave Noncie said, -Do come soon.-

-Don't worry, I will.-

She saw. Florence saw how her hands shook.

What is she doing? Giddy over a man she hardly knows. Wiggling her shoulders and her head. Would her sister be able to jump free fast enough, before he hurt her? He was that type. Spot him a mile off. A man with his own ideas. Yet she wished for her sister that he might be okay. Nothing else around, and why shouldn't he be okay?

45

*E*difice pictured how his home once looked white as dove wings, shuttered in dark green, and the porch with turned ornate spindles that held up the curved mahogany rails, now rotted. Three swings had hung, one each for him and his sister and a larger one for his parents, and where they gathered in the summer evenings, gently swinging, gently waving to the passers-by.

Everything about his life was better as a child. But poor as he was now at least he owned four acres of land that ran back of the Logans' land and the meadow all the way to the Green Mountain forest, the meadow where his still was hidden and another five acres a mile or so down the river. Wood-cutting land. Yes, he was lucky.

As he put on his boots and coat and wool hat he told his wife, -Going cutting wood.-

But he never told her much. The words they had spoken he could collect in an eggcup.

He had brought his bride to this house right after the wedding in the church on the hill. Was she pretty? Yes and no. Not your Rubensesque type. Not a lot to hold onto except for the front of her. What did that matter? He was going to see a naked woman for the first time and he had dreamed of all the ways of touching her, all the ways to kiss and how the softness of her inner flesh would soften his past sorrows.

He was just about to have his twentieth birthday. Gerty was nineteen. He was glad to be her protector with her mother dead five years before and her father murdered three years after that.

When he was eighteen his father had sent him to Harvard. He had been a quiet boy, sneaking into dreamy thoughts, listening with one ear, yet able to respond when called upon. Nobody from his village had gone to college except a couple of girls to normal school to become teachers.

But at Harvard he couldn't understand his classmates' slang, the kind of kidding and references to things he didn't get. Smooth fast talk, continual smiles. Slaps on the backs. Pale faces.

All of them seemed taller than he, men in long raccoon coats, like old Mr. Logan. They sang slurred, raucous songs in the *yard* keeping him awake, partying every possible chance, it seemed. Drunken weekends and yet they arrived in class bright-eyed Monday morning. In those days he had never tasted liquor.

A fellow in his house mocked him, -How come you were named a building, Edifice?-

-My mother like the sound of Edifice.-

The fellow walked away. Edifice knew he would tell the others and the laughter would begin and Edifice had not told all the truth, that his parents really liked the connotations of Edifice, strong and upright, withstanding storms and head above the crowd.

He wrote his father. *"I'm a fish out of water. Everybody here has soft white hands. I beg you to let me come home."* His understanding father let him. Maybe he was lonely for Edifice too. And his father only lived for two and a half years after that.

He would enclose Gerty into safety forever, that had been his promise to himself.

He had ordered new sheets from sears robuck and was in anguish over whether they would come in time. But the day before the wedding the Sears Robucks' truck swung into the driveway. He ran upstairs, tearing the brown package and releasing the folded cotton, soft as milkweed down. Before he made the bed he shook the hooked rugs out the window. Dusted, swept and did it all again.

The whole village filtered into the church. The weather was so fair that tables had been set up for the reception on the church lawn. Dancing in the church basement went on most of the night, but he and Gerty left.

He carried her upstairs that night. Light, she was. His heart flying against her simple wedding dress. When they were dating she had been chaste to the point of retreating when he barely joined his lips to hers. But that only made his fire bloom wilder. Wait, she kept telling him when he tried to embrace her. Wait, she had said, as her small mouth, the size of a mouse's seemed to disappear whenever he came close.

He lit the candles in the wall sconces. When he opened the windows the room seemed to rock gently from the licking candlelight.

He laid her on the bed and leaned over her to undo the buttons of her dress and on the first button she said, -What are you doing? Leave me alone.-

He stood up, almost falling backwards. What did she mean? Did she just need a little time? -Perhaps, you'd like to undress yourself. I'll wait outside.- He shut the door and paced the wide creaking floorboards. but after a number of minutes Gerty hadn't summoned him. He knocked. She didn't answer. He slowly opened the door. She was in a flannel night-gown. His heart was on the loose. He crawled in bed and started moving his fingers to lift her gown.

She screamed, -Stop it.- He tried a soft touch to her cheek and she screamed again. This time loudly, hysterically, jumping out of bed and running around the room like a lunatic.

He tried to calm himself and then her and finally he asked -Do you not know the facts of life?-

Her screaming turned to laughter or crying laughter or something he had never heard except raccoons' fighting in the night. Silence stunned him and then her sarcastic voice, her cheeks taut. The tiny mouth rip-cording the words. -How dumb are you, you think I haven't seen a bull and a cow, rabbits and dogs and all the rest.-

-Then what is the matter?-

-Nothing is the matter. I just want to be left alone. And no sleeping in my room, neither.-

He was shocked beyond thinking. There was no concept he could fall back on, count on. The emptiness was a sudden death too devastating to find a way into his brain. His knees shook, then his torso, like that day when he came upon his dead mother and touched her cheek, sending the icy cold up his arm to his heart.

He found his threadbare sheets and made a bed in the room that had been his as a child. The room she took over had been his father's and mother's. Though he had known from the beginning Gerty was not what he had imagined or dreamed as his great love, she had been the beginning of hope, the beginning of rescuing himself from the time he had rescued her.

The next day after his dazed sleepless night he found her in the kitchen. Perhaps she just had to get used to the idea. They ate breakfast but with few words. He didn't even want to bring up the wedding and how lovely the day had been and all the flowers people had brought and how life would be better now that she was out of that shack, the shack of her father's murder.

Edifice took long walks up in the woods, thinking, hoping, and not knowing what to do. But as the days and nights went by he stopped knocking on her locked door and the hurt festered and grew deeper. His longing for love and sex was cutting cut deep. He thought about taking a drink of liquor to console himself. Though he had never taken a drink, not even when the cider was hard.

Weeks went by until he asked her, -Why did you marry me?-

-What do you mean?-

-What do I mean?- He slammed his fist on the table.

It was true he had never said he loved her nor she him and had a different reason for marrying her but she couldn't know that. He hoped she didn't know.

-Why won't you let me try to make you happy in bed?-

-I'm happy that you aren't making me happy in bed.-

She rose from the breakfast table and announced she was going to feed their few chickens. She looked at him as if he should follow along and help. But at that moment he decided he would never go anywhere with her again, not even to the chicken coop. He could have had their union annulled, but throwing her out to the wind he couldn't.

He thought of his father and how many times he had wanted to talk to him about why he was marrying Gerty, but his father died before he had proposed. Gerty had no place to go, no other relatives. She had no skills except to hunt. How he came to loathe her. And oh how he wished he didn't spend the rest of his living time loathing her.

s Papa watched Persons walking with Florence toward the barn he was tempted for fun to perform his own grandfather's ritual with Persons. Well, better not, he might tell old hawk-eyed Hugh. Papa slipped through the gate to the south corner of his garden where the sun was heating up the stone wall. He unbuttoned his trousers, pulled them and his underwear down and sat his bare ass in the loam. What luxury. The tickle, the warmth. As much pleasure as almost anything he could think of. He shut his eyes and wriggled. He could hardly bring himself to rise but when he did he knew the time was right for planting the tender crops, since no dirt stuck to his ass.

-Lay your hand flat on the earth and see if it comes up clean,- is all he said to Persons later.

-Sure does.-

They found a few leftover tools, a shovel and rake, and began turning the soil, pulling the weeds where he had already made a row for early seeds... peas and spinach. Papa was in a talking mood; real glad to have Persons to listen.

-I owned a mill. I made a name for myself for knowing a lot about flour and I lectured at conventions of millers around our country and in Canada. They knew that I had knowledge about grains, all kinds of grains.

-Grains? Grains of wood?- Persons stopped.

-No, like wheat.-

-A kid I knew died in wheat.-

-Died? What do you mean?-

-Up in the silo, sank down too deep. He couldn't get out and the heat fried his brains.-

-My goodness. Terrible.- Papa dug a bit and then went on, adoring to have an ear, -My mill, back in Kentucky ran on a water wheel, on the Pecane River. One of the largest water wheels in the county. Big as to the top of our house.-

Persons nodded.

Papa thought he wasn't getting the drift. Making the idea simple he said, -The mill has big millstones. The bottom stone is fixed and the top stone was balanced on a spindle, which was raised, or lowered.- He stacked up some flat stones to show Persons. -Both stones were corrugated, like the bottom of cardboard boxes.-

Persons stopped digging to listen.

-The wheat was scraped, rather than bruised. The wheat to be ground entered the mill by a great big hole in the top stone and was carried out toward the edge, then leaving in the form of what is called meal down holes round the outside of the bed. By raising and lowering the top stone, the meal could be made as fine or as coarse as you'd like.-

-Is that right?- Persons yawned.

But now Papa didn't care. He wanted to relive aloud, and here was someone who wouldn't stop him the way his girls did. -The mill wheel on the river made the stones work.-

Persons was staring off at the distance. He said, -I heard of this man who got killed in a mill, a sawmill up in Randolf, got his hand caught in the saw. Took it clean off, like a butcher on a shank and he bled to death right in front of his buddies.-

-I'll be.- Papa pointed to the shovel for Persons to continue digging and he himself stopped to light his pipe. -I was famous. I had knowledge and I liked to help other millers and I was invited to speak all over the world.-

-You said that.-

Papa stared at him.

-Then the fire. At first no one saw the fire. Only as big as my thumb nail. Low down, bottom floor. Trickles of flames into the spilled grain on the floor. Then suddenly raging, high as the highest trees, engulfing my mill. We ran out, all of us just in time to see the whole place blow up like a huge balloon exploding. All of my mill collapsed into itself. Heaps of ashes drifted in the air and when the sky cleared the whole town came to see. Nothing was left.-

"Wow," Persons said.

-Then we moved to Chicago.-

-Did you know they can burn people to ashes,- Persons said, -and then scatter people to the wind because they ain't people anymore?-

Papa shook his head, wondering how many morbid stories this kid had stored in that cranium of his. The weird thing was, he wasn't gloomy and Papa around Persons wasn't gloomy either, even when recounting the fire. It almost seemed like somebody else's fire. Though he did think now and then about the poor mill-hands losing their jobs.

When the kid trotted into the house to get a drink of water, Papa stood at the edge of the garden that overlooked Mount Glebe and a hillside with young evergreens in rows. Stood there enjoying as a wind swayed a clump of birches. Made him dizzy. He sat down on a rock to rest.

Now was the time for cleaning the old tubes. He brought up something, spit it over to the side and sucked, hard as a baby, on his pipe. What was going to become of him? He had always been a man of hope, of enjoyment, but he thought of his friends again, his club where he lunched almost every day and talked of the state of the world. Discuss and argue. Use your brains. That world was disappearing here. What did they call it? Out to pasture.

CHAPTER 11

*N*oncie was calling for Florence to come.

Although napping in May's balmy air that poured into her window, Florence was glad to be awakened. She was having the awful nightmare about Irving finding her. Noncie was yelling from the bathroom, -The dogs. Don't you hear them?-

-Who let them out alone?-

-Probably when Persons and Papa went to the village to get milk. Florence, please go.-

-Why can't you go?-

-My hands are in the gel.-

Florence pulled on her oxfords. -What good is it to try and soften your hands in this place?-

Were the dogs yapping from the same place where Borie was killed? Could the culprit be there again? But she had to go. Times like this, wanted a drink to ease her mind. Two months dry, her festering craving only got worse, pitting her stomach into an ulcer.

She would sneak. Soundless. The path was no longer muddy. She was a bit more fit from walking up and down the hill to the village. Cautiously closer to the frantic barking. She jumped as she screamed. -Please don't shoot.-

Edifice McHuron stared at her.

-Please. Oh Please.-

He held up his empty hands.-I don't use a gun. I don't own a gun.-

She looked at the ground wondering if he had dropped it quickly so she wouldn't see. The dogs worried at her feet.-What are you doing on our land?-

-I was looking.-

-At what?- She backed away.   At her? Would the dogs protect her
if he came after her to do... in her sternest voice she said, -Get off our
land.- She wanted to say, you killed our dog didn't you? *Be careful. Don't
get him angry. Set him off if he were a murderer.*

-Look lady, we don't exclude around here. People walk anywhere. My
land abuts yours.-

-You better go.- She said softer this time. Papa had reported how
many guns hung in the McHuron's house.

-I was looking at your trees.-

-To steal because everybody around here steals?- *Stop this. I've got to
get out of here alive.* She continued backing, keeping the dogs with her.

-I want to offer you something.- Her heart pitched. Why had she
come here alone? He came   toward her. Would he throw her on the
ground? Kill her afterwards? She turned and ran. The dogs, upset by her
tone, tried to climb up her legs.

Edifice followed, calling, -If you let me cut some trees I'll bring you
half, all split if I can have half for myself. My land is hard to get at.-

She was trying to take it in. She didn't answer. Kept on running.

-You'll need wood for next year.-

-I have to talk to the rest of my family,- she called back. Didn't need
to call back. He was right behind her.

-I'll follow you down.- She ran, stumbling over rocks and roots. He
was as close as the dogs.   He whispered, -*Tempus fugit.*-

The dogs had stopped barking. She looked over her shoulder to see
where he was. He was no longer following. But in his eyes was a warning.
Her heart kept a quicker pace than her feet. Kill? She didn't really believe
he'd kill her. No, some other kind of death from this man, something in
herself.

Edifice felt that about her. She was peculiar enough to gall him. Gall
drove him after her, not down the path but to the side until he couldn't
see her anymore... through brambles and slick green grasses, over the
stone wall that led to the lane past their house.

The truth was he hadn't needed their woodlot. He just was snooping,
came to sneak past their house. He could get enough on his own property.
A stupid idea to offer his time cutting just so he could trade it. Okay, face
it. He had become increasingly inquisitive about them. Mostly her. Some
secret, not dead, but living in her. She didn't even look like anybody he
knew with her soft plumpness, her ribbony hair, black, shiny as a kitten's,
and her simmering eyes that in certain lights turned black-blue, like a
bruise. What had bruised them?

CHAPTER **12**

*P*ersons had slipped into the family like a new pet. Since Noncie realized she was only interested in a baby he became background to her, like a servant. Other things were on her mind. Damn, Hugh had arrived when she was in the village and she missed him. She barely controlled the urge to get in the car and race after him.

She put the groceries on the counter. -Does your supervisor like chicken?- She asked Persons.

-You mean Hugh?-

-Yes, does he care for chicken?

-No, all of us takes cares of the chickens.-

-I mean does he like to eat chicken?-

-He doesn't like to see blood spattered and heads chopped off and the chicken with his head off runs around like he's alive.-

She pursed her lips and waited until he was finished.

-What is his favorite food?-

-He likes a lot of butter, like me.-

Maybe she should fry the chicken, golden brown in butter, hoping she could do it right. Look it up in the White House cookbook. Florence and Papa's ears perked up.

Persons smiled. -You going over there to eat with him?-

-Oh no. I want to invite him here to dinner.-

A grin came across his small face and he jumped up and down like a five year old.

Noncie handed Persons the telephone and he asked the operator for the Children's' Home. She had rehearsed him carefully.

-Hugh, guess what? I have been learning to cook.- Pause. -Miss Noncie's teaching me, though she's learning too.-

Noncie quickly took the phone away. -Hi, we'd like you to come to Sunday dinner and see how Persons can cook now.-

-Why is your face red?- Persons asked her. My God, she hoped to heaven Hugh hadn't heard.

-That's very nice of you.-

-Let's say two p.m.- She was thinking that was plenty of time after any church service he might be attending.

Papa hearing, pinched Florence's arm. Florence nudged him with her foot. Good, is what they felt. But then he thought, Florence and he would be left alone if she moved out. He didn't want to imagine the house without Noncie trying to keep it all running right, her practical sense, her company.

Yet there were times when he dreamed of hurtling out of here, go on a trip, a cruise, an African Safari, but he was a liver-lilied, not enough courage to escape. Yeah, sure, like he could ever leave his darlings?

Sunday came. Florence kept the kitchen stove fed with wood. Each day she had meant to tell them about Edifice McHuron's offer to trade wood for cutting. But didn't want him around and anyway summer was about to bloom. And they would only need a little wood for cooking.

Every day she walked up that path with Persons and the dogs just to be sure that creep wasn't on their property and to gather fallen limbs to drag home. Papa had bought them a new ax, which nobody had tried yet.

On Sunday Noncie ran around the house, seeing that everything was in the best order. There was a lilac bush heavy with flopping blossoms at the beginning of the driveway. She carried the abundance like a bride, hugging them against her bright blue linen dress.

She filled two crystal vases, placing one on the long dining room table and one on the coffee table in the living room. She shut the door to the study where Papa paid the bills, corresponded with a few old friends, kept pictures of his tennis team in high school, his mill with all the hands in front, and one of Florence and Noncie as little girls in the Chicago park. He threw away the pictures of his wedding. Why, Noncie didn't know. Not a bit of order to the room. Important documents were at the lawyer's office back in Chicago. His money? Noncie had no idea.

He sometimes napped on a chaise longue they recently bought at an auction. Florence had painted the room red, even the floor, and touched up the floor before she'd gone up to bed last night. She often stayed up later than them, having trouble sleeping, no more nightcaps to help. She paced the floor or sat in the living room reading circle of hell in *Dante's Divine Comedy*...for some reason she refused to explain. Maybe, somewhat like witches in fairy tales she had read over and over as a child. Maybe the fear of hell kept her from pitching backward into her own hell.

The table she graced with amber Venetian glasses. Papa's gold-rimmed plates and the hand-wrought silver flatware, wedding presents, that he seemed not to dislike and wanted to give to a colored servant when they moved. But Noncie begged him not to. -Give her the silver-plated. They aren't worn.- So Papa did and the servant's happy tears slid down her cheeks.

Before Hugh arrived she went to the hall closet where on the door Florence had nailed up a mirror above the shelves with all their lipsticks now, and eyebrow pencils, pomades for their cheeks, a French eyelash curler, belladonna to widen their pupils, though Florence was using them up fast, piling them on as if icing a cake. Why? So her face would be hidden?

But when Noncie made herself up she panicked at the lipstick she had chosen—too garish—and rushed to scrub it off with cooking oil and start afresh.

She combed Persons' hair a couple of times. Papa stopped her. She was making him a ninny. Instead he gave the boy his Vitalis for checking his wild strands.

Persons careened down and out the door when the Ford drove up the driveway and Hugh, big slow moving Hugh, stepped out. Persons remembered to take him around to the front door and Noncie escorted him into the living room, hardly able to look at him.

-Would you have a little wine?- Papa asked.

How could he? Florence thought. So he had hidden a bottle just in case.

-Oh no thanks. I only drink a little at weddings or such, I mean not at all now with Prohibition.-

-We had this last bottle in our wine cellar long before Prohibition.- Noncie broke in.

-Lovely lilacs,- Hugh leaned close to smell.

-Do you like flowers?- Noncie asked, with a skittering voice. –I hope to figure out how to grow some here. In the city we called the florist. But how lovely to be able to cut my own.-

-Are you happy here?- He asked.

Florence quickly said, -We all love it here.-

Noncie said, -The countryside is like England (*though she had never been there*) lovely simple people. I mean uncomplicated.-

-Not so uncomplicated.- But he didn't enlarge.

Florence couldn't move her attention from the bottle. She grabbed it and ran to the kitchen. Noncie jumped up after her while mouthing an excuse. But when she ran into the kitchen Florence was pouring it into the sink.

-Good girl,- is all Noncie uttered and tenderly touched her shoulder.

Noncie announced that dinner was ready and Persons rose to express his glee, -Baked potatoes, string beans with peanut butter and me and Miss Noncie fried up a chicken. First wiped it dry, salt and peppered it. Dipped each piece in flour and dropped it into the hot butter. Slurp, sizzle, spit.-

Hugh smiled at Noncie.

Florence said, -Delicious.-

-Yes, indeedy, delicious,- Hugh echoed.

Noncie only dabbed at her food, too on pins and needles.

Persons served the dessert all by himself. But he broke in as Hugh was complimenting Noncie, -Nope, Miss Florence and I made the cake.-

Was this kid going to ruin everything? Noncie brooded. She'd like to get rid of all of them and have Hugh alone. When the meal was over she said, -I'd love for you to walk outside with me and maybe you could suggest what flowers to plant and where.-

He stood up and Florence caught Persons's arm so he wouldn't follow them,

-We'll clear the table and Papa will make after-dinner coffee for when they come back.-

Noncie led Hugh out to a meadow across the lane. -How are things working out with Persons?- He asked softly, leaning toward her.

-Just wonderful. He is such a good boy and of course I've had lots of experience as a social worker.- She hesitated over her lie before saying, -Making kids happy is the most important job in life.-

-Yes indeedy.- They walked deeper into the high grass. -A social worker. We have a lot in common. That was in Chicago?-

-Yes.- She wanted to change the subject.

-I'm impressed. I mean so difficult in a city. The problems must be overwhelming.-

-Yes indeedy,- she said kicking herself for copying him. -So where do you think I should put the garden?-

-This is a beautiful spot right here. Sun all day and perennials grow to giant size in Vermont. It's the cool nights.-

-I thought I would have a sliver of a moon-shaped garden.-

-Original. You're original.- He studied her.

She studied him, a foot taller than her, his swinging expressive hands, preacher-like.

-I would be happy to come see how things are doing. You have such an eye for beauty…along with being a beauty yourself.-

She could not choke out a thank you.

They walked farther from the house. He told her about delphinium, bottle gentian, musk roses and trillium she could dig from the woods, along with lady slippers. The way he said the names tickled her ear. He stopped close to her. Moisture seeped all across her skin.

-Maybe the gentian should go here where they would have space and seed themselves. Do you have a wet spot?-

God in heaven, what was he talking about? Did he know?

-Like over here,- he pointed, -looks bog-like but not too wet.-

She could hardly take it in.

-You can get the seeds down at the grain store. And I could bring you Shasta daisies next time, phlox and bee balm. They won't bloom for a year.-

- How can I wait?- She lifted her eyes to his.

-I know.-…He did not turn from her eyes. -But country people always wait. We're not in a hurry.-

My God, he wants me.

He took her elbow as they walked up the steps to the house. His fingers holding tightly confident as if he'd held her many times. –I will come back next week. Will you be here Wednesday afternoon?

The coffee was ready in the living room. But Hugh was missing, searching out the bathroom without asking. Noncie signaled to Papa to follow him and explain it was not toward the kitchen but up stairs. But Papa did not get to him fast enough and they heard a holler and they all charged to his study.

Hugh had opened the door and stepped right on the floor, which was still sticky from Florence's touching up.

-So sorry,- Noncie groaned. Noncie knelt and untied Hugh's shoes, and Papa helped take them off and he was able to step onto the safe dining room floor.

-Florence was supposed to put a sign on the door,- Noncie said, which was not true.

Persons said, -Your shoes looks like stepping in slaughtered blood, Hugh.-

Florence ran with the shoes out to the shed to get the turpentine and removed the paint. When he thanked Florence for removing the paint his mouth no longer had an appealing comfortable look.

After the coffee and fragmented conversation, and lingering embarrassment he said, -I better be going, thank you.- He turned to Noncie. - So enjoyable. I mean it. -

He put his arm around Persons so they could go to the car together and alone. Noncie stood at the kitchen door, her head way to one side to see better every footstep of Hugh's retreat. When he opened the car door he turned, found her and smiled so enthusiastically that her hands involuntarily lifted to her chest to keep her heart from hurtling to him.

After Papa and Persons had gone to bed Papa heard his girls in the kitchen. -Relax, so he stepped in wet paint.-

Papa sat up, but too weary to go down if a fight escalated. Then he heard drum rolls of laughter, followed by the soprano giggles, the way they so often solved their differences. He lay back down, sighing. Everything will be okay. He wanted everything to be okay so that he could sleep and so he wouldn't start thinking of his own sorrows and the lost love of his youth.

The next day Florence stopped by the sad little grocery. Seemed like less on the shelves each time and Miss Wilcox wasn't too interested in staying open many hours. She slept back of the counter on a canvas cot, snoozing away until mid-day. Had to wake her to get some service. Though if they knew the price the customer might leave the money. Florence called out. No sound.

Miss Wilcox sat up -For godsake what do you want? Can't you see I'm sleeping?-

-We're running out of toilet paper.-

- Don't you have a sears roebuck catalogue?-

-Yes, but...- Was she serious?

-I'll sell you two rolls to hold you over.- And then she quickly escorted Florence, taking her arm, right out the door. –Londonderry has a lot of toilet paper.-

As she hurried away Florence thought, good for Wilcox. Nobody was going to take away her freedom just for money. Why had she let Noncie and Papa take her freedom away? What a weakling she was, came here with no hope of indulging. This place was dry as a bone, or was it? Get rid of that thought. She was good now, three months and eleven days. She stopped at the post office to pick up her monthly letter from the lawyer with Irving's alimony check.

Just before the bridge she spotted McHuron walking toward her. She walked faster, not taking another glance, but when she stepped on the covered bridge, -Hello,- came from behind her.

She pretended not to hear him, counting on the klump, klump of the wooden boards.

-Have you talked over the firewood with your family?- He was next to her, stroking his beard that looked trimmed.

-No thank you,- she told him even though she hadn't asked them and wasn't about to.

-You're making a mistake.-

-I've made plenty of mistakes in my life.- She thought he said, me too, but they were near the grain store and the voice of Mrs. Browning yelling into Mr. Browning's deaf ear, quickly obliterated his answer. Florence pretended she needed something in the grain store.

When she came out, Edifice was gone, thank God. At the hill she opened her letter and had to endure an emotional freeze that Irving Polver was still alive.

CHAPTER 13

*D*on't bring anything, Irving Polver had told her, not even panties. But she had slipped two new pairs into her pocketbook. And she couldn't leave the cameo that her father had placed around her neck on her sixteenth birthday eight days before, the day she'd finished high school with highest honors.

At a graduation party Papa had invited all her friends who beamed at her but nothing about them mattered. Her eyes were fixed on the sky, waiting for the last of summer light to fade.

Noncie and Papa were asleep at last.

Everything wonderfully exaggerated, the sweltering air, her prickling fear, and overwhelming joy. Dangerous territory, a serious grownup, a creature like none other in the world. Rich black hair and tiny mustache, flat oval lips and asymmetrical eyes, the brown of mink—-holding his hand, running for the taxi.

He paid the taxi from a roll of money.

-Did you write your parents a note?- she asked.

-Look kid, men don't write notes to their parents.-

-How are we going to live?-

-I inherited enough money from my grandpa to take us from heaven to hell and back for the rest of our lives and for all our household staff when we build our home.

Little shivers pinched down her arms.

She had written a note to Papa and Noncie. But erased it. Started again. She couldn't explain her behavior. And down deep a smidgeon of truth bubbled up. Papa didn't approve, never would approve of Irving. And of course she was under age. But she felt bad about Noncie not being able to help plan the wedding, pick the bridesmaids' dresses, the flowers.

Help her pack nightgowns, lace slips, chenille, cashmere suits and splendid evening gowns for her honeymoon.

She didn't think about her dead mother, gone five years before. She felt a distance from her anyway. Something about Papa's coldness toward her mother...that would take more years to understand. Florence's note to Papa and Noncie said: -I'll telegraph you soon as we arrive where we will be living after Irving and I become husband and wife. Love to you both, Florence.- But she crossed out Florence and signed, Flossy.

Irving had brought a small suitcase. When they had settled in their train seat she said, -I thought you told me we were buying everything in New York?-

-This is for our trip now.-   He unbuckled the leather bag with three bottles and two silver goblets.

She squealed as he pulled the cork and the champagne splattered over them, -A blessing, a baptism for you.- He poured and his lips kissed hers so abruptly he nearly spilled the bottle.

Although she thought she couldn't drink any more he opened another bottle. She had never felt like this, well maybe once when she had had a high fever with measles... dizziness with increasing   upsetting velocity.

-I can't drink anymore.-

Come on kid, keep up. This is our night to kick society in the butt.-

They sat up. He hadn't ticketed them into a sleeper and told her why. –Because we're celebrating until we get to the Plaza Hotel in New York City, and we can sleep it off for days. Maybe the Plaza will be our permanent residence after we go to Maryland to get married.-

But her nausea was full blown. She ran to the tiny bathroom in the swaying train and threw up over the floor and toilet and felt obliged to wipe them clean with toilet paper almost throwing up again from having to clean up. Back in their seat he had fallen asleep and she did also lying against him, thrilled and queasy at the same time. She had run away like a wild unstoppable horse jumping its corral...eyes flashing.

Is this a castle?- she asked as they entered the Plaza.

He raised his eyebrows.

They slept all day, rolling into each other's naked bodies and that night he said, -Now you are no longer a girl.- And she thought she was in an English novel. She couldn't remember the details. Too hung over. He wasn't brutal or anything like that, but he conveyed to her that she was his. She was his object and she loved being his object as he vigorously took her, but did he actually say, -I'm ramming you to the quick.- Or was that a distorted memory?

Money poured out of him. He was drunk on money and drunk on booze and the very next day they hit every important store in town including Tiffany's and a well-known boutique on Fifth Avenue. Clothes were made, clothes were delivered and tried on and altered. A hairdresser came to their suite. Irving said, -do something about her forlorn hair.-

Afterwards Florence put the curling iron to her hair but kept it on too long and some ends were burnt into scorched hay so he bought her three new hats. Irving decided on a tailor who spoke only French but Irving could respond in French. Florence was allowed in the fitting room and watched as the measuring tape measured the inseam and she shut her eyes against a storm of desire.

Two days later he bought a car, a Rolls Royce, and drove them to Maryland where they became man and wife and then sped right back to the Plaza. If her father found her he could drag her home, annul the marriage for being under age. But she didn't worry too much. This was a big city and she was in a swim of headiness beyond fear.

Irving taught her to be a connoisseur. He tested her memory. They analyzed the flavor, running the wines around their mouths to sensitize their taste buds. She had rebelled slightly, just slightly, because one day she was too under the weather. She cried. All of it was too much for her to fathom, but he coached her, complimented her.

-What a girl. Look how you can hold your own. You'll soon be up to capacity.-

(whatever that meant). Five whole days it took before she even telephoned Papa. When Papa heard her voice he tried to control his angry tears just so he could find out where she was.

-Oh Papa, I'm a married woman.-

-You waited five days to call me? Noncie and I called everybody we knew. Irving's own parents hadn't heard hide nor hair from him.-

Papa didn't tell her he had called the police and hired a detective.

A pause. -I'm Sorry, Papa, but we are having the time of our lives.-

-You know full well what I think of him. I'll see to it he goes to jail for kidnapping.-

-Oh please Papa. Please don't. I love him.-

-You sound drunk.- His voice was breaking.

-Don't be silly. Irving is here and we're going to dinner. He's holding my new silk coat. Papa be sure to water my cactus plant.-

-Wait, Noncie wants to say something.-

-Oh honey, please come home. Papa is nearly having a breakdown, I beg you.-

-Don't worry, we'll come back as soon as I'm of age. I'll call again real soon. Don't you worry. Please, you and Papa don't do anything. I'll call you every week now.-

When she hung up she felt a long moment of twanging pain.

More than a month went by, living like that, and instead of calling home she wrote letters, afraid to hear their voices, all with glowing reports, theater, opera, dinners, aged wines and sending her love with abundant kisses.

Some days their feet never hit the floor, never out of bed, but she couldn't recall their lovemaking. Only that his body was a heavy mass on her, where he often fell asleep.

By Christmas she was into her cups as much as he, couldn't wait to get some liquor in her, couldn't wait to get to the nightclub and talk to other partygoers, other rich people, imbibing bums. When they shopped she sent presents to Papa and Noncie and their cook and even to the dogs, little coats to keep them warm, woven in Labrador.

God, what a wonderful life. Hadn't crossed her mind what she had become. She thought she was just a gay party girl, knock them dead with bright talk and humor, school girl uppity tales and she charmed the pants off the men with her intelligence and he, Irving, charmed the girls dancing with them and she beamed at how the girls were wide-eyed over him. She had a prize and they knew it.

She wondered if Noncie and Papa realized that Chicago didn't hold a dime to New York? But she longed to see them. Thought about them more and more. She wanted to show them New York. Someday maybe Irving would let her bring them to New York.

Christmas day she telephoned. She had telegraphed them 100 red roses.

Noncie said coldly, -100 roses instead of you? That's supposed to make us feel just dandy?-

And Papa couldn't help his sobbing, -I promise you I won't touch Irving, Just come.-

Florence held the receiver away so she wouldn't hear his sobs.

-If you loved me, Papa, you'd want me to be happy.-

-Come on,- Irving shouted, -the cab is waiting.-

-Papa, got to go. Merry Christmas.- She hung up and said to Irving, -Call the room service, for a quick one.-

-You telling me what to do, slavey? Okay, a little drink.-

As she drank a great relief washed over her. She pushed the word happy around, letting the liquor thin her anxiety and swallow up her haunting thoughts. That night she woke shaking. She could not remem-

ber exactly what her father or her sister looked like. But there was something that seeped into her soaked consciousness, something wonderful.

She thought of the right moment to tell him and changed her mind
every day and decided suddenly in the cab they were taking uptown to a
Harlem club. At 110th street she blurted out, -I'm pregnant.-

He was silent.

-We're going to have a baby.-

-The hell we are.-

He was silent all the way there and all the way home and in the club
she saw him from a distance as if she were bird watching through the
wrong end of field glasses. He had danced and stumbled with one woman
after the next and one irate husband had punched him in the stomach
and Irving crumpled to the floor. Smaller into the distance he became, yet
poignant was his handsome face and she wanted their child to have his
face. She wanted their child to look just like all of him. He would get used
to the idea. He would love the idea.

He didn't dance with her that night, but she didn't care. She was not
feeling so hot. She drank little. She knew he'd need time to digest that he
was going to be a father and allow his brain to have an overnight rest.

The next day he said, before they had had enough sleep, -Get dressed,
nothing too fancy.-

-Where are we going?-

-You'll see. Something exciting.- He took her hand to pull her along.

Her heart was beating fast. What exciting event was he taking her to
now? To purchase baby clothes, maternity outfits? Way down in lower
Manhattan. -I've never been here,- she said.

-Right. Something different.-

-What's here?-

He didn't answer but took hold of her arm as if escorting her across a
dangerous gully.

They were in the warehouse district. He knocked on a metal door and
a man opened it. Irving shook his hand. -This is Florence.-

The man was dressed in a white coat. She knew then. She turned to
run. Irving thrust himself at her, holding her around the waist. She
screamed and wriggled. Another man, with a huge neck and huge arms,
grabbed her up. She kicked and screamed, -No.-

Irving slapped his hand over her screaming mouth. –Stop this. We'll
get arrested.-

The man in white opened another door. –It will be okay. Done before
you know it.-

She screamed into Irving's sweaty palm.

The muscle man laid her on a cold metal table. She scrambled to the edge, but Irving rushed to hold her down. She tried to sit up.

Push, break away. Pull her mouth free she screamed.

-Shut the fuck up,- Irving said. -You're in goddamed trouble and we're fixing it.-

The other man strapped her across her belly.

–Why? Why are you doing this?-

-Don't worry. You'll be good as new.- The man in white said in a calm voice.

I'm going to die, she thought and cried for her Papa. He won't even know where I am. The other man pulled her knees up. The man in white pulled off her panties. She struggled, tried to kick him but he succeeded and threw her panties on the floor. Irving covered her eyes with his hand. -It will be over in no time.-

-It's our baby. Why are you killing our baby?- She screamed.

Irving slapped his hand down on her mouth so hard she couldn't move her head. She sobbed in muffled gasps. The muscle man held her knees apart until her hips felt broken. Irving turned his head to watch the killing.

She thrust her knee into his face. Irving's rampant rage became so swollen it burst like an enormous cyst. He squeezed her legs back farther, holding her knees to her chest until she gasped.

A freezing instrument tore at her some deep place, some place that would never heal.

She barely heard the executioner murmur. -There, there. There, there. I got it. Here it comes.-

Gushing blood. Plop into a pail. Irving forcing whiskey down her gagging throat. More blood. Baby blood. Reeked of the freshness of new life. All over her, the floor, the executioner's shoes.

She could not remember the executioner's face. Was he in black, though wasn't he in white? Didn't he have a black hood over his face and wasn't a cleaver in his hands? Didn't he chop up the baby? Throw the bits in a pail. Pail and all into a dumpster…

In her dreams his instrument grew larger, sharper, a guillotine. Their baby's head rolling down streets, across fields, floating in a red sea of blood.

He wiped her down with gritty towels. Cramped and weak, they made her stand, and in such pain she couldn't speak. Irving rummaged in his briefcase for a clean towel and stuffed it into her panties, which he had picked up off the floor and didn't even shake out before putting them on her.

He patted her head. -Like new.-

Back in their room Irving said, -Good girl. Champion girl.- He poured her a drink without ice. She would not look at his eyes, even his face. And the next day filled with pain, body and soul, he said, -Come on Florence, we'll going shopping, get you all new outfits and throw away the past.-

She didn't budge from bed, turned her face to the wall. -Okay, I'll get them myself.- He slammed the door behind him.

She stuffed another towel in her panties. She grabbed what money Irving had lying around. Terrified that the doorman wouldn't find a cab immediately and terrified Irving would find her at the railroad station, bring more men with knives. Inside the station she found a shop. She bought a scarf for over her head and another for her shoulders. She left her new fur coat in the ladies room.

As she waited for the gate to the platform to be opened there he was, looking for her. Was it Irving? Why was Irving everywhere? All the men were Irving. Wobbly and bleeding she made it into the train.. She found a seat and waited to be captured. All the way to Chicago, all the way to their apartment, not until she was inside the door and collapsed into Papa's arms was she free. No, not entirely. Would Irving come and kill her? Yet it didn't matter. He already had.

CHAPTER 14

*N*oncie sighed at the thought it would be a whole week until Hugh came again. Keep the house in perfect order. But her vision made it difficult to spot dust. She asked Florence to help and she gladly whisked a cloth around, singing off tune to the rhythm of her flitting.

Florence was amused at how Noncie acted like a doctor eliminating a dread disease, so fervent was her dedication to attacking dirt. She rearranged her new displays of stoneware. She filled a large Bennington crock with apple blossoms from up in the orchard.

It occurred to Florence that Noncie revealed herself in painting the living room virgin white and over that she laid a big black male bear rug...in hopes? Only trouble was the big black bear was dead. She felt sad at the thought. Yet she remembered her bedroom floor painted hopefully with bright, plump apples.

Florence wondered about herself deciding on blood red for Papa's study. Maybe because of how she felt about men, a big red flag, a stop sign. She loved trying to be psychological. She had recently read some of Freud.

That afternoon she took Persons and the dogs up into the woods where she had seen Edifice. She peered into the thicket, just to be sure he wasn't spying. No McHuron. He probably really did hide a gun that day when he heard her coming. She would feel better if she had a gun.

The air was brightly filled with warmth and a breeze through the infant tree leaves pulsed, sighed and calmed her.

-Persons, what are you doing? Take that out of your mouth.-

-It's spruce gum.-

-Sap.- she scolded.

-Try it, please.- He held her a sticky glob. -We all chews it.-

What the heck. She chewed slowly. The flavor was a combination of mint and burnt coca. She laughed. –Not bad.- He laughed too, showing the gap in his teeth where some was stuck.

A gun. Yes.

She seized Person's shoulders, turned him around, back to the barn. He followed her through woods, the crunch of twigs, last fall's leaves, and over sharp rocks, fast. The dogs ran ahead of them, turning now and then to see if they were coming.

She asked Persons if he knew how to use a gun.

-No.-

-Me neither.- But two days earlier she had seen a pamphlet lying on a beam in the barn next to a rifle. –I think we're going to learn-

-Yippee-

-Let's keep it a secret until we know how. okay?-

Persons jumped up and down.

-After you learn you'll never go hungry. Shoot yourself rabbits and deer when you are grown. You will never be hungry.-

She read him the instructions. -Load a Muzzleloader by inserting lead components into the bore way of the muzzle. This necessitates the shooter's fingers to be directly in front of the muzzle during most of the loading process. It doesn't take much imagination to realize what could happen if the gun should accidentally discharge during loading or cleaning.-

Persons was biting his lip. -Use a mark on the ramrod to make sure the rifle is not loaded. Wipe the bore free of oil. Measure the powder charge and pour it through the muzzle. Lubricate the bullet. Seat it. Cock the hammer and slip the cap over the nipple. Keep the muzzle pointed away for safety. When ready, shoot.-

-I don't think I can learn that.- He fidgeted.

-We'll learn it together. We can practice up in the woods shooting at a tree. Good thing powder doesn't rot like apples.- She had found a box full.

-I know somebody got killed by a gun up in North Dummerston. Kyle's brother Simon shot him over a game of Parcheesi. That's why I never play Parcheesi.-

-We will be very safe with the gun. I promise.-

The gun felt odd in her hands, too big and heavy. She had never touched anything that felt that foreign or powerful. Made her want to be reckless. Made her want to have a drink.

They sneaked some straw from around Papa's garden, tied it to make a loose target in a tree crotch. She hid the gun in the woods . Florence told

Noncie and Papa that Persons was helping her give the dogs a run every day.

They practiced how to hold the gun up against their shoulders and how to place their head and eye to see the target. She stood behind him with her hand on his other shoulder to give him confidence. His bones were small, unformed like his mind. She wondered where he would go after leaving them. She hoped not so far that they wouldn't see him.

CHAPTER 15

*H*e was figuring the village was empty and quiet when he made his way up to the hill. Suspecting he was fooling himself, Edifice traveled different routes so nobody would know what he was up to. For a while he and Gerty had a cow. He bought it when he came home from Harvard and when he proposed to Gerty. He figured a baby would need a cow. Later he used the cow for an excuse to go up that long hill to his pastureland each day. But the cow died a few months back. Now it was more dangerous.

Behind bars? Made him hyperventilate just thinking about even a speck of liberty stolen. But nothing was on his breath. The purity of vodka. And his fellow villagers had their own problems, trying to get enough food for the next winter and no real income…mostly shooting or trading help. A roof leaked they'd go over and help, needed to depend on one another. Edifice almost fell off the Prichard's roof, being too much in his cups. But there were some who wouldn't do anything for anybody and some with grudges that Edifice didn't even know why.

Today just as he was going up the meadow he spotted Dr. Peabody. Toughest bird ever and he was never going to forgive her for what she'd done to him. After nine years he could still feel pain. Nothing bothered Peabody. She could pull up her boots, make her way through snow or rainstorms, and wade through mud or water with her worn physician's black bag, looking like a bank robber.

Up on Glebe mountain a snowy day where Dimmy John was cutting trees with other men a huge elm fell on him, mangled his leg and right there on the spot she, gave him a shot of whiskey, pulled out her saw and while the men held his shoulders, sawed his leg off and quickly lit a candle and cauterized his stump. Dimmy John fainted. One man threw up but all of them were in awe, admired her and thought of her as one of the

72

men, even Dimmy John. They glorified the slight-built courageous woman. Whenever somebody described some callous way she handled them inevitably someone else would answer, -Well, she saved my life, or she always gives my kid a lollypop.-

As she had grown older, maybe fifty now, the topknot on her head was tighter and higher but also fuller, like a well-made bird's nest. People liked that she was plain. -Lie up there, Mr. or Mrs., girly or boy,- never their name.

Edifice thought of her as a car mechanic. Patients were chassis, carburetors, combustion engines and exhaust pipes. She was a little more personal to Gerty and called her by name.

He could spot her far off, her stride as wide as long clippers cutting at the air, and her man boots, to which she attached tiny bells, jingled wherever she went. Some kid got the nerve up to ask her why she wore bells, and she answered with the grin that showed her upper gum. -Girly, I wear them to warn all kinds of birds that I'm coming.-

Whatever the hell that meant.

Edifice felt very differently about her, but she was the only physician for miles. The day of the accident, nine years before, Edifice had been splitting wood with his ax and the ax slipped and when he had cleared the blood, he saw that his finger was dangling.

-Lay out your hand there.- Peabody had pointed to a table beside the examining table. She was positioned in such a way she blocked his view. She told him it would hurt a bit. He thought the stitches. But after his holler he stood up and saw her throwing his finger in the trash. Blackness took him and he nearly keeled over.

-What did you do? What did you do?- He hollered.

-Couldn't save the damned thing.- (like it was too rusted or worn out.) He staggered to the door. His mind in paralysis.

-Wait a minute Mr. I got to bandage it.- But he skidded down the steps, holding his finger wrapped in his shirt tail and leaving a trail of blood like Hansel and Gretel. He reached the end of the street when Tom Long, his good friend who had moved away now, found him and rushed him home to bandage him and made him stay a bit.

He thought about Tom. They had skied in their long Norwegian skies, out to see the owls or woodpeckers, just to be in what they loved, never tiring of the family of mountains that they rediscovered each season, each day as the sun slipped shadows across them or swift clouds shimmered over them and gave them the illusion that the peaks were gently shaking.

Looking at nature now pointed out his loneliness...the oppressing fog that hit the valley at a running pace. Lonely young waving grass. Every bud, every bird chirping had some birth of expectancy when he had none.

When he sat and read he felt better. He tried to save enough money from selling wood to the Flood Brook School so he could buy books from a catalogue. Actually he felt contented a lot of the time. That was his nature.

But Florence Logan was causing him unsettling discomfort, her pretense of elegance and her haughtiness. He pulled at his beard and sat up all night in the rocker inside the shack of the still, drinking himself to sleep.

The next day on his way home he rested against the walls of the covered bridge when Florence Logan walked by, looking feathery-soft and round as a partridge. He blocked her.

-Hello.-

She spun around with a look of panic. -Why are you always in my way?-

-That's awful rude for a lady.-

-What do you want?-

-What's your hurry?-

-You're standing too close.- She shoved him in the chest. -Out of my way.-

-I wouldn't be too impolite if I were you. You might need more wood someday.-

She rushed on but so shaken she had to stop on the other side. What was she having here, an apoplexy attack? Where did he get it? He didn't smell of anything but there was no question anymore.

CHAPTER **16**

$\mathcal{P}$apa filled his pipe with Virginia tobacco. Afraid of using up the best Dunhill's from London and maybe not being able to get more. He used the good stuff when he was feeling low. Bellowing out a cursing session might also relieve him. When Florence and Persons were walking the dogs he stood under the big thorn tree across the lane to his garden. He swore out the explosive words he had learned from his mill-hands.

-Goddamned, fuck, bunghole cunt, shit,- when he couldn't go farther with the list he started over again. What brought this on was thinking of his dead wife. He envisioned those two women Clara Brighten and Olivia Seward. Olivia became his wife. Although the women had lived in different towns, each knew he was squiring the other. His buddies envied him with the beauties and getting away with it. The awful part was he thought he was in love with both.

He just couldn't make up his mind. They didn't look a thing alike. Clara was a redhead, not the flaming kind, the kind that looked like a cross section of a cedar tree. He could still remember her mint-sweetness when her face brushed against his, her lips pressed his.

For more than two years he was tortured by loving them both. He could see in their eyes they were also. Each time he came home from a date with one he decided she was the one. But the next day his feelings would be confused. One day at his flourmill window he saw Clara walk by, her pungent red hair, fluttering ribbons in the late afternoon light. She was holding her father's arm looking up to his face with such tenderness. Clara, the unadorned beauty, pure, innocent and filled with love. He realized he loved only her.

But when he arrived home that day a letter was sitting on the hall table. He wished he had never read it. Oh God, how he wished he had not believed the contents, had understood the conniving.

75

Without knowing he had betrayed Clara.

He was a betrayer. Take Florence. He should have hired more detectives to capture that despicable Irving. Why hadn't he? He had indulged her, hurt her character. He was a weak father, gave in. He had let that bastard ruin his daughter's life.

Papa dug an angry hoe around the beans. Yet planting gave him a sense of hope and soothed his longing for his friends and culture. When he wasn't depressed he thought his life now meant something, something noble by rescuing his darling Florence.

*P*ersons wore his new blue jeans that Noncie had bought him. She was working on keeping him neat for Hugh. She hoped Hugh wouldn't notice how difficult the chiaroscuro of bright days was for her. She had to tilt her head this way and that, like a listening bird, since only her peripheral vision was left.

She had rearranged the furniture so when she sat opposite him she wouldn't have to look directly at the sunny windows yet they would give pleasant light to her features. People told her she looked stunningly young in spite of her prematurely white curls

When he knocked on the door, six days since the last time, she sauntered to answer. Don't seem too eager.

-I brought you something.- Hugh handed her a box full of plants.

Delphinium and Shasta and a few coreopsis.-

She beamed and laid the box on the kitchen table as she explained that Persons was out in the barn with Florence.-

-I'll see Persons in a bit. Let's walk out in the field to look for trillium or lady slippers and figure out where to plant these.-

As they stepped out the front door, he touched her arm. From that gesture, that big smile she visualized another garden, one at the orphanage with Hugh and her making rows, kneeling together in the loam. She would have said a fond goodbye to Florence and Papa…but of course inviting them every Sunday to dinner to play with their baby.

They were standing in the field opposite the house when he said, -How gracious everything is here. - He leaned toward her, -mostly the company, that is present company.-

Noncie's mind leaped like a young colt. Perhaps it was here that they would live and he would commute to work and Papa and Florence would move back to Chicago. She and Hugh would sit here in this house with a blazing winter fire rocking the cradle.

-Let's sit here.- He pointed to a fallen log near the edge of the bog, out of sight of the house. When he sat next to her, their hips touched. Her breathing stopped and started with a small gasp.

He asked, -Do you mind if I ask you something?-

-No.-

-Have you ever lost a love?-

-No.- She wouldn't tell him about the failed attempts of love.

-Though you never get over the loss, lately I feel differently about my wife. My grief is not raw and painful. It has filmed over like a scar. While her spirit has invited me with her. I'm accepting she is gone but not lost. Am I making sense?-

-Yes.- But where was he going with this?

She brought me to the Home. She was the one who wanted to work there and now I have to, no want to, carry on her work in commemoration. I promised to be father to them all. And slowly I am, I think.-

Her heart sinking, -You love her still.-

– I'm lonely.- His eyes were scanning hers.

She couldn't speak…the expectancy.

He picked up her hand. –It's wonderful that you have come here to live -

Her face was hot.

-Persons is special to me. I don't know why. Perhaps something about his trust. My wife and I didn't have children. There was something amiss in her, the doctor told us. We were very sorry, I think particularly me. The boys were enough for her." They stood up.

I'd like to come see you often. Is that okay?-

-Yes. Oh yes.-

He leaned toward her, his lips touching hers when they heard Persons calling, -Hugh.-

Hugh pulled away and rushed toward him. Noncie, slow to rise out of her trance, followed.

Persons came running from the barn and shouting -Hugh, Hugh.- He was swinging the rifle. Hugh stopped. Noncie stopped just behind him. Florence ran toward Persons, her arms out and shouting, -Stop.-

Nobody knew how it happened. Was his hand on the trigger the whole way? Did he mistakenly pull it? All they knew was that Hugh cried out as the bullet struck him. Florence leapt toward Persons, Noncie toward Hugh.

-Drop the gun,- Florence shouted. Persons dropped the gun as they all surrounded Hugh.

-Where are you hit?- Noncie cried.

He held his leg to stop the rush of blood. Papa heard the shot and ran from the garden, saw Persons crying and the others helping Hugh into the kitchen. Noncie grabbed a towel and knelt to press the cloth on his wound just above his ankle and when she withdrew it she discovered, he had only been grazed, thank God.

-I didn't mean it, Hugh. Miss Florence was teaching me so I could kill rabbits to eat. She told me it was a surprise, not to tell. I just wanted to...-

Hugh touched his arm to show him he understood. Noncie collapsed on a chair.

-Miss Logan taught you to use a gun?-

Florence said nothing.

-You told him not to tell,- Hugh shouted at Florence.

-Yes she did,- Persons said. -You weren't supposed to know, yet. A surprise.-

-And you. You knew about this.?- Hugh addressed Noncie.

-No, I...-

-You were supposed to know what was going on.-

-Miss Florence played with me the most,- Persons said. -I think she liked me the most. Miss Florence took me up in the field to practice every day.- Persons snuffled and rubbed his eyes with his knuckles. -I wanted to surprise you. I couldn't wait. I wanted so bad to show you, Hugh. I wasn't going to shoot it. It was the gun, not me. Not me. It just went bang.-

Bandaged and his shoe back on Hugh stood up. He looked at Noncie, not Florence.

-There is no good sense in this household. And we were lucky this is all that happened.-

Florence said, -Don't blame the others, it was me.-

-Persons go get your belongings please,- Hugh said. -We're going home.-

Persons eagerly obeyed. -This won't happen again,- Florence said. - We like him so much. Nothing like that will happen again. – She felt sick for Noncie.

-Certainly not,- Hugh said. Noncie was too mortified to stay near him. She went with Persons to help him pack. She said -I'll miss you, Persons. -

Persons said, -Thank you. But mostly I'll miss Miss Florence.-

Hugh opened the trunk of the car. Persons put his suitcase in. Noncie stood on the kitchen steps. Persons waved to Papa and Florence on the lawn. Hugh was looking at Noncie as he stepped in the car. He shook his head, not in an accusing way but with sadness.

-You ruined...- Noncie said to Florence. -Do you never think or have any kindness for anyone else? You've wasted your life. And you killed the one chance I had.-

Noncie ran upstairs to weep.

The next day Florence walked up into the orchard to lick her wounds. Not until nearly dark did she return. Trying to think about how to fix what happened and knowing she could not. Her hair was a scramble of tangles, her skirt torn. Almost dark she slipped into the house.

Noncie was sitting with her head in her hands.

-I'm so sorry.-

-Maybe he'll think it over and...- Papa said, trying not to believe the truth.

Noncie did not answer him.

The silence went on for days. What could be said? Breakfasts and lunches, which Florence hardly ate, were excruciating. And Noncie took to her room all afternoon. Maybe this was the way they would live now. Hurt, hurt, hurt, hurt, Papa thought.

Florence thought, what use was her life? She must think of some way to live. She thought of helping Papa in the garden but when she entered the gate he didn't talk much and when she asked if she could help him, he said, -No thank you.-

She retreated, holding her hands together as if to comfort herself. That afternoon she filled her pocket with money. She left when they didn't see her, careening fast down their lane and out to the hill road. She walked slowly past the mansion house.

She paced up and down the two-block street. A few people greeted her as she passed. But her eyes were peering everywhere. Everywhere, everywhere for him. In her growing desperation she began spinning and pacing faster.

She thought she saw him way at the end of the street toward the cheese factory. Yes. There he was, thank God. Good he didn't see her. She followed his ambling and snatching gait in the distance. Just past the factory he turned abruptly as if he suddenly made up his mind where he was headed, up and across an empty field.

She looked carefully about hoping that nobody noticed her. Up the long slope she watched him go behind some trees. She took a deep breath and climbed, frightened that she had lost him when he appeared again. This time he was running over a bumpy hill and down the other side.

Out of breath, up the slope and over the rise she spotted the roof of a shack. He slipped in and shut the door. On cat's feet she approached, but stood outside, waiting to store up bravery before tentatively knocking on his door.

Who in the world would be coming here? Edifice's heart and body lurched to peer through a crack. Couldn't believe his eyes and yet he had wondered if someday this wouldn't happen. He opened the door. –What are you doing here? This is private property. What do you want?–

-You know.-

-No, I don't.- But he knew perfectly well.

-Please.-

He was going to make her say what she came for and then refuse her. She had been so haughty with him but most of all her coming was dangerous.

-I want what you're making.-

His anxiety was growing. -And where did you get the idea I was making anything? Who said I was making anything?–

-Nobody.-

-Then what are you here for?-

-I need...please,- Florence begged.

He leaned against the door jam, crossing his ankles and looking at her. -Go.-

When she looked like she was going to cry empathy grabbed him. Alike the two of them, listening to the same music, the needle scratching the record into a groove of no escape.

-You say what you are here for or I'll shut the door.-

She couldn't get the word out. They looked at each other. -Vodka you must be making. I don't smell it on you. I just see it on you. One drink, that's all I want. Of course I won't tell anyone.-

-One drink? Is that right?-

-Yes, I just want one drink. I don't crave it. I just like it, I mean once in a great while. I'll pay you, of course. -

One drink, who was she kidding? -I don't have a glass.-

-That's all right. I'll drink out of the jug.-

-How would I know how much you drank in one gulp to be able to set the price?- he teased.

-Come on, any price you want.- Fear was squeezing hard on her.

-Okay, how many swallows would you want?- He wondered if she'd leave lipstick on the top from gobs covering her lips.

-I don't know until I start swallowing. How much will it cost per swallow?-

-Forty bucks.-

-I could buy this whole village for that.- She laughed with sarcasm.

-Sorry.- He didn't want her here again.

-Okay, I'll buy a whole jug,-

-No jugs... I'm not selling you jugs so you can carry them through the village with everybody hanging out the windows.-

-I told you I want one drink.-

-One drink today.-

-What do you think I am, an alcoholic?-   He opened his mouth but decided not to prolong any of this.

-Okay, today, that's it. It will cost you one buck no matter how much you go at it. Be quick about it.-

-You going to drink, too?-

-You mean because we're going to drink out of the same jug?-

-No,- she hesitated, -because I hate drinking alone.-

He took off his cap and ran his fingers through the mash of his thick hair. He reached over onto the makeshift table, sawhorses and a slate slab, took off a jug and passed it to her. She looked at the jug... the poison... as if this would be her last drink, and death would come immediately.

She wiped it with the palm of her left hand. She put it to her lips and sipped. She closed her eyes and let the liquor ripple down her esophagus, down through the parched tunnel to the long empty station, and home. Right now, that's all she would think about. They passed the jug back and forth.

-Why are you really living here?- he asked after they were mellow.

-We like it here.-

-Bullshit,- he said.

-Don't talk that way to me.-

-Hey, lady you're on my territory. You rob a bank or something?-

She stared at him.

He took a long swig to cinch the flames attacking him. What was the mystery about this woman? He wanted to know but he also wanted to get her out of his life. He was in a pickle now that she knew about his still.

The afternoon light was fading. He was sitting on the steps, she on a rock. He staggered to his feet. -I have to go. And you shouldn't come again. I mean that.-

-Don't worry. I only wanted one drink.- She believed it.

-You go first, the way you came.- She put one foot ahead of the other in staggering care. She had to take her time in order to sober up.

He watched her, feeling something. Was it sympathy, or a mirror of himself? Was it, because he understood her, even knowing nothing about her?

CHAPTER **19**

$\mathcal{F}$or good luck Papa swore under his breath.

-What did you say?- Noncie asked. -I couldn't quite hear.-

-Nothing, just coughing,- he called back from his room.

Florence hadn't risen. She had come in late afternoon and climbed straight into to bed telling them she had one of her terrible sinus headaches. Not until noon did she arrive in the kitchen for some coffee.

-So,- Noncie said, -drinking it black?- The cow creamer was staring at her from the middle of the table. But Noncie didn't really care what she might be doing. This was the first she had spoken to Florence in the days since the gun incident. -Why did you teach him to shoot?-

Florence almost answered, *for the stars.* -So he'd be able to shoot his own food. So he could grow up and be independent. That's all I wanted. He sneaked the gun before I could …-

Noncie waved her hand to stop her. -I've got to live, don't I? I wish you had never been born.-

-I wish I hadn't been born either,- Florence said.

-I wish I hadn't been born, either,- Papa said. Florence smiled then laughed, not from the irony, or even relief, but for the ridiculousness of the three of them. Noncie began to snicker. They laughed together as insiders, as a unit, and the formidable dark began drifting away. Noncie served them bacon and eggs and cornbread in the pan to keep it hot, laying it on the dish towel on the table.

She laid on top the silver serving trowel with L carved on the handle.

Florence thanked her. –You're the best sister.-

Florence thought, only one mishap. Just one slipup. She was really a changed person. I'm dry. I'm okay. She wouldn't go near Edifice McHuron again. She'd had her little detour and was back on the road.

She thought of her love for basil. That was it, she would start an herb garden for Noncie's cooking.

The garden would be designed to look lovely until late fall. She'd dry herbs in the barn. Some to hang in the kitchen. She planned the garden out near the barn, nearer the house than Papa's. Florence could see him from hers. He was out working all the time, his skin bronzing in the high sun. From a distance she sometimes didn't recognize him. He looked straight and handsome and she imagined him a young man strolling in the evening with his cane, and tipping his hat to other strollers, women drawn to him.

She had just the right spot to make a garden and she would tell them…all for Noncie. Though he was awkward with her still she said, - Papa, maybe someday we can have another boy from the home. I miss him, like you do.-

-I hope so.- But there was hesitation in the word hope.

She found a string, laid it on the ground in a circle and placed sticks to show where a path would be. But digging wasn't easy even though her legs developed muscles from walking down to the village and back. Good, she thought, Five days had gone by since the jug.

Down to the feed store to pick up some herb seed she spotted Edifice coming out of the store.

She rushed up the road. Thank God he didn't see her, but fragments of his low distinctive voice was playing an old tune in her.

As she passed his house she thought how he was like his house, dry rot which spread unnoticed…that could spread to her.

CHAPTER 20

*N*oncie woke eight days after the gun accident, jumped up, looked out the window into a field of neophyte plants from Hugh and decided she was not going to have a ruined life. I will not think about Hugh. I will do something with my life, not think about them or him. Yesterday in the post office, when Papa drove her down, she saw a sign. She hadn't realized that Papa would drive her any time, three times a day if needed, so he could see the postmistress.

VOLUNTEERS FOR OLD HOME DAY.
See Loretta Crocker.

-I'm going over there,- Noncie told Papa who stayed, leaning over the counter, and, in order to keep the postmistress's attention, asked for -Two penny post cards, please.-

-You bought two yesterday. You must be writing up a storm, Mr. Logan.- Okay, she knew his game. -You keep track?-

She pursed her lips. She handed him the two cards and he slid the money in her hand, touching her thumb. Just getting a whiff of her breakfast breath, bacon and maple syrup laced with the sharp smell of coffee, gave a flooding tingle to his lower parts.

He wasn't dead yet.

Loretta's stone-faced little girl answered the door, then moved aside to let Noncie in. An older girl swinging her body and her long hair and wearing an apron came from the kitchen.

-Is Mrs. Crocker home?- Noncie asked.

-I'm Mrs. Crocker.-

-Oh, you look so young.-

-Thank you.- She waited. -You came to see me?-

-I'd like to ask about Old Home Day.-

85

She let her arms relax -You got relatives from here?-

-Relatives? No.- She hoped she hadn't answered in a shocked tone.

Loretta nodded. -What would you like to know?- Noncie felt like saying, do something to help mitigate my sorrow.

The girl was hanging on her mother's legs and looking at Noncie with intense green eyes and a frown of disapproval.

-What do you do at Old Home Day? I might like to volunteer.-

Loretta beamed. -Oh everybody waits all year for it. Those who have moved away come back .- She went on to describe the day. –A parade, supper, crafts and the main event, a water fight between the firemen of Londonderry and us. Would you really like to help us?-

-Yes, I would.. Could I decorate?-

-Decorate?- Loretta Crocker looked puzzled.

-I mean like the supper tables or along the street with buckets of branches or flowers? I'll cut them from my garden and maybe ferns from our woods.-

-If you want to,- Loretta said. -I guess we never thought our street needed it, with the parade. But sure.-

Some perennials that had been there for years around the Logan house were blooming, like peonies. Noncie also had planted her garden with the plants Hugh had brought, trying not to cry as she planted. As the shoots appeared she tried to think of them as life's new beginning, but they punished her with the memory of Hugh's mellow eyes and strong chin and his over-accentuated lumbering ways, and the moment he told her she was beautiful…and the greatest sorrow of all, the child she knew she would never have.

The day before Old Home Day the three of them bought maple syrup buckets for the peonies. It looked like rain. -You know what happens to peonies. - Noncie moaned.

-How about umbrellas?- Florence asked.

-Umbrellas?-

Noncie trying to have charity toward Florence once again said, -That's a good idea.-

Papa and Florence were the ones who bought the umbrellas up in Rutland, wiped the store clean of them. –Sorry,- he said, -all they had was black.-

-That's creepy,- Noncie said.

The morning of Old Home Day dark clouds blurred the tips of the mountains. There was a big possibility of rain. Noncie tried to figure out how to keep the umbrellas standing up against the wind. She asked Florence, whose mind was good at figuring.

-Sure we'll circle the peonies in wire and wire the umbrellas to the circle.- Papa and Florence worked from seven to eight A.M. But just as they finished the sky cleared brilliantly.

Papa whined, -I almost resent the clear sky after all our work.-

-This way we have enough umbrellas for all the funerals for a lifetime.- Florence giggled as they folded them away.

-That's a nice thrifty thought,- he said, knowing full well she had never been thrifty.

She grinned at him, even though she was fast becoming a wreck. It had almost been a week since she had fallen off the wagon. But her craving came in bursts, like interludes of punches in her stomach or just behind her eyes, unhinging her. She sat in her herb garden, which helped....chewed on the tiny chives and new basil. She picked some to brush her teeth, the way she used to. Breathe in the herbs, let them escort her to a distance far removed from longing.

Now there was not a cloud to be seen. Sweet air rushed down the lavender mountains blending with coarser wind spilling down from Canada. Loretta came out of her house and thanked Noncie for her contribution of buckets overflowing with blossoms.

Noncie dove into the project, turning the flowers this way and that, straightening them, being sure the buckets were holding the water. Yet all the while wondering if Hugh would come to the event, even though he was a town away.

From inside the church the parade started up. Girls with antique hats dripping with feathers. Women with tucked bodices and lace petticoats, hiked up with ribbons. And one tall lanky teenager wore his grandfather's bright red long-johns underwear, peppered with moth-eaten pinpricks. The grandchildren were standing in line laughing their heads off. A goat cart with three boys, blue ribbons flowing from their hats, a parade of girl scouts and one very old civil war veteran, dragging a leg and leaning on a hickory cane. The last to come were three men dressed like Abraham Lincoln with top hats.

When the parade was over people lined the street quickly. Florence stood on a slight rise to have a good view of the strange, frightening main event.

Papa couldn't believe how small the fire engines were that drove up and parked about thirty feet from each other in the middle of the packed-dirt main street. Children ran in and out of the crowd, hooting and playing, dogs leaping after them. Two men shooed them away and pounded stakes at the side of the road to mark the goals.

God in heaven, there he was, Edifice on the team of five men from Flood Brook that were fighting Londonderry. Florence stepped back into the crowd where he wouldn't see her as he skittered down the bank to the river, carrying the hose to sink it into the water.

The two teams assembled. Les March, the referee, stood in the middle of the two sides waiting to blow his whistle. The men fidgeted, nervously. They were dressed in firemen's rubber overalls and thigh-high rubber boots, but with no protection on their heads.

Edifice McHuron stood out in front of the Flood Brook team as leader, the four others behind, holding the flaccid hose and pointing it at the Londonderry team. Durham Cork started the pump to draw the water and called, -No hitting the face or head.-

Edifice held the nozzle, waiting for the signal before he turned on the water. The pump for each team whirred loudly, ready. Florence would flee around the corner or deeper into the crowd as soon as the fight was over, frantic not to run into him.

Edifice glanced quickly around and spotted the bird with the wispy hair in front of Loretta's house. Brutal masculine adrenaline surged at the sight of her.

The crowd stepped back as the cotton duck hoses filled— the powerful, clumsy, snake stiffened making the nozzle waver almost uncontrollably. The men tightened their grips.

How serious they looked, Florence thought, what a bunch of fools. She despised male showoff games and she was taking no sides. She meant to watch both teams, but the only team she watched was McHuron's. No, the only person she watched was McHuron.

Les blew the whistle.

The teams pointed the nozzles toward the opposite team as the water frenzied into geysers, and then into blistering hurricanes. The stream throttled the men and filled the street with a roaring flood.

The blast hit Edifice in the solar plexus, knocking his breath away. Breathe. Don't fall. He'd never been a front man. He had drunk only a little the night before. But the force of water from the other team unhinged him. He tried to keep the nozzle focused, but it wriggled, taking all his strength just to hold on. The four men behind were struggling to help, leaning forward to withstand the blast, trying to hold the hose from wobbling. The men were forced to lean against him. How long could he stand up?

It was impossible to see, the opposite team was out of control, couldn't see well enough to direct their gushing spray and bombed Edifice's cheeks and mouth. Keep breathing. Keep your eyes open. He gasped and gagged against the fury. His head rolled forward into greater injury. Point the nozzle. Into what? A wall of water. The men behind him leaned farther into him, their feet planted into a sprint positions but listing against him too heavily. Clumps of pain. Can't keep his eyes open. His head fell lower and lower. His knees drifted apart. Too much pain to feel pain now. He never heard the shouting from the standbys. Then one brief moment he heard his name pulling him from a near blackout.

He could no longer lift the nozzle. He fell on his face and his team dominoed on top of him. He couldn't move. He couldn't breathe. He was dying. But he felt something. He dragged himself, out to the grass and threw himself down. The rest of the defeated team staggered to their feet, dazed. The crowd screamed "Londonderry," over and over but Edifice could hardly take it in or care. He shut his swollen eyes.

My God, Florence Logan was kneeling beside him, leaning over him as the pain of his wretched body overwhelmed him. Blood oozed from his hands and nose. She took a handkerchief from her pocket and said, - What a horrible mess you are. Meaningless brutality. Should be outlawed.- She wiped blood pouring from his nose.

He pushed her hand away. -What are you doing? Get away from me.- -Showoffs. Savages. Look at you.-

He tried to wobble to his feet, but he was too weak. When she stayed leaning over his flattened, excruciating body, he said as forcefully as he could muster, -Stop. Get.- Her attention was the last straw in the humiliation of his defeat. The whole village would be taking in this scene.

She backed away. He pulled himself first on his knees and then onto his feet. Suffering and hunched over he moved toward the fire engine and the rest of his team. They shook hands with the Londonderry team. Then slapped one another on the back.

Florence noticed that standing across the street were McHuron's wife and Dr. Peabody with arms across her chest, both of them glaring at her. Neither one of them had come to Edifice's aid. Maybe she had done wrong, had put him down in front of everyone?

No, she did right, the others did wrong allowing this craziness. Not helping, not being kind to him, the one hurt the most. Florence bit her lip and rushed after Papa and Noncie, who now were walking toward the church for supper.

Papa was feeling good. He liked the whole exciting event. He put his arm around Florence, —Flossy, dear. That was kind of you to go to help McHuron.-

Noncie was already ahead as villagers passed to compliment her on the lovely flowers. -That is very nice of you,- she kept saying and for the moment Hugh had left her thoughts.

CHAPTER **21**

*P*apa slid through the opening in the stone wall to his garden, carrying tree branches to stake his tomatoes and beans. He sat at the edge of the garden unspooling his memories, some running down the gullies of mawkishness, some deeply romantic…his lost love. At last came the harsh ones, slinging him into a clog of sudden depression.

Bentley Burke had been his best buddy. They ran the mill together. He carried Papa's ideas to fulfillment, digging up places to sell their flour, putting on the gladdest face you'd want to see, even in lean years. After the mill burned and Papa moved to Chicago they visited back and forth once a year but now they were too old, too far away and there was little to say in correspondence. What could he report, the weather and what sparse crops grew in this cold climate? He couldn't really tell about his daughters and his own secrets, now and then, wanting to dump his life in the river or out a window.

Yet the visions of the past faces, colored and white, came to comfort him, times hiking along the river, fishing or picnics with girls and telling stories of adventures. And his buddies in Chicago at the club, joking, playing pool, arguing politics. No cards, however, against his stiff-back Scottish heritage.

Yes comfort came by letting certain memories filter into his thoughts. Ray Castle. Babcock Church. He had named his dog Babcock after him. A Negro man, Lancaster Jones had shoed his riding horses and they leaned against an old oak and talked about horses, the gait, the nutrition, even the horse's personality.

Romana Leibengut, Mary Adams, Leroy Davis, Donald Harris, Jenny and Anna and Katherine and Elizabeth Memphis, whose singing was heard at every wedding. He was thankful he could still recall their faces, the color of their hair. He could recall the rhythm of their walk, their laughter, but most sounds of their voices had faded and only a rare conversation fertilized his memory.

He thought of the word fertilize and went to dig up some compost at the south end of his garden... and then there were the words of his wife, Olivia, spoken that night, the wife he had thought was decent, kind. But what she confessed at their sixteenth anniversary made his life with her an evil falsehood.

Worse, far worse were the words that were never spoken between his real love, Clara and him, the words he wanted to say and the words he wanted to feel back against his lips. Why couldn't he recall her voice? The heartache for lost Clara seemed worse in his old age or maybe here in this place where he had time to reminisce the heartache was fiercer. Yet ironically the memory of Clara's sweetness sustained him. Her memory sweetened his life.

He had placed an envelope in the desk drawer in his study with the instructions for the cemetery in the Presbyterian Church yard in Sheldon, Kentucky. Please place my remains as close as possible to the grave of Clara Beaumont.

The girls wouldn't have a clue why. He sat on the stone wall surrounding the garden taking him back to that church's Sunday school room. He had loved the dank, civet odor of the basement. Faded Miss Stesser was the teacher, the leather Bible limply molded to her lap, her small mouth pinching out each word, most of which he couldn't hear. Her voice was also faded. But he had loved the sound which floated him into daydreams.

Each student was given a Bible after confirmation. He thought of his as a good luck charm. Way back then he had begun to flip the pages to find the answers, like playing roulette, didn't make sense exactly. He liked the idea of reading to his daughters, as if it *did* make sense. Maybe when he was gone they would take up the practice. He liked, no wanted, them to have a legacy from him and sadly it didn't look like it was going to be in the form of children.

Reading made him feel tapped into magic. Just that morning he had opened the Good Book and came upon the story of Judas hanging himself upside down. Would he ever do such a thing? All these thoughts made him tired. He decided to take a nap right there on top of the warm stone wall, to mellow his old bones.

CHAPTER **22**

*F*lorence invited the dogs to her sunny bed to have a petting feast.
She had to lift tentative old Jessica. Tonya and Babcock head-
longed up and Florence sneaked herself into the middle of them. They
knew the privilege. She didn't always ask them up because their muddy
feet soiled her silk bedspread, or their brush and brambled fur tore at the
threads, but she had become very lax. Who the hell cared? She was ill with
need and guilt. She loved them because they were dumb, and she could
confess everything to them. Forever forgiving, forever accepting, loving
eyes fixed on hers and their eager tongues a salve. But not enough. Nothing would stop the memory of Persons running, pulling the trigger and
Mr. Possiblity stepping in the car and leaving…her sister's chance.

In the afternoon she dressed in a skirt she didn't like, muddy brown
and put on a dingy mauve blouse. But she stopped at the door in the hall
with the shelves of makeup. Couldn't help this habit. The mirror told her
again her lips were strange. Below her lower lip was a puffy line she was
born with. Made her lips look, she felt, way too big for her face so she left
that lower edge untouched. Beneath that was a tiny rip of a scar she hid
with powder every day. It was where her two bottom teeth had cut
through her face as a child when she fell face down on the curb to escape
her nanny who was taking her to school, which she hated.

She said goodbye to no one.

Hurry, hurry. Not fast enough, as if she were chugging over spikes in
the field, scrabbling and clawing her way up from a dry cistern. Lugging
her body like a ton of boulders, pebbles piercing her ankles. Nothing
would be fast enough. She needed help. Her stomach was screaming, her
gut an abyss. Would she remember how to swallow…or even open her
mouth?

Where was the place? Did he move ? Was it a fantasy? Deliria tremens She was panting and running. At last, there, the tip of the oasis, the roof of his shack in view. *Now rain will come and the desert will bloom.*

As she approached she neither heard nor saw signs of life. A trembling hand knocked on the door. No response. She paced back and forth. Sat on his doorstep, her dry tongue swelling. She decided to try pushing the door. It gave way. On the floor lay a stack of books, on a shelf a line of jugs and in the corner the silent still. She lifted several jugs. Empty. Then she found a full one.

-What do you think you're doing?- She spun around, saw him coming in, dropped the jug, spilling much of it on the floor. With swiftness he rescued it.

-Don't say anything- she cried out at him. -I was going to leave money.-

-Instead, *you* leave.-

-Can I at least make some appointments?-

-Don't you get it? I can't have you here.-

-Then can't I buy a jug, please? You hide it some place and I'll pick it up. I'll pay for it now.-

-Way too dangerous. I could go to jail, Prohibition, remember? Worse they would smash my still.- He took in the whole of her, a faded dung-colored skirt of soft creaseable linen and a blouse the color of dusk, open at her breasts. What was happening to him? His eyes fell on her gobbed lips. A sudden drunkenness before he drank, a skittish recklessness dizzied him. And something else merged, which he wouldn't dare name, some unacceptable something.

He said, -Leave. I have things to do.-

He waved his right hand at her and she noticed his half finger again and shivered with the hurt of it.. -Just one swallow.- Her voice was steady, not begging.

Struck his heart how her eyes looked pained and trapped.

-One swallow.- She tried.

-Only if you take off that fake mess on your lips. Can't tell who you are.-

He tossed her a sort of rag towel hanging on the edge of his chair. She threw it back at him. He quietly said, -Good day, madam.-

Her dignity sent her out the door. But her adrenalined body, couldn't take it. She opened his door again, took the rag from his hands and wiped.

-More,- he demanded.

She rubbed them. Looked down at the stain of red in the towel. The sight undid her, was a concrete sign of the injury coming to her from what she was about to partake.

He handed her the jug. She took the longest swig he had ever seen and handed it back and he drank much more, just to secure the upper hand.

She sure didn't like him but must tolerate him anyway.

-Goodbye,- he said. Worried about her staggering down the hill for people to see. What had he done? Really foolish move of his.

-Wait, here's a dollar,- she said. He took it and held the door for her to leave. He followed and shut it behind him.

-Where you going?- She asked. -I got business.-

-What kind of business?-

-Would I tell you that? It's bad enough you know about my place. Never again. I don't have enough to share and way too dangerous.-

She didn't answer. The mellow spirits took her fluttering away from battle. She felt nestled in a friendly haze as she maneuvered down the slope. He stayed behind. She knew he was watching but when she came to the woodlot she peered back and saw that he was headed way off to the left, away from the village. Since his back was to her she decided to follow him.

Maybe he had a stash somewhere else. Could she turn a criminal, a thief? Edifice turned right, then left and headed onto a washboard dirt road that soon became narrow, with spines of grass in the middle, from disuse. She kept a distance, her walk uneven and she could see he also was a bit staggery. Where the heck was he going? Maybe he had detected that she was behind him and he was leading her on and into danger..somewhere that he had hidden a gun.

He seemed to walk slower, or was she catching up? The road now was all grass, hardly leaving the space between the woods on either side for a vehicle, but there was a faint signature of car tracks. He stopped. She saw ahead they had come to a brook, about twelve feet across but swollen into rapids. Emboldened by her alcoholic brain she went within four feet behind him.

In a sudden move he swung to face her. -Boo.-

She jumped.

-What are you after?-

-You got more. You lied. -

-Why should I even answer you, but no.-

-What's that over there?- She pointed across the river and up a slope to the beginning framework, half hidden by trees, of a small building. The way he looked at her frightened her. But the way she looked at him also frightened him.

-It's just a fishing cabin I'm building. Nobody knows about it and you better not tell in case I get in the mood to let you have more.-

More, he said more. Yet she backed away, spooked. Could he be building a place for nefarious things. Sex?...kidnap...torture, murder? She ran back down the lane. She ran. But glanced back seeing him watching her retreat with a puzzled smile on his face.

CHAPTER **23**

*I*n the afternoon Papa and Noncie drove to the village to buy milk. He walked to the grain store to pick up tender seeds for his garden. He had dressed and shaved. He never went to the village without his suit and tie and didn't care that he saw no other man dressed like him. He was going to remain civilized.

He also liked the idea that he looked good so when he stopped to get the mail from *her*. Maybe eventually he would accept life here because of his and Noncie's mission and because of the beauty of nature . But he worried too that his civilized ways would fade.

When Papa came out of the grain store, watching him were three men sitting on the defunct platform of the railroad station. He didn't like the looks of them. Low-life…slumping, swinging their legs, mud on their overalls.

-Say, Mr. Logan, come join us.-

Papa hesitated. They must be putting him on, laughing at him. He felt awkward in his suit. A man stood up and pointed to a place beside him. What the hell, though he first dusted off the boards.

One spit chewing tobacco from the side of his mouth into the road.

-Too bad about your dog.-

Papa's neck stiffened. –Know who did it?-

-No.- The man said.

Another one spit and nodded his head toward McHuron's house.

Papa answered. -My daughter ran across him not long ago

and when she confronted him he told her he had no gun and didn't

hunt.-

-Maybe, maybe not.-

-But you aren't sure?- Papa asked.

-Didn't see it happen.- The man admitted.

The tall, pot-bellied rummy sorted in his pocket and pulled out a small leather bag with a draw string. He opened it and passed the bag. Each of the men took a smidgen and he offered the bag to Papa. –Have a chew.-

Papa thought quickly. Better say yes or what would they might feel insulted. He thought of chewing as a habit of the lower classes. He looked at the bag and slowly reached for a pinch. My God it burned. He wanted to spit without chewing.

-Like it?- The one who gave him the bag asked.

-Not much,- Papa admitted and spit.

-They all laughed, Papa laughed with them.

-Sometimes takes getting used to. Look at this,- the youngest man said. He lifted his pant leg and showed him a false leg just above his ankle. -Peabody cut it off. Saved my life. Took a while to get used to, though.-

-I'll be,- Papa said. He liked being with these tough guys. He hunkered down slumping like them. But he knew he couldn't break through all the way. Too ensconced in his outer, formal, screwed up gentlemanly ways. He wished he could sneak out, be an alley-cat at night, have beer buddies, and get into fist fights. He took another pinch and arched his spit.

-Papa?- came a voice.

Papa jumped up trying to wipe his mouth while walking briskly to Noncie.

-What were you doing?- She asked in a tone of disbelief.

-Nothing.-

-Who were they?-

-Nobody.-

-Nobody?-

Why had he said that? They were much of what he envied.

CHAPTER 24

$\mathcal{T}$he next day Florence left saying she would get the mail and take a small grocery list and let Papa and Noncie have the day. She rushed up the hill, banged on the still's door. No answer., Banged again. Nothing. She sat on the step to wait but after fifteen minutes gave up and trotted along the grassy road. When she came to the brook, there he was sitting next to the brook.

-You're a persistent bugger aren't you?- he chided. -You came back to get something?

-No just to see—- she paused not knowing how to finish.

-You mean what I'm building?- knowing full well that wasn't it.-

–Just tell me, please, you building another still? -

He acted as if he hadn't heard her. –Lots of rocks to step on. I'll go first to show you.-

-What are you talking about? I'm not doing that.- And why was he pretending to be so nice?-

-All this way and you aren't coming?-

-Has this place got what I want?-

-Depends on what you want,- he teased. -I'm not showing you unless you want what you want bad enough.-

-What did he mean? No, I...-   she was leery as hell, but fear would never be crippling enough to keep her away from the jug.

-I got to get the planks across.-   He pointed to his scavenged knot-holed boards on the bank.

-I'm taking this board over and when I get to the other side you can start, if you want.-

-You got some of the juice on the other side?- She asked outright this time.

-I might have a bit left in my jug.-

Her heart squirreled around. Thank you God. But she was a liability alive. Yet a little in his jug! He had some! She had to ford the rapid. Never been in a fast stream like this. Stumble? Crack her head? Why would he want her to see what he was up to? This was not good. Where had her sense gone?. A poisoness snake paralyzed her will. She was in the vortex of a magic spell, ready for a heightened thrill.

But play along, don't infuriate him. He could be another Irving, light a little match and he'd incinerate. This was nuts. She was supposed to go across this rushing, whirling brook? Alone? But she wasn't going to ask for help, or show him any weakness.

He came back to pick from the stack of boards and lifted one to his shoulder. Stepping deep into the swirling eddies carrying the board threw him off making him stumble over the slippery rocks. A flash of a balance only. His knees buckled and he leaned forward, flopped quickly, the board under him becoming a slide on the white water. He was gone. He was gone. She doubled over and shut her eyes. A second later she opened them. He was only a few feet from the bank on the other side; the board had caught on an overhanging tree and in one quick strong movement he was able to climb onto the bank and pull the board with him.

He spun like a soaked dog, shaking off the cold water. She shouted, - It sure seems water is out to get you.-

He didn't like that one damned bit, but he certainly wouldn't give her the satisfaction of knowing. -Maybe together we can make it.-. He came back for her, wondering why. Why in the world was he getting her more involved in his life? He couldn't even stand the woman.

She thought, why had she teased him again? Maybe to show herself *his* weakness.

-We'll get some branches for walking sticks and hold on to each other. Okay?-

She wondered about her flopping skirt but she couldn't hold it up and hold onto him and the stick also. At least she had on her practical walking shoes. What the heck, so she got wet. The irresistible urge to fling it all, headlong into adventure. His arm felt as solid as a heavy branch but supple like the skin of ripe fruit.

They stumbled onto the other bank and scrambled up the worn scoop of land that made a path. Sopping and cold Florence said -Oh my God we got to ford the river again to return. -

-Unless you want to stay here.-

I'm crazy, she thought, but still fear couldn't stop her longing. He led her up beautifully made steps, flat rocks imbedded in the hillside, jutting out free from the ground, a cantilevered stairway, slightly curved to the rhythm of the hill. She stopped to admire. -Where did you get such perfect rocks?-

-You really want to know or is that rhetorical?

She nodded.

-Years back herds of sheep roamed, keeping the meadows abundant way up to the mountain tops. Now with the sheep gone, because Australia sold lamb cheaper, Vermonters stopped having herds, so now the trees are closing in again. The herders had built summer shacks to tend the sheep but after a while nobody used them. They went to ruin. These rocks came from one of those shepherd foundations back in my woods. I've been carrying them and chiseling the edges round for nearly a year. I own this land from my father.-

He sounded normal. Yes. He did. But so had Irving, even when he took her in the cab. Even when he pretended they were out for a big adventure. Never mind that kind of thought. Just keep going.

At the top of the twenty stone steps and across some flat land deeper in the woods, mostly hidden, stood a sturdy framed-out structure. The place was small, maybe fifteen by twenty feet with no walls or roof, just roof boards without slates. On the salvaged uprights were woodpecker holes and black water stains.

Her legs began to stiffen. This was the frontier. People took the law in their own hands, and her family didn't know where she was. She figured she'd better talk. -My family knows I took a walk up the hill. They will come looking. They will see the lane here.-

-You're scared as a rabbit aren't you?- He was grinning.

-Of course not.-

-What are you really here for?- He faced her square on, her slightly oval black misty eyes.

-You know what I want and the only reason I have anything to do with you.-

-Watch yourself.-

What was wrong with her? Be careful. Don't talk anymore.

He thought of going for it, toying with that, put her in a tight hole, but decided against it, knowing the seriousness of her need. -I'm telling the truth. I only make the stuff back at the still. And only a smidgen is left in the jug here.-

She didn't answer. She skipped quickly down the beautiful rocks to the water's edge again. He caught her arm. – I have to go.-

-What's gotten into you?-

Her breathing jumped a notch. The river seemed colder and her feet like ice. The rapids washed the hem of her skirt against her legs, making them weak. False moves, almost falling, an unstable rock with slime.

-I'll help you across.-

-No.-

He grabbed her arm. She jerked away just as she climbed up the bank on the other side. But walk, don't ran. Her panic might excite him. Was he following her? She didn't want to look.

Petrified. But at the end of the lane she turned. He had not followed. Out of breath, she stopped. He was not in sight. I'm alive. She stood in the sun to dry off and empty her shoes of water. She felt a drift of calm filter out her fear.

CHAPTER 25

*N*oncie turned her head this way and that to be sure. Yes, yes he was there, Hugh walking down the street past the post office to his car. She walked as fast as she could without stumbling in the bright sun, but he stepped in the car and was gone up the hill past the church, spinning his wheels. *I will not weep.*

And she was going to do more than survive, try and do more, help herself while helping others, find a way to improve the village. She had been thinking about the bridge, how rickety and out-of-date it was, and realizing what good would come to the village with a new bridge. The next day she composed a letter to the Governor asking him to consider a new bridge.

Noncie visualized the celebration, the whole village helping make the town beautiful after the new bridge was built. The adults would dig and fertilize for a park and the children would spread seeds. Children from the Orphanage. Hugh would bring them (couldn't help herself).He would know she was not just a home body taking care of the house and Florence, but contributing to society and maybe....

She posted the letter. The postmistress raised her impressive eyebrows.

The next day Florence scrambled up the hill.

Not there. She rushed to the cabin. As she ran closer she heard the sound of a hammer. When he saw her he stopped and came across the brook. Stood in front of her with his armscrossed.

-Just a nip,- She begged.

-I did bring a jug today but I've been thinking I have to know a few things about you first. I want the truth. You didn't answer the truth yet. Why are you people really here in Vermont? Your old man rob a bank? Or did you? Your sister a German spy?-

-We like it here.- He tightened his arms and widened his eyes.

She couldn't tell him. She didn't believe it. She could have stopped on her own, not have to dry out in isolation here. -My sister and father were bored, needed a change and it's cheaper here. I came, sacrificing my own desires in order to make them happy and of course see some new scenery. It's easy for me here, I have an internal life more than they do. I like to read.-

-Just like that? Up and go along with them to this dump?-

-Dump? Why are you in this dump?-

-I'm here to drink. Where else would I be able to boil it up? On the streets of New York?

-Your wife drink?- The fact that she mentioned his wife startled him, as if he hardly remembered that was what she was. He didn't want to talk about her but said, -No, she doesn't do anything. Hunts, makes meals. I don't eat her shot meat. I eat fish or quail you can pick right off a branch. But mostly my meals are pure liquid. I'm an alcoholic.-

She looked at him, amazed at his honesty.

-I'm not,- she said.

-Well, I'll be.-

-I'm not.-

-Let's start over. I want to know the whole truth or you get nothing from me.-

-I'm a social drinker, just like a little now and then. And I don't like drinking alone, as I told you, and I know you need money. Again, I'll pay you whatever you like.-

-I'm warning you, if you don't tell the truth you get nothing. I see how uncomfortable your sister and father are living here. Say it out loud why did you come to Vermont?-

She said nothing.

He turned to go back to work.

-I...- She stopped.

-Well?-

-I'm an...we came to get me away...I wanted to come too... to be cured.-

-Say it, Cured of what?-

She whispered, -alcohol.-

He was touched by her confession. -All right. Come across.- He tried to take her hand but she pulled away saying, -Don't touch me.-

-But only one swig,- he said. She had made him feel guilty, convincing him she wanted to quit. He should help her, not give in.

After she had swigged some quickly and he did too, she said, -I'll work free on the cabin for you know, now and then.-

-You work?- He laughed.

She bit her lip and plunged, -Wait, I'd really like to learn about carpentry, never mind the swig.- She thought if he just let her work he would give her some. Like every day, like all the time. She didn't see meanness in him. -But before I work here I also want to know something, -Did you kill our dog?-

-I told you I don't own a gun.-

-How do I know you're telling the truth? If you don't tell me the truth I won't work for you.-

He laughed. -You aren't working for me.-

-Okay, what's the story? Why don't you use a gun, if you don't?-

-I don't have to answer that and as for you being a carpenter, even out here in no man's land women don't hold a hammer unless to pop their husbands one.-

-I have nothing else to do. I like learning. I'm really good at learning. I'd like to learn to drive nails and saw planks, fit things together. I'm good with my hands.-

-I'm sorry.-

-I could be useful.-

-When did those lady arm muscles have a chance to swing something heavy? -

-I played tennis when I was young.-

-Goodbye.-

-Please.- She could feel tears roaring against her eyes.

With his back to her he felt what it would be like for him to be down a dry well. But he also knew he was in dangerous territory, danger he wouldn't even admit to. -You have to do things right.-

He watched her wipe her tears away. But this was no good. She could screw things up for him. And he'd have to stop and show her how to do everything. Why was he giving in?

She felt the thrill of coming downstairs for Christmas when she was nine and finding what she had most wished for, a brilliantly yellow canary that opened its throat and caroled her into trembling.

-Why did you let me follow you here?-

He didn't answer. He didn't even know himself. He walked a few paces with her as she left.

-You go that way. I go this,- he said.

-I'll be here tomorrow,- she said, wondering also why he had given in.

The road was slashed now with striped shadows stretched by the waning lemony sun. When he started to leave her, turn up the hill, he whispered almost to himself -Your lips are naked.-

But she heard.

Edifice climbed the drive to his home and quickly slipped into the leaning barn entrance but didn't get far, backed up. Threw himself on the ground, while his stomach, coming from his heart, drew up in cramps. He rolled in agony back and forth on his hips, his face crushed into the grass. Without his permission his feelings were unclogging like a branch falling over a spring dam. He was trying to wage against unpredictable, out of control weather flooding him with no life-preserver, and no bank to cling to. When he was able to sit up and move he knew he must not let this happen. He must not think about Florence Logan, dream what he was dreaming. The black hole of the gun long ago had destroyed that.

He pulled himself to his knees and to his feet, but the cramps had not left completely. He wiped his mouth with determination. He opened the door to the kitchen, smelled the rank venison Gerty had shot, and retreated to his room without eating.

That man, with his thick muscles and sturdy body she would easily be able to stay neuter about, the way she would a man servant. He would be difficult to get to know anyway, hiding behind that beard and the expression of his eyes shaded by the umbrella of his blond hair. She could ignore him as a person, just get what she needed from him. But he wasn't like any man she'd run into. The fact was he was a different kind of a bum, not a bit like Irving, a flashy, suave, bum. Yet didn't all men have something they wanted to steal from women?

Anyway he was probably a hidden pansy. Look at his wife, and with no kids, no doubt in a marriage to cover up. Pretended around Florence he was a hunk of a man. That was it. She was glad she had solved it. A business arrangement she and this Edifice would have. She would never have to worry, feel ill at ease about him. Yes, a business arrangement. But she must be careful to keep this from her family. Go at different times. Not stay all day. Sometimes go in the afternoon. Sometimes morning. Imagine, in this God forsaken place she would have a steady reward.

The night was cool. She climbed into her bed but shutting her eyes could not shut out the voice that was neither rapist nor neuter nor pansy. She had heard his whisper so penetrating that her skin puckered. –*Your lips are naked.*-

CHAPTER **26**

Where do you think she goes every day?- Noncie, agitated asked Papa.

-She told me she just likes to walk to clear her head.-

-Her nose is red when she comes in.-

-Exertion.- Doubt rushed in, even as he tried to counteract Noncie's pessimism.

-Maybe we should follow her.-

-And if we discover that she has found a source what do we do?-

-She wants to stop.-

-But..- Papa said, -Follow her?-.

-We could lock her in her room until she dried out and then talk to her.-

Papa was considering. He was stimulated by the idea. -But we have to have more proof.-

-But how?-

-Staggering or making no sense.-

Noncie blew up -I've got to have a better life. I've got to do something. Get my mind off her. She's driving me crazy. Years and years of crazy. If only I would get an answer about the bridge.-

-Yes. I'm sure you will soon.-

-Would you drive me to the orphanage to see... Persons?-

-Your eyes are worse, Noncie?- he asked gently.

She didn't want to tell him. –Just want your company.-

They drove up the long driveway to the top and Papa said, - I'll sit here.-

Knowing whom she really hoped to see.

-You sure?-

When she knocked the cinnamon smelling woman called out, -We're all in the yard.- Persons came running.

-How are you?- she asked.

-I'm real good.-

She handed him cookies she had baked.

-Oh thanks. Oh thanks. Where is Miss Florence?-

-She stayed home.- She didn't really know where she was but certainly wasn't about to bring her.

-I want to see her.-

-Is Hugh here?-

-You came just to see Hugh?-

-No, no. I mean of course not. I mostly came to see you.-

-Why without Miss Florence?-

-Is Hugh busy?-

-He goes out. He visits kids. Goes to meetings.-

-So, he's away today?-

- He had to go to a meeting. Hugh is teaching me to read like Miss Florence.-

She hesitated as if Hugh might suddenly appear. –Give Hugh some of the cookies. Tell Hugh I came by to see...you.- She took his hand and patted it. –So you are learning to read, how nice.-

-I don't shoot guns anymore.-

-Of course not. You have no idea when he'll be back?-

-Who?-

-Hugh.-

-No, maybe supper. I help him cook sometimes.-

-I'm so glad.-

-Are you going stay here for a long time?- He had finished about two-thirds of the cookies.

-I..- but the door bell rang and Persons went to open it. Noncie stood up, her heart rounding a corner in her chest. But Papa walked in, spoke to Persons and turned to Noncie, -Well?-

-Hugh is out and Persons doesn't know when he will come back.-

-Suppertime, I bet,- Persons said.

-Tell him, hello,- Papa said as he took Noncie's arm. –Goodbye Persons. Good to see you.-

Noncie said, -Tell Hugh I'll come again to see you both.-

As they started for the door Persons said, -Be careful. Last week on that road a tractor hit a car and the tractor turned right over on its back. The man was dead. There was a lot of blood for miles around. Papa doesn't drive a tractor, does he?-

-No. Good-bye Persons. Don't forget to give Hugh some cookies.- She started out the door then came back to hug him.

She was miserable, knowing she wouldn't have the nerve to come again.

CHAPTER 27

*J*e wasn't hammering. There was no sound. He appeared at the door, not smiling. He must stay aloof as he watched her cross the brook that was low now.

-I have something for you.- She drew a paper from the pocket of her royal blue skirt. Inside the cabin she unrolled a drawing, nothing to lay it on. The only table of chipped enamel was too cluttered with tools. -Do you mind?- He removed two killed jugs, a dipper and an enamel cup, two pieces of good silverware, an ax, a hammer and some kind of a rag. He put them on the floor. He couldn't figure out what the drawing was about.

-You see you could attach one end of the two cables onto that strong tree and then attach the other end to the willow on the other side, high enough for the momentum to take you past the middle before you have to pull.-

-A pulley across the river. Never thought of that.- He was lying, humoring her. He had been lazy about constructing one. An on going laziness could easily capture him. -What's this?- he asked, pointing to a sketch down in the right hand corner.

-That's the seat. I thought you'd know how to build that the best and what to build it out of and how to attach it to the cable.-

-That's kind of you to think I could.- But she hadn't caught his jibe. His face was leaning over the drawing, though he wasn't really studying it. He was thinking. How much was she going to involve herself in his goings on? He had had a night to think it over. For so many years now there had been no change in his life other than the weather. Even though he did not want this empty life, it was too hard to fill, and with what?

-How big you think the seat should be?- She asked but she kicked herself for playing the dumb feminine role.

He scratched his beard. -I'll think it over.-

He definitely must be a homosexual. No real man would have let a woman give him a mechanical idea without some kind of a fight, or pure dismissal. -But I'm not leaving you the sketch unless I get some steady... -

He swiveled around. She was so close to him that he whiffed the sunny moisture of her skin. He pulled away. -Okay, it's a deal.-

Wow, she couldn't believe it, just like that. He gave her the barrel stool with the seat worn into an impression like somebody fallen in the snow. He reached behind him and brought out his Vodka and handed it to her. -Wait a minute here, don't gulp it. Make you sicker than a skunk.-

-Yeah? I guess I should slow down. Right, I'm not used to drinking like that.-

He rolled his eyes.

She asked him, -Do you mind telling me. Do you earn any money? I mean, how do you live... and your wife live?-

-Like I said she lives mostly on killing and a garden that she tends and that I eat too. And also I forage in the woods for mushrooms and berries.-

A picture came to his mind, Gerty, sitting at his father's great old oak table in the kitchen, tearing the venison, bearing her teeth, groaning with happiness just to ridicule him for not eating.

-Why don't you shoot, or do you?-

-How often do I have to tell you I don't own a gun.-

-Tell me why.-

-No.-

Tell me why.-

-No.-

-Why won't you?-

-End of subject.-

She paused. She drank. She looked over at his wooly face, becoming familiar, as the land around her was now becoming familiar. -I want to be cured. I'm really trying to work on it. I bet you want stop too.- She sank into silence and he didn't answer. She had thought all alcoholics wanted to give it up, knowing how immoral it was.

–If you don't have a gun why did you give up shooting?- She would like to get off the stool and lie down, let the vodka reach every niche in her body.

- I can't tell you.-

-Tell me.-

-No, I won't.- The sound of his voice had a swirling, staccato rhythm as the alcohol swam along her bloodstream. She slid off the stool and lay on the floor then he lay down, not next to her but across the room.

He closed his eyes remembering, remembering the first time he was aware of Gerty. She was

In a class below him, serious and shy. Then when she was nineteen and he was twenty and her mother was dead like his own mother but her father was alive and she lived alone with her violent father. Edifice took her square-dancing a few times in the basement of the church and she was agile and sort of pretty with long brown hair, but she never smiled. That was the beginning. He didn't want to remember more. He fell asleep.

CHAPTER 28

*J*ust as Florence crossed the bridge there stood Gerty McHuron at the edge of her porch leaning against the maple tree that was holding up the roof. Her skinny arms were folded over her gross chest. And she was watching every step she took as she passed by. But Florence looked straight ahead. Creepy lady. What was her problem? She wished Edifice would tell her about his wife. Something weird. Gave her a shiver. And why did he stay with her?

Next day Florence wore her Panama hat and her yellow cotton skirt, not a good camouflage as she went through the village. When she found the lane leading out to his river-cabin she quickened her pace. She felt her body was less bloated and leaner now. She had thought of buying overalls up at Rutland. But what about the bib? Made it hard to pee. Never peed in the woods in her life. She had held it in the last time at his cabin. And how do you wipe yourself? Maybe just shake, use a fern or do a little squatting dance.

He looked as if he had been waiting down by the brook.

-Skirt?-

-I don't have anything else.-

-You can't work in that.-

He walked toward the cabin. Was he dismissing her? But when he stepped over the threshold he turned. –Are you coming?- Inside he handed her a pair of blue jeans. -You can change into these each time you come.-

-Who are you kidding, fit me?-

He handed her a piece of rope. -Tie them good and tight with this.- He gave her a plaid shirt and turned his back for her to dress.

-I picked out trees to attach the pulleys on either side and not too high so we can load up the building materials. I'll nail boards for steps on the tree. The pulleys are a bit rusty. They used to pull hay up to my barn loft.-

-How do we get the rust off?-

-We spit on them.-

At first she didn't know he was joking, until his eyelids crinkled.

-Oil them.- he went on.

-You ever hold a hammer?-

-No.-

-Ever use a screwdriver?- She didn't have to answer. The way he asked wasn't insulting. He showed her and she helped nail boards to the back wall. A loud siren blew.

-What's that?-

- Every noon from the Flood Brook firehouse.-

-I guess I should have brought us some lunch,- she said.

-I'll get us some.- He waded in the stream. He signaled for her not to talk. What was he doing staring down at the water, slipping his hand beneath, but not moving, keeping still for minutes? Then he jumped up holding a wiggling trout. Rushed to shore and laid it on the mossy bank in front of her.

-How did you do that?- -

-It will take me years to show you everything.-

-You arrogant...-

-I was only teasing.- But he also was keeping her away as much as pos-sible.

He built a fire and she helped gather sticks.

She asked him, -You hungry?-

-I'm always hungry, with my meager cash, in winter, it's hard. I get thin. Mostly I live on what vegetables Gerty has canned. One winter was so harsh I tried to eat the inside of bark like a beaver and a road killed porcupine.- His eyes wrinkled again.

-Oh sure – But she couldn't tell if he was telling the truth and she couldn't tell if he was thin or not in ill-fitting clothes.

-I can bring you food,- She said.

-I'm okay-

-I've never eaten really fresh fish She closed her eyes, concentrating on the sweet buttery taste. He passed the vodka but both tried to control their intake so they could keep working. Her fingers, thumb, palms had never been this fulfilled as when using the hammer. She felt the sound through her fingers, maybe the way a pianist feels when pounding the keys into a triumphant sound.

The sun coming on them from a break in the trees wooed them into stretching out and sleeping on the mossy bank. The only time she had ever slept in the open was while sunbathing on the beach of Lake Michigan. But that was not like this, dissolving her tired muscles into deep sleep, and total peace.

When they woke he got his nerve up to ask her, -Were you ever in love? I don't want to pry unless you want me to.-

She turned toward him. -I'll answer if you answer what I asked before, but I'm phrasing it differently. Do you love your wife?-

-No, I don't and she doesn't love me.-

-Why are you together then?-

-Your turn first,- he said.

-Then you will tell?-

He nodded.

She couldn't tell why but she felt okay about telling him. She started. Paused. Was silent. Couldn't tell him looking into his eyes directly. She had to turn her face away. -I never mention his name out loud. I ran away with him and got married. I was sixteen. His name was Irving. We lived at the Plaza hotel in New York. He was wealthy. He taught me to drink. We drank in bed. We drank at bars and at dinner.-

The vodka had made her words slow and the slight slur made her southern accent appear. She told him the whole story, every engraved detail. The warehouse, the men holding her down, her own husband holding her legs. His hand over her mouth so she couldn't scream. The pain and the spouting blood. Her running away, running back home, never seeing Irving again. Never wanting a man again...she emphasized that, do not ever again want a man.

He watched her face until she turned toward him –Horrible,- he said. He wanted to throw his arms around her but couldn't after what she said about men.

But he took her hand a moment as if to help her across the void.

She didn't ask him any more about Gerty that day.

They sat in silence. He thought of a wounded bird he once nurtured that never flew again.

CHAPTER 29

When she left, walking fast down the lane for home, he felt nausea coming on again, but this time for her. Sorrowful creature. God-awful suffering that ruined her. Irving had locked her into a prison of alcohol. How could anything or anybody free her? Time takes nothing away. There is no such thing as the past passing.

Even with their shared ruination he felt there was no common ground between them, even though he and her ex-husband, were both killers for opposite reasons. Yet she had more of a sense of *being* than he did. Come into village life and try and work at learning something completely new. She had carved out her own sense of justice against that bastard by being brave and doing what she damn well pleased, in that sense liberated.

When Florence arrived at the other side of the covered bridge toward home she adjusted the skirt that she had changed back into. She looked up the road and again caught Gerty McHuron standing on the porch but this time waving for her to come. Florence hesitated and then thought, what the hell. She climbed the rutted driveway. When she neared the porch Gerty talked in a soft voice, probably so nobody passing would hear, -You think I don't know what you're doing?-

Florence took a deep breath. -And what is that?- Her heart clenched.

-I'm warning you.-

Florence gaped at the straight powerful face with slightly cracked, skinny lips and a bob of hack-sawed hair. Her eyes shone like something peering from the woods at dusk.

Gerty McHuron launched so fast Florence couldn't get it.. - Comeinherewithyourface fullofstuffand tryingtohorneinwhen you got no right suckingaroundwhereyouaren'twantedand socializing withother people'shusbandslikeyou havearight, notnotsocializingshackingupandoffy-

116

our pinsbringingyourcity whore ways, wanderingaroundlikeyou are get-
tingitandIcouldgetyouin jail in onesecondyoubetter behaveyoursellady-
fortroublewillbewhatyouget.-

Florence said loudly, -I have to go.-

-You stay put. I'm not finished.-

Florence didn't move, but only out of fascination -I know what you're
uptoyououtherewithyourfuckinways he evenfucking against the law
weareuprightpeople around here andIcoundlheredon'tyougonearhmany-
moreandI'llhavethetwosofyouarrestedonthespottwocountst-
wocounts.*getwhatisadulteryandtheother*.Youdollandhinkhe'ssometeddybea
riwasntohehasn rightan dneitherdoyouespeciallyyoucomingheewithit-
piledonyourfacelikeworsethnanywhoreanywhereon-
thisearth.oingtostayfallenorunfallenitsmineImmarriedtohimandyouain't
evergettinghim.

He is a killer.

Florence left her while she continued ranting. What could that
woman do? She hadn't mentioned the still. No, she couldn't do them
harm. Could she? By the time Florence reached her lane she was amused,
thinking her patter was like the nightmare song in Gilbert and Sullivan's
Iolanthe.

As she trudged tipsy and out of breath, a hellish heat came over her in
spite of the gusty wind that moved overhanging branches of maple and
elms sway at her like giant fans.

She didn't want Edifice McHuron, But Florence could not smother
the thought that Gerty might do them harm after all, go looking for the
still, call the law or pump them full of bullets from her stash of guns.

A storm was coming up over Glebe Mountain, the sky bruised
black and purple. She hurried along the lane. In all that gobbledy-gook
that poured out of Gerty did she grasp her last words? Did she hear right?
The word killer, that Edifice was a killer? She must have meant killed
their beloved Borie. So he was a big liar. Did he also take Borie from the
church and do something with him? As lightning slithered across the
mountain she ran harder and rain leaked slowly out of the clouds. No,
she meant a human killer.

But why should he believe his wife? And she wasn't sure she heard
right. But that was it. Florence was through drinking with him. She did
not care that she might stop not out of her own strength of character, but
plain old fear.

CHAPTER **30**

*T*he thunder and lightning had moved on. But the rain continued in a soft hazy language, trickling onto bending tree branches. Edifice found the place and knelt to pull the weeds away from his mother's grave. Because his father was buried in the cemetery by the church he cleaned up around the church yard. And now that the church was empty (except for an occasional funeral or wedding, Les March told him he couldn't pay him but he mowed the graves anyway. When he visited his mother every Sunday, except in severe weather, he felt he was going home, like their traditional Sunday dinners. He opened the rusted box next to the grave where she had kept her sketchbook.

Why had his mother left him without saying a word? Why had she died so suddenly? Then his sister left him to live far away and his father died. No enduring loves in his life. He knew why he stayed with Gerty in spite of despising her. Wasn't there a Chinese proverb that if you save a person you are responsible for them for the rest of your life? He couldn't just throw her out. Tried to believe it wasn't just because of what she knew and might know, call the sheriff…but out of charity.

He wouldn't remove her but he would remove the house from around her instead. Take it with him and reconstruct a semblance of his happy childhood, away from her. As he knelt by his mother's grave he recalled that she had not been loving, that is, not physically affectionate. Her affection came in words. She praised him. Her eyes gleamed and her voice rolled over him like a blanket. Made him be better than he really was because of her belief in him. Her bright enthusiastic love could soften and often eliminate his boyish meanness and anger. She said while tucking him in bed, -I love peace, and hope you will grow to love it also.- He laid an Indian paint brush blossom on her grave and sat for a while in the misty rain, looking down at the rambling mansion of his birth, the wreck and symbol of his life.

He dredged up that time his anger at Gerty had boiled up so bad that he rattled his truck over the state line to Haborsville. He had known about the place since he was fifteen, everybody knew. A cold winter night, ten years ago, he put chains on his tires and headed out, clanking those thirty miles, steering with one hand and tipping the jug with the other and singing to keep up his courage the old Welsh hymn that his father used to sing: "Guide me O thou great Jehovah, pilgrim through this barren land."

He parked the truck right in front of the house. But when he cut the engine he saw steam coming. Opened up the hood. My God, he had a radiator leak. In the back of the truck he kept a bucket. He knocked on the door, a Victorian house with a haunted-house look. Barely could see light through the shuttered windows. A big woman, tall as he, answered. The hallway was lit with rusty dregs of light. -Make yourself at home- She pointed to a doorway of a parlor.

-No I just wanted…-.

She broke in -You can tell me and I'll point out the right one. They are all experts. Not much business on a night like this. You got your prick, I mean pick.-

He glanced at the glowing rosy half-dressed girls like manikins posing in a window with sober dead faces until his gaze fell on each one. Then as if he had pulled a cord, the face lit up with an incandescent fantasy smile. He quickly turned his eyes back to the big woman as she said, with suspicion, -What's that bucket in your hand? You up to something? We don't allow kinky.-

-I don't want anything but water for my truck,- he heard himself say. - My truck radiator is leaking and I got a long ways to go tonight.-

-This is your first time isn't it,- she said with encouragement.

-I just want water, if you please.-

-And exactly why did you come to this house?- She crossed her arms over her broad, mannish chest. -Lots of houses along this street. Just to spy? You some sheriff or something?-

-You were the only one, the only house with lights,- he lied. She snatched the bucket from his hand.

-You stay here.- He turned and faced the front door. Didn't look back at the girls. Ruminated on the fact that he had sung that old hymn he hadn't thought about for years, like his mind had already been made up. He just couldn't join a down-and-out sex-imprisoned human being who didn't want him, who maybe hated him. But he wished he could. He sure wished he could. He was dying there in the hall with the ache.

The madam came back. She had rethought her anger and said pleas-
antly, -Now you go out and fix your radiator and come right back.- She
patted his ass. Made him jump.

-We'll give you the fun of your life.-

He thanked her and put the water in the radiator and the bucket back
in the truck. Turned one last time to look at the house. Cured himself for
ever coming again. Yet he could not forget the silky girls, silky garments.
For many months afterward he fantasized their rosy skin while doing
what seemed necessary, yet made him sad, holding his longing in his
lonely hand. And afterwards the shame of having ever wanted those poor
creatures.

Now he thought, walking into the village from his mother's grave, that
he wouldn't know how to make love to a woman since he never had.

CHAPTER 31

—*Y*ou been drinking. - Noncie banged down the pot where she was stirring a stew.

-Where did you get some?- Papa asked.

–We gave up our lives.-

-You're a broken record. Nobody put a gun to your head. -

-You're right.- Noncie raised her voice. -You're the only one with a gun.-

-That was an accident,- Papa said. -This is getting nowhere, and..-

He reached for the Bible. He read from his random selection. "There is no decree or statute which the king established that may be changed..."-

-Will you ever stop that nonsense, Papa?- Florence left the kitchen, but loitered in the dining room.

-"After this I saw the night visions..."- Papa read on.

-You destroyed not only my life but my last chance,- Noncie screamed at Florence.

-This has been said and...- Papa slammed the Bible shut.

Florence called back. -He wasn't much if he didn't come courting you afterwards.- She was getting a fierce headache and staggered toward the living room to lie down on the couch.

Goddamn, she is soused, Papa admitted to himself...but he turned to Noncie, -Give it up...and.-

He thought, *I should go on a cruise and find a woman. Leave them to hell.* But later he thought, *why can't my sweet girls stop egging each other on?* Then he said to Noncie, -Isn't it time to make up with Florence?-

Florence fell asleep, tumultuous sleep, lying sprawled on the bear rug, never having reached the couch.

Perhaps she heard them talking, or was she half dreaming? Was Noncie saying,

-She's found another Irving. Worst of all I heard he was in jail once.-

-In jail? What for?-

-Heard it from the postmistress.- She took off her apron and sat in a chair opposite him.

Dismal shits, Papa thought.

Noncie went on, -We never had a single criminal in our family.-

-Not true. Not true, Aunt Jean was on morphine and was committed to a prison-like institution.-

- Yes, I know that story, not a real prison. And she was allowed to keep her maid. And the maid sneaked in the morphine tucked inside the bun on her head. Even though Aunt Jean was locked up, she was happy as a clam until she died of an overdose. Prison. That's a good idea. Let's lock her in her room for three days to dry her out. Then we might be able to talk sense into her.-

They schemed quickly. -Let's hope her stupor lasts,- Papa whispered.

Noncie pulled up the kitchen scatter rug. They tiptoed into the living room. Her mouth open, she was yanking snores from her throat. Papa had her feet, Noncie her shoulders. Florence gave them one long rasp, but never opened her eyes. She really was asleep. They rolled her onto the rug.

-Boy, she's heavy as green wood,- Papa whispered, wondering how they could carry her upstairs. He was too old for this crap. Florence's arms fell out the sides of the rug, drifting and slapping each riser. They half set her on a step each time to catch their breaths. Noncie wasn't sure she could make it. Papa wasn't sure he could make it.

Part way up Noncie dropped Florence's rear end and Papa nearly fell backwards, grabbing the banister to save himself. She thought she had hold of the rug again but her hands slipped and Florence bumped her way down a few steps. Papa kept backing up to save his balance and her.

Florence was semi-awake now. She glanced about. Where was she? She giggled -You two giving me a ride, what fun.-

-Yes, Flossy,- Papa whispered.

She drifted again into oblivion.

Three more steps. At the top they slowly dragged the rug down the hall to her room. -One two three,- Papa said, -lift.-

With one last heave they laid her onto her bed.

So peaceful, Papa thought with envy, since he had many fitful nights. Noncie made sure the potty from the attic was in her room, a pitcher of water and a glass before they left. Papa took out the iron key from inside and locked the door outside.

-She'll wake up and think about her life.- Noncie rubbed her hands together. Her eyes had tears of hope.

Florence didn't wake until noon the next day and didn't think about her life. She had heard enough through her fog. She had heard their scheme. She swung from depression into outrage. They had no right. She paced the floor. Looked out the window, too far to jump.

Noncie came with a tray of oatmeal and warm maple syrup, but she almost dropped the tray. Florence was sitting naked on the bed . Noncie had not seen her naked since she was a child.

Get some clothes on,- She shrieked. She left and locked the door. She did not know why she shrieked, was it the realization that Florence's body was beautiful, rounded and adult, so adult?

Florence hugged herself at her simple revenge. She didn't touch the tray. Lunch came. This time Papa brought it. He took one look at Florence who was still naked but sitting on the bed with her legs open. He dropped the tray smack onto the floor. She called through the door, - How long are you going to play this game. I can play mine as long as you like.-

-As long as it takes for you to reform, rethink your wasted life,- Papa called back.

Noncie came and whisked the potty away to empty it. She held her nose. She thought how low they had slipped. Instead of raising Florence up they had lowered themselves into chambermaids.

-It's your turn next.-

-Whoope,- Papa said.

-I'm serious. I'm not doing it next.-

Shit, Papa thought, appropriately. At the end of the second day Papa couldn't go on with the scheme. He knew she was naked in there and he couldn't bear to look. He unlocked the door and swung it open but she rose up and walked toward him, sticking her breasts out at him.

He practically killed himself running down the steps and yet smiling at her cleverness. She had won by understanding how ingrained was his decorum and at the same time she humiliated him because she knew he believed in the worthlessness of such precepts.

In the kitchen now with coffee in her hand Noncie said to her. –Mc Huron was in jail.-

-Why are you telling me that?-

-I heard it from the postmistress,- she said.

- Florence is never going to see him again.- She doesn't want to drink. She told me and she told you too.-

-That's pie in the sky.-

The next day Florence sat in her herb garden, feeling good and with no headache. The mint was high, oregano, parsley, chives, and bunch onions with their curled purple tendrils were up.

Cold turkey. Maybe she would take up something like hooking rugs or writing poetry. She promised them both again.

CHAPTER 32

*A*s Edifice was walking past the cheese factory Landman saw him through the never-been-washed window (so that thieves wouldn't see what good cheese he made and break in he told Edifice). He rushed out with a dish in his gnarled hand to give Edifice. How he loved the rubbery neophyte curds, so delicious Edifice could hardly talk. His stomach had been aching with hunger.

-Been up to your mom's grave?-

-Do you remember my mother well?-

-I sure do. The Decoration Day hunt when everybody was going off to the one soldier's grave from this village. You were too little or do you remember? She invited the children in the village, maybe thirty of us before the flood took lots of them houses. Remember the hunt?-

-My sister and I helped her hide the prizes. We made the lemonade.-

-Your mother spent days tying together the ribbons, didn't she, and then wove them all over, across the bridge and in backyards and up the church and Lovelace's barn and ended up a different place every year. The kids had to follow the ribbon together to the end and there in a huge basket was the candy, one piece for each child.-

-She made the candy for weeks,- Edifice said. –My sister and I helped.-

-Nobody was left out.-

Edifice could taste the dark nuggets. They rolled the sugar candies and dipped them in the melted chocolate and laid them out on buttered waxed paper.

Landman wondered if he should go on with this, since Edifice began to look sad. But Edifice said, -One year she bought thirty-six or so bantam chickens and each child got to take home a chick.-

-Bantam because they would be laying children sized eggs,- Landman said. -We all never forgot that. They were pets and we named them. I named mine after your mother, Eliza. She was different, your mother, like you, Edifice.-

-Thank you,- Edifice said.

-Two of the Smither kid's chickens got eaten by Browning's dog and the Smithers didn't speak to the Brownings again. I'm not sure if that was why.-

Edifice knew where Landman's account was headed. -That is until Jud Browning and Clorisa Smithers fell in love and got hitched. Then came the grandchildren and all of a sudden the families began speaking again. -Hate flies out the window with those cherub faces flies in, don't it?-

-Maybe that's why I'll never be forgiven,- Edifice said.

Landman didn't ask what he meant. He gazed at him. -Why do you stay in this village? You got brains and strength enough to go anywhere. I don't even know why you stay with her. Although it's none of my business.-

-I got a history, a past that is sticking to me like fresh tar.-

-You with a history?- He gave Edifice a friendly slap on the back. -Anyways I know, even a humble place like this can get into your veins, I know.-

Edifice believed his friend knew little about him. Yet some he must have put together, like why he didn't hunt anymore.

-You're a good friend,- Edifice said.

-Likewise,- Landman said.

CHAPTER **33**

Dear Miss Logan,
  Your letter sounds like a good idea. I'm glad that you wrote me. I would suggest you have a town meeting and take a vote and send the results up to me. As you know these are difficult times and our state budget is hard put but we will look into it.
  Yours truly,
  John Metcalf, assistant to the Governor.

*T*he town meeting was set for August 15. Noncie became increasingly tense. Rumors had circulated everywhere, sides taken, simmering anger. Some of it was laid on her. How did the word get out? Must be the postmistress steamed open her letters.

The new bridge would be not only for the town's well-being but also for hers. It would be a gift to the town, pull them up, and get them going. Noncie crossed her fingers, very worried that the vote would be negative. Progress was not something the villagers cared about.

Recently when she walked across the covered bridge the light through the slats made her dizzy. Her world was becoming more and more smeared like dyes in a wash. The panic that overcame her was not just having the world around her fade, but fear that she would not recognize Hugh from a distance. Why was she thinking such thoughts?

As she was leaving the bridge she almost bumped into a baby carriage parked outside the grocery. -I'm so sorry,- she said to the young mother but what she had meant was sorry that she had come across a baby.

Noncie brought home a letter to Florence. Who? She realized it was from Irving's lawyer. She read it and said to Noncie, -Irving is dead. There will be no more alimony.- Then the lack of alimony was not what struck her, but that maybe she would not have to think about him anymore, brought on by the monthly reminder. Hatred, love, lost youth that she had worn like a tattered dress, she could now discard. But she would be totally dependent on Papa...a kind of prison. Maybe she could sell her diamond ring from Irving, thrown in a box in her bureau.

-Heavens,- Nonce said, -I always worried that he would trace you down, kidnap you or kill you.-

-You did? So did I.-

Noncie hugged her, pleased not only about Florence, but hope for the bridge.

Florence wanted to say how remorseful she was about Hugh but was afraid to bring up that distressing subject. And she felt dismal about Noncie's longing for a baby.

One day later there it was in her mind and invading her heartbeat. She filled her pockets with herbs to eat for relief and wondered where she could buy chewing tobacco. She laughed at herself, the picture of herself chewing with the men sitting on the station steps and spitting out of the corner of her lips.

The Herbs were just herbs. Maybe she was just born with a stinking sewer of a character, ready to go to his cabin, ready for death. Couldn't help it, better to die for what she loved, that beautiful taste in her mouth, than never to have died at all...whatever that meant.

She opened the door where she had all her cosmetics on racks, lipsticks of every possible color, eye shadow, round tiny beauty mark pasties for her cheek, powders and wax for her eyelashes, which were still long and fetchingly thick, unlike her hair. She had plastered her face, including two layers of different colored lipsticks.

Good, Noncie's mind seemed fully occupied on the bridge. Maybe she would leave Florence alone. Although Florence wondered if Noncie could change anybody's mind around here if they didn't want a new bridge, which seemed likely, too much trouble, disruption and what for? They were getting along without it.

Florence put on her best white linen dress with the tatting of rosebuds on the sleeves and bodice. The dress lilted just above her ankles, showing her white hose. The outfit slimmed her plump figure. She pulled down the hatbox and found her panama.

She slid by Papa, who was sitting in his Adirondack chair in the yard.

But then he said, -You look beautiful. You have a style. Where are you going?-

She smiled at him. She knew her smile was one of her best features. She went on her way, waving to him.

Fast walk. She had figured out a different way, in case that knife of a woman was laying in wait for her. Across Hullet's field, down Barnett

Samuel's lane, then down a dip that people called fern valley and out across an empty lot where she grabbed onto a rope, she had once noticed hanging from a tree. Children swung to the opposite bank of the narrow part of Flood Brook. She knew if anybody saw her they would faint at the flying lady in a white dress, but it was the only way she could get across without ruining her shoes and dress. She had saved her lovely linen dress from touching the water. The skirt billowed in the breeze. Right over the river she flew.

When she landed she heard laughter and turned back to see the two young Proudy kids in a fit of giggling. She ran then, up through the scrubbed looking birch woods seeming and into the waving summer field to the left of her destiny.

There in front of the still, lying on the grass in the sun, was Edifice. Asleep, or pretending. She stood over him and he suddenly he opened his eyes and gasped, but said nothing, no greeting, nothing. He sat up.

-I've come for a drink.-

-Who are you?- He asked in disbelief over her makeup. His own face above his beard was flushed, his heavy eyebrows pulled together, his mouth in a twisted mock. -So, where have you been?-

-Could I please buy a drink?- She tried to act official, though she wouldn't have much money anymore.

His eyes on her lips, he said, -Where have you been? Two days? You been sick? Not coming to work anymore?-

-I'm fine. I just want a drink, thank you.-

-What's wrong with you? I don't know you, look at you. You better leave.-

-I'm not leaving. And this is who I really am. Period.-

-I don't think so.-

-Well it is.- She pulled a dollar bill from her crocheted purse. He stood up and tensely, solemnly, walked into the still and brought out a jug.

-You already know I'm not selling you this unless you wipe off that mess.-

She was furious and aroused. Her face scorching, as they stood, feet apart, like duelists ready to lift their weapons.

-No,- she said. He turned back into the still and slammed the door. Inside he thought of what she was wearing, all that finery, like English ladies going to the races, her flesh ripe and golden with baby freckles rushing up and down her arms and that face, well it was the underneath face, the pug nose, the large glistening black eyes and cheeks as soft as new mushrooms, her swan's neck which he pictured bent back, exposed for kisses. Why was she acting so cold?

She called out to him -I'd like to have a drink.- Trembling overtook her.

He opened the door. -You don't get any until you do something about your face and tell me what's going on-

-I won't.-

-Okay you're a stranger. Too dangerous selling to strangers.-

She said nothing. They looked at each other. She turned and walked away, came back, pulled her handkerchief from her pocket, paused. Then slowly, her hand continuing to shake, wiped her face.

He thought she's like a child trying on her mother's makeup, she smeared some on her cheek. He was filled with the charm of her.

He disappeared into his still for what seemed a long time while she paced up and down, then appeared with a jug against his hip. She sat on the step and he handed it to her.

-When are you going to tell me what's going on?-

She took a long satisfying swig. Then he took one without wiping the top and waited until she asked for another. They began to mellow out, the two of them in the afternoon sun, sitting on the step, and she was just far gone enough to say -I know something about you.-

-And what is that?- He moved closer to her in spite of himself, loving the faint rich odor of the perfume she had dabbed at the back of her ears.

-I know something bad about you.-

-Well, I'll be, that couldn't be. I'm perfect.- But he felt unnerved.

She drew a breath. –you're a killer.-

He swallowed before choking out, -Where did you hear such a thing?-

-Your wife.-

-I can't believe...she couldn't have. She hardly talks to anybody. Why was she talking to you?- The muscles in his neck tightened.

-Are you a killer?-   He stood up, knocking over the jug that neither one righted as the liquor spilled out on the steps, flooding onto her dress. He jumped up and down in a frantic dance, kicked a log over and over. He picked an ax on the wood pile.

-No.- She tried to stand and run but it was too late. She was too woozy now and her panic was making her hyperventilate into profound trepidation.

-She didn't tell you that.- He threw the ax into the log. –Where did you hear that?- He was squeezing her arm. She stared at the ax. Could she grab it from the log before he did? His squeezing seemed as if to keep himself from falling.

-Tell me.- She dared. -I'm good at secrets. I didn't believe her. It's not true. Of course not. She just wanted me to leave you alone. Now I don't walk past your house.-

-She told you what?-

His squeezing hurt her. It was too late to run, too drunk. -Let me go.-
He slowly released her. -Please tell me.-

-She talked so fast I just think she said, did I know you were a killer?-
The beat in Florence's heart was looping as Edifice's face came close. Then
he sat on the ground and rubbed his beard.

-I didn't know she knew.-

-It's true?- Florence wobbled her way slowly away from him. Alarm
arose just enough to take hold of her legs. She ran as best she could. She
got as far as the worn path down the hill. But he was chasing her. Almost
upon her. He caught her.

-Sit and I'll tell you. Nobody else knows. And you got plenty of reason
not to tell or the river will dry up so fast you won't even smell it disappearing.-

-I'll stand.- Irving had taught her one other thing beside drink, always
be ready to run.

-Gerty lived up on this hill, an only child. Well, there had been
another child, who died in some strange incident. Found her drowned.
Maybe murdered. That's what I think. They were so poor they didn't even
have proper walls, tar paper walls and a plank roof. Her mother died also
under weird circumstances and her father didn't tell Gerty that she was
dead for a long time. Said she had run off, but we all knew better. She had
no way of leaving. My father tried to give them money, knowing how
poor they were, that is, tried to, but her father swore at him and threw my
father out.

-After her mother died Gerty lived alone with her father and came to
school with black eyes or cuts, claiming they were accidents...like a hoe
she stepped on hit her in the face. It was true I hunted then and one day
bright with fall leaves I climbed to hunt up the slope where later I built
the still. Not far from there sat the tar paper shack where Gerty and her
father lived. Never had enough money to clapboard the place.

-I was turning to go home without any game when I heard screaming.
I stopped, ran toward the sound. Saw them. For a second couldn't catch
who they were. Then I saw it was Gerty and her father. Screams from her,
as if her flesh were tearing, her father was pulling her hair and slinging her
against the house. "I'm going to kill you," he shouted.

I leaped down the slope. Gerty had wriggled free and was running. But
her father grabbed up an ax from the chopping block. His lard arms raised
high, lifting it above her head as she tried to escape around the corner, but
he was almost upon her, yelling with villainous anger. I lifted my shotgun
and pulled the trigger as involuntary as breathing. The bullet traveled
without me… no, with all of me.

-The ax flew from her father's hands to the ground. He fell face first, his legs sprawled. I had bombed a hole through the center of his body. I had killed him.

-Gerty turned. She glanced at her father on the ground, his blood erupting out his back. Only a moment. She didn't look where the shot had come from. Maybe she hadn't seen me. I don't know to this day. She stepped over her father's body and took off into the forest the other way.

I ran back up the field. I turned this way and that to find the best place. Came to the cliff of rocks. Where? Where, I kept looking? I found a flat spot and dug a shallow ditch with a stick, a rock and my bare hands, replanting the grassy sod over the grave of the gun.

I didn't think she saw me. I ran the other way. No, I didn't think she saw me. She never even alluded to that day. Yes, I buried the gun and never used one again. I walked slowly to the village way off in the woods and by the lane near the river where the cabin is.

-The sheriff came to the village. Nobody cared that her old man was murdered. Some people may have thought Gerty did it, but nobody said anything. Most people thought her evil father should be dead. When the sheriff asked me I told him I didn't own a gun. -

-Gerty was in high school and I went off to Harvard that fall but didn't stay and three years later I married her. Why? The only reason was that she hung in my conscience like a dangling sword. I felt responsible for her the rest of my life. -

Florence gasped.

-She doesn't want you around me because you threaten that I might throw her out and she would have no roof over her head. Or land to hunt on or have a garden. I believe all of her is hatred that came from the blood of her father, dead or alive.-

-And no children.-

He looked away. Shame roared back in him as if Gerty's rejection proved his worthlessness.

-She never, not once let me get near her. But I'm now glad, glad she's not the mother of my children.-

Florence sat on a rock and he stood above her -So she just wanted to use you and you took it?-

He flushed with anger. -I don't think you know what it's like to kill somebody.-

-You've made her your punishment.-

-That first night she threw me out of her room but the next night she came in my room in some gauzy nightgown to torture me. I fell for that come on but she ran away screaming. Maybe she wanted to see if I would rape her or beat her like her old man did. She locked her door after that. Sometimes I bit my hands into bruises. I was only twenty-one years old.-

Florence rubbed her eyes, held her head. -Oh my God. Is that why you began to drink?-

-It is.- He looked at her, the image that was riveting him was her exposed lips, the dance of her lips as she talked, pulled laterally, pursed, bitten, and somber.

-My husband taught me scorn, estrangement and contempt. He taught me how to lose my girlhood and my humor and good will and most of all taught me to drink.-

Edifice knelt beside her and very carefully placed his lips on hers, keeping them there to stop the bleeding of her memory…of his memory. She didn't let his lips go until she felt faint from an unfamiliar unsettling of her own feelings.

-You didn't just come up here for vodka alone, did you?-

CHAPTER 34

*H*anging on the apple tree was a deer. Gerty must have shot it on the Logan's land. Illegal this time of year. Edifice had to pass the creature bleeding out to get into the house. He couldn't look up or he'd see it swinging and he couldn't look down or he'd see the rubbery, visceral-slickness of the blood slowly spreading.

He would stay the hell away for the skinning, gutting and cutting up the creature. He knew she had once borrowed a saw for the bones from Peabody…the saw Peabody used to sever a hand or a leg in emergency on a woodsman.

Gerty hung the pieces of deer here and there to age, even though it was summer. That night when he came into the kitchen to make coffee and fry up a few mushrooms to put on bread, she sat at the once shiny cherry table. Her venison cooking smell, layering the air with flavors, that particular smell of the wild he would never get used to.

Gerty sat eating, pulling and shredding the meat, mocking and insulting him.

-So what you doing with her?- she choked out with her mouth full.

-Who the hell are you talking about?-

-The woman with no hair to speak of.-

-I'm not doing anything, with anybody.-

She ate for a while.

He savored the delicacy of the chanterelles, shutting his eyes, as he had done as a child over his mother's lemon squares.

-I know what you're doing and I'm warning you what I'm capable of. Oh, I'm not going to shoot you or nothing. I got the law on my side. Lots of the law. Just snap my finger and they come racing. Racing and happy because there is so little to put their teeth into around these parts.-

-Call them for what?- he dared.

She didn't answer.

He finished his plate in private in the parlor. He came back, washed his dish, took his coffee and strode into the attached barn and tore out a nice old window with square panes. He would wash it in the river.

He'd lived with her unspoken threats but now she was speaking them. If she dared get him arrested he would divorce her, sell the place or let Florence move in there, if she wanted.

Then where would Gerty go? Nowhere. No home and she knew it.

He put the window into his truck, packing a moth eaten blanket around it.

Florence was dressed in overalls this time like Papa's, and he started, -What the hell...- Stopped himself. —-What is that you got on?- He was coming from the garden with a handful of baby carrots, proudly holding them up like candles.

-I wanted to look like you,- Florence answered. But left him quickly so he wouldn't ask more and ran down the lane, stumbling a bit in the overalls that Edifice McHuron had given her and were too large.

He rushed into the house, threw the carrots in the sink and opened the Bible fast. Anxiety pierced him each time now before he opened the Bible. This peculiar habit was his addiction. He was really counting on the good book to help him predict or make sense of each day, a little like rubbing a magic lantern.

This one seemed apt: *seeing they may see, and not perceive: hearing they may hear, and not understand.* Was that his relationship with Florence? Could he do better by her? But how?

He reclaimed the carrots, wiped them dry but something occurred to him when Noncie arrived. He lit a match and tried to light a carrot, like a candle.

Noncie took off her gardening hat and squinted at him. She wondered, was he really going cuckoo? -What's that about?-

-Better than burning a cat or dog or...-

-Or what?- She moved close to him. -Papa?-

-It's a burnt sacrifice to our Lord... I don't know why exactly. But God has a way of creeping back in when you've thought you locked Him out.-

Noncie decided to pay no attention to him. Always had been a bit odd, which obviously

Florence had inherited.

-Papa, in that case at least start praying for a sturdy new bridge.-

-Good idea. The damned carrot wouldn't light anyway.-

She had too much on her mind to pay any more attention to his silliness.

Florence took the new route. Across the rope strung from a tree over flood
Brook. The same kids saw her, dressed so differently and said, -That ain't the same person, is it?-

But on the other side she slowed to a contemplative walk. She was okay with the kiss. Thinking about it, she figured Edifice and she kissed only out of serious need to comfort each other from their harsh pasts and that was that. Simple.

The pulley platform was tied to a tree on the opposite side of the brook. Yet he seemed nowhere. She called out, -Edifice.-

No answer.

She waited and called again. His truck was parked before the river. Heck, I'm going into the water. She rolled up her overalls, but only a little way into the brook she fell. Nothing hurt. Just soaked and mad that her nice panama hat tossed and danced down the riffles.

When she reached the other side she spotted him downstream. Wearing her hat.

At first when he saw the hat and didn't see her he panicked that something terrible had happened to her. He met her as she climbed up the bank.

-I love my hat on you, makes you look like a gentleman farmer.-

He continued to wear it, dancing about doing a "step and fetch it," act, holding it close to his chest and singing, -What's in the bag?-

-I brought us some lunch.-

-Well, I'll be.- He started into the cabin and explained -I'm about to attack the sheathing. That's the covering over the framework inside here. It's going to be diagonal so it doesn't get too boring. I haven't got many boards yet. I have to tear more out. I have a window though.-

-But there's no opening in the wall.-

-You cut through the wall, frame it out and stick the window in.-

-No kidding.- She walked around the room, jittery and excited.

-Yep.- He stared at her backside. -You wet your pants?-

She turned in shock.

-From the brook.-

-Let me help you take them off. I'll give you mine.-

She didn't dare try to unscramble her surprise. –I'm okay.-

-But you'll be so uncomfortable working in wet clothes.-

-No thanks.-

-Why?- He waited.

136

-Okay, but no looking, promise.-

-I promise,- he said.

When she turned her back on him and she heard him come toward her. She didn't move. His hands reached around her shoulders from behind and down her front to slowly undo her overalls. A tingling sensation enveloped her. She didn't move as the overalls fall to the floor.

He whispered, -Florence Logan, I don't know how to do this, but will you let me try?-

Chapter **35**

*Y*ou have to help around here,- Noncie said. -I'm not going to be the only scullery maid, sister

Florence was drifty. More than drifty. She sat at the table not moving. Noncie plunked the bowl of unpeeled potatoes down in front of her. Florence's hands had always been dexterous and sure in spite of drink but now the new kind of intoxication made them erratic. She was overwhelmed with feeling. She peeled in hunks and jabs, leaving deep crevices in the flesh of the potatoes.

-What are you doing?- Noncie picked up the bowl.

-We were not brought up to do this.-

-Where's the maids in this house?-

Papa came in and thinking, they were fighting or would fight again, used his latest weapon. He rushed upstairs to the bathroom and came down fast as he could. He sat in a chair near Florence. He filled a bowl of water, and laid it on the floor beside him. He pulled from his pocket the shaving brush and squiggled the soap on his right leg where he had lifted his trousers. The girls watched, speechless as he began shaving. Florence's giggles rose into hilarity, spilling out with gasps. She couldn't stop the beautiful feeling of life. Noncie finally gave in, bursting into her own deeper almost soundless laughter.

As for Papa, oh how warm the old man felt toward his amused girls.

Edifice used to think about the fate of mankind and the fate of the nation under The Depression. Now he thought only of their fate, Florence and his, a daytime worry, a nighttime worry, a waking at dawn worry. He stopped on the way home and leaned against a maple tree near the path and shut his eyes to see Florence's face in ecstasy to feel her breath at his neck and memory of her hollows and spheres, the small of her back as it curved to the knob of her tail bone, her sloping shoulders and cone shaped breasts. Her pomegranate cheeks and rosy chin, one eye more hooded than the other, the slight convex curve of her belly and long arms and long flat wrists and a wide girth of thighs. Her slender hipbones, her mossy mound below. Had he touched every inch? Of course he hadn't. It would take him a lifetime.

He would have to practice and practice until he knew her by heart. But even in their magnificent lovemaking he was afraid she did not feel as he did. Just a roll in the hay for her. Would she think differently the next day….or, or. Why was he not allowed in his love the purity of ecstasy?

As he walked into his kitchen Gerty looked up. She slammed her dinner down on the table. He wasn't afraid of her anger. She wouldn't dare tell on him about killing her father, if she really knew. There would be no proof and she would be considered a suspect since she had been the one abused. But what he did fear now was something vague, something awful she could do to Florence.

He cooked himself some rice and ate in silence. But while he ate she leaned over him and said in a clenched whisper, -How dare you do this to me?-

-Do what?-

-I know she goes to see you and you do her. I'm your wife, you bastard.-

-My wife? My wife? I could have us annulled.-

-You better reconsider that remark. I could tell on you what I figure you're making.-

Although a little shocked he didn't want to bother fighting with her. Wasn't worth trying since it had taken so much energy just to keep peace inside himself, hard to keep his temper -How dare you harangue me when you have never ….never let me. Don't even think of threatening me, or Miss Logan, ever or else.- He left the room shaking violently, leaving the bowl of rice to thicken and turn cold.

Like a tree Florence was, with her years of layered rings, hidden until the tree was cut down. He knew he was naïve but she was anything but naive. Skittish as a Morgan horse, unpredictable as the weather…that was okay. He loved any kind of weather, the silence of nestling snow, contentious summer storms, wet leaves of fall, and the chattering of naked limbs in the forest. The only certain thing about her was that she would come for the juice, no doubt about that. Yet each time, since that first making love, he felt she was his beloved. But when she headed for home he plunged into the depths of despair, still afraid she did not feel the same about him.

Five times Florence had come to him. This would be the sixth, he watched
and tore at his beard and crossed the brook many times to peer down the path when he heard
her he quickly turned to hammering or sawing, while his beating need for her almost toppled him.

Her voice, soft and elastic, called out his name through the trees as she scrambled onto the pulley. He couldn't help his quivering, silent panting, rolling heart, and a tightness rising in his brain. He pictured her puff of energy, hopping here and there, the way her mind searched to learn. She had picked up carpentry just like that, retaining what he showed her and now ready for nuances, like dovetailing. He smiled, that was what they were doing with each other.

This time he rushed down the bank and when she landed off the pulley she jumped into his arms, throwing her legs around his waist like a youngster and he carried her up to a new place—each time it was a new place. This time under cool leaves as their bodies flamed.

If raining, they used the mattress on the floor of the cabin. They sank into the luscious cool. He kissed behind her ear, letting his tongue lap the edges. He sneaked the tip deeper into her curly vessel of her ear. She cried out from the thrill and when he heard, his tongue touched faster, then down her neck. Down her breasts, her belly. Kissing, lapping quickly, slowly as if gliding on powder snow.

Then sober, church-like came their final phase. He must hold off temptation. He stopped to simply hold her, waiting for her to cry out in need for him. He rocked her back and forth deeper into the leaves.

Afterwards she whispered, -I never knew this. I didn't imagine feeling like this, this love.

"I know."

Later he asked her, -Do you think of him anymore now that he's dead?-

-Yes… I bless him.-

-Bless him?- His heart sank.

-For steering me to you.-

-But what if we didn't drink anymore? Would you still come here?

But her body had relaxed into a sudden sleep. His head lay between her breasts.

The closeness of her surrounding flesh reduced his eyes to mesmerizing comfort. He wouldn't allow himself to think of the two of them as doomed, or having some inevitable danger.

Or not loving each other anymore.

The blast of the noon whistle woke him.   -We must finish the roof,- he said, -before cold weather.-

The roof so far had boards and was ready for slate shingles. He had brought a few slates each day he pulling them form the barn, some over the woodshed. Florence followed him onto the cabin roof and he showed her how to place and tuck and secure the slate. One third of the roof was done now.

She turned, felt a little unbalanced and almost fell off, distracted by his short thick naked body, his heavy muscles connecting so smoothly they seemed like finely sanded wood. She thrilled at the small parts of him, his dark hands and neck that had been exposed day after day to the sun, ornaments on his otherwise birch-white skin, his hairy chest, his exotic stubby feet and what she felt was the most sympathetic face she could imagine. She was overwhelmed with love.

He said, -Hungry?-   He led her to the brook. -Very still. Kneel right here on the bank.- He took her hand and placed it palm up on top of his. He steered her, dropping their hands slowly under the water, to a large trout that matched the gray brown of the brook.

Once under he clamped her fingers on the slippery fish. She screamed. It escaped.

-You'll learn,- he said and he reached and caught one, not as big as the other, and threw it up on the bank. She was bending over the water washing her hands. He caught a glimpse of her globe-buttocks and moved soundlessly toward her. He took them both gently in his hands. She crumpled at his touch, letting out a moan of surprise and surrender.

-You doomed little beast,- he said.

They made love the second time that day at the edge of the water in the hush of lavender mallow as the dying fish flopped for air in the rhythm of their own final gasps.

CHAPTER 36

*P*apa was often puzzled by what bugs had attacked his garden and what damned animals tore at his vegetables. And here in mid-July and the nights were already cool. Good for that new-fangled vegetable originated in Italy, called broccoli. Good for spinach. But the peas were sluggish and the beans were miffed and stopped climbing the poles.

Some days his blood also was sluggish and his body bent and his hips ached and his neck had a crick. Today he felt good but lonely. The stab of it came, wanting youth, longing for Clara all these forty-six years.

He closed his eyes. His fingers drifted up the back of Clara's neck. His fingers against the cord of her spine in memory of their dancing. Oh you whom I did not marry. You my only love. Maybe he needed some spiritual overlay to his life like the love of God. Ridiculous. Yet maybe that was why he read the Bible to his daughters, truly hoping the randomness of God's hand would open a path for him.

He wished he could be with somebody like God who had no faults. He was sick and tired of Florence's deception and Noncie with her new addiction, the bridge, waiting for the town meeting. Some days he caught her pacing the floor and embarrassed when he caught her. But he was able to get some relief by just having a look at the postmistress and glowing fantasies.

Vestiges of his daughters' childhood brightened him by his recall, rocking them, reading to them, acting out the characters, walking them long hours in the park and playing hide and seek. All these years of loving just now grew deeper bringing him to wiping his eyes.

After all he had far worse faults. He had memorized them all. Said them, like a counting sheep mantra to put him to sleep. But they weren't a confession. He was very attached to his faults, allowing him the inconsistencies in existence. Oh how he'd like to go public with a big juicy swear fest, or go to bed with the ironic postmistress.

The high sun got to him. He lay down on the warm dirt of his garden and sighed. He undid his trousers. He pulled them slowly down to his ankles, looking around to be sure no one was in the vicinity. The girls had gone to town. He wiggled his bare behind in the loam. Light and fluffy was the earth. He sank in, shutting his eyes.

-Oh,- he said aloud. It was warm, but cool just below the surface, like the lovely feel of the new-ground flour in his mill. He rolled his ass and testicles into the sweet softness. Laying back now in the soil, looking for a brief moment at the glorious blue sky, he shut his eyes and slowly undressed the postmistress.

His hand, now racing smoothly over his stiffness, was her hand. Barely touching. Expert fingers. The familiar swelling sound in his chest. My God, her lips down there? A circle of pressure. Clamped and smooth. A race to finish. No, don't end yet. Now the phantom hands, one on either side, tugged, almost brutally forcing loose his mountainous desire.

Small groans of agony. His showering stream, no longer straight up, fizzled, but felt as it always had, the only thing worth feeling on earth.

$\mathcal{N}$oncie was ready though tense, sweating at her temples which made her white hair crimp tight as hydrangeas. She looked over at Florence, her eyes in a smogged focus, as if struggling to make out a certain star in a dark sky.

-Are you coming with us dressed like that?-

-Yes, I am.- She smiled sweetly at Noncie and straightened her overalls.

-Please change. We have to show who we are. How can you go looking like poor white trash?-

-This is me.- Florence raised her hands to her chest.

-How could it be? What are you turning into? Please change your clothes,- Noncie begged.

-Just get in the car. We'll be late, Flossy, - Papa said.

They both obeyed. Noncie tried to put Florence out of her mind.

She could not believe how many people arrived at the town meeting. Parents with children in arms, toddlers who couldn't be left...No nanny or maid. Old men and women, middle-aged, and even a few stray high school kids. She realized she knew most of the faces if they were close enough but not all the names. Just then she saw the only beard in the crowd. Edifice McHuron, but not with his wife. Gerty was standing, not sitting, over against the left wall near Dr. Peabody. Noncie and Florence sat down, Papa in the middle. -Can't you sit a little away from us?- Noncie asked Florence softly. -We're trying to make an impression here.-

Florence whispered back, -It's the debate not the clothes that will make the impression.-

Papa looked over at Florence. She was really his blood and bones, that Florence. Left of center. Stubborn. A screw loose even when she wasn't drunk.

Horace Hibbard slammed down the gavel. His round protruding nose and his grunt of a voice reminded people of the pigs he raised. He was well liked, shared some of his pork with any widow that gave him a smile.

He said, –The meeting will come to order. We are here to discuss whether we want this new cement bridge or to keep the covered one. Seems they will build the new if we vote yes.-

Les March, the schoolteacher, stood up. Horace nodded for him to speak.

-If we have a new bridge we could have a better school because the state would make us a better road and that would bring in more work, like maybe another sawmill and the like and that would be more money for more than one teacher.-

Horace nodded for Tom Overlace to speak. Angry, he called out, -you hankering for competition with my mill?-

Les answered. -That's not a bad thing. There is plenty of wood to go around.-

-It's not the wood. It's who buys the wood with no money to spare.-

-It would be good for all of us.- Sonny James said from the back of the room.

-Good for sending us packing.- Tom Overlace shouted.

Horace was nodding at Jenette Rodale. –Yes, it would be best for the kids to be out of a one-room school. My two boys are smart and don't like to listen to the same thing again from the lower grades. More people settling here would add to the school.- She sat down quickly, blushing.

Edifice's friend, Landman, rose to his feet. -I'm for keeping the covered bridge, keeps the snow off. I was once in a storm with my horse and buggy and we sat there until the wind stopped. It's a mighty handy thing, a roof.-

-Who has a horse and buggy much these days,- Peter Hill said with a chuckle.

-Not everybody owns a tractor like you,- Landman continued, unruffled as a lake on a calm day.

-You all know I only got a horse and buggy.- Dotty List's voice showed she had been insulted. -I'm for keeping the old bridge, too.-

-The covered bridge isn't safe,- Digs Browning answered.

-It can be fixed, those underpinning rocks shift a little every year but they could be reinforced,- Landman said. -It lasted through the flood.-

-I want the old bridge too,- Prentice Wilnot said. He was the ancient man with few teeth, too old now to make much of a living off the land. His wife hooked rugs with stiff slow fingers and sold a few at Old Home Days in several towns. -I played ball on the covered bridge in bad weather when we were younguns, Blogette, you all remember him, and Digs and me.

145

But Digs, being on the other side wouldn't look back at Prentice as Prentice stared lovingly his way.

-And Blogette died up there in the woods, maybe you all remember? We was walking with him and taking the dogs to look for birds and we had had quite a meal together before hand and...-

-Thank you, Prentice,- Moderator Hibbard interrupted grunting kindly -We're glad you spoke about wanting the covered bridge. Next?-

Noncie stood up. -I think you all know how I feel about having a new bridge, how much it will improve the town, make life better for us all.- She sat down.

But Prentice hadn't sat down. -And out of the blue sky this bird dives at Blogette, a crow it was and made Digs' dog, Nelly Anne, run away and Blogette dies on the spot, from fright,

Dr. Peabody told us and...-

-Yes,- Hibbard interrupted again and pointed to the postmistress. –The covered bridge has to go. You all know that Hayden Johnson takes his fancy go-to-races Morgan horse across to ride up to Bellow's meadows and when the horse gets to the bridge the creature lifts his tail and lets lose with great happiness. It's clockwork. The covered bridge is his poop-ing place.-

Great tittering rose up. Papa laughed out loud and catarrhed. Some-thing so adorable about her using the word pooping.

Prentice started again -And the bridge has a memory of what's-his-name, lived over on Hill Road or Thomsonburg, don't remember what he did, but something...- His granddaughter tugged him to sit down.

Hayden Johnson rose, -I have seen you,- he said to the postmistress,- Go and scoop up the manure and race to your window boxes to give the petunias their dinner.-

-Just to clean it up, you old coot.-

-None of that,- the moderator said with a grin.

Papa beamed at her.

Prentice had wiggled free from his daughter. -I remember now, he got mad at old Brown and laid logs across the bridge so he had to move them to get across. Big brutish logs and full of slugs.- His daughter pulled him down again.

-We'd have to pay more taxes for a new bridge,- Ezra Hill's brother Edward called out from his seat.

-Please stand when addressing the meeting,- Hibbard said with a grunt.

-Snot,- some kid called out and people turned to see who, but couldn't tell.

-You don't pay taxes anyhow, Edward Hill,- his wife said.

-You going to humiliate me in public?- His face crumpled into deep lines.

-It's no secret,- she answered, -That we don't got the money.-

Diane Cross said, -How about mud season? What's a cement bridge going to be

like in mud season?- Heads swung around to the right to look at her. She hardly ever talked. People said she lost most of her words in the 1929 flood.

-Same as any other bridge, I suspect,- Horace Hibbard said.

Francis Davidson stood. -You can't square dance on a cement bridge. Too hard on the feet.-

His son, Roger said, -But Dad, we don't have to dance on the covered bridge anymore. We do it in the church basement now.-

-Confining in every sense of the word,- Francis answered.

Millicent Jones, holding her corn-haired bright-eyed baby said, -My pappy died on the bridge coming home from sugaring. I don't ever want to see it torn down. It's like his memorial.-

Linette Roar, who had been leaning against the piano in back, said, -Well, if the walls of the bridge hadn't been there people might have seen him from the grain store or along the main street and saved him.-

Board Gazette said, -People could stand up on the rail and throw themselves in the river to you know, kill themselves.- He crossed himself, even though he wasn't Catholic.

-You could jump off a roof and kill yourself too,- Tilly Toussaint said. She was known for her comebacks, and her hot cross buns on Good Friday.

Snickers rose. Horace Hibbard hit the gavel.

-How did all this bridge stuff get started anyhow? Some outside influence here. That isn't right,- Prentice said from his seat where his daughter had hold of his arm so he couldn't stand.

People looked over at Noncie. Red flamed her face. It was to help them. Couldn't they see that? But she decided to lay low, not to antagonize. It was then that Edifice McHuron asked to be heard. The audience turned politely.

Florence could see that the people respected him, knew he had brains. -As you all know I have lived here my whole life but I'm a first-generation immigrant from Massachusetts.-

They laughed.

-The point I want to make is the world is changing, like all our villages. Times are rough all over. And those of us who didn't desert our community are struggling. We can't help that. But we have this beautiful bridge that was originally built by the Lovelace family, right George?-

Across the room George nodded back. -Your great grandpa was a wonderful craftsman, hand-hewn pegs axed by him. The slate roof from the mines up at Rupert collected by sleigh teams one winter. It has stood now for nearly 100 years and babies have been wheeled across, women walked and men on horses and old folks hobbling to church...- he was getting into it. -It's our bridge of life. It's what has kept the two sides of the town a family. How could we cut it down and bury all that went before us, all our history?- He sat down and there was silence.

Florence stood up and addressed the moderator. Noncie put her head down. In her soft voice that drifted like snow across the rapt audience Florence said, not looking at Edifice who was a number of rows back, -Edifice and I have talked this over many times and I agree with him but I have an idea. Why don't we keep both bridges?-

She sat down and the whole place stared at her, hushed.

She looked over at Gerty McHuron and saw the fury on her face but assumed Edifice would be proud of her, didn't realize what she had done, telling the world and particularly his wife that they were bound to each other, talking over all that mattered. A hum grew and a restlessness, at first small, then like a gust of wind rustling the leaves. Horace banged his gavel.

-Mr. Moderator,- Tyler Taylor said, as if Florence's confession brought it to mind. -People kissed their first kiss on that bridge.-

Hayden Johnson stood. -How dare you talk about kissing? I caught you sneaking down underneath the bridge, hiding out with my wife. How dare you brag about lovers and the bridge.- Hayden leaped across the room at Tyler and punched him in the jaw and Tyler, a big strong woodsman, punched him in his solar plexus. Hayden folded.

The people nearby stood up to watch and a couple of men tried to stop the punching but found themselves in the midst of the punches themselves. Pandemonium. The moderator slammed the gavel harder, which sounded like a mere whisper beneath the shouting and scrambling. The fight erupted along the aisle. a chair across the room. People tried to stop the fighting, but more fighting erupted as some tried to escape. Folding chairs crashed and smashed into the crowd. Screams. Entanglements, flailing arms and ramming bodies as they rolled out the door.

Noncie stood up shading her eyes as she did against the sun, but now as if to understand what was happening. And Florence and Papa jumped up.

Florence rushed behind the crowd, looking for Edifice. Had he been trampled, hurt? She heard two fighters on the road, yelling in violent voices. The hall was nearly empty as the villagers stood about outside the door watching the fight continue down the road.

Horace Hibbard rushed out and called to the people. -Please stop and come back in for a vote.-

Slowly almost all the crowd returned.

Florence looked around and then outside again. Edifice was nowhere. He'd left. He didn't care what happened to her, caring only about how people stared at her announcing with no uncertainty they were lovers, caring only about his reputation.

Horace Hibbard said, -I think we can vote now. Only a few people are missing.- All those in favor of a new bridge rise. He counted 34 for and 22 against. He hit the gavel. -The new bridge will be built.- Noncie broke out into a cheer, along with many others.

CHAPTER **38**

*T*hat night Florence slept in her work clothes, shoes and all. Well, it hadn't been right without talking it over with him…to spill their relationship to the whole village, no matter what the villagers had assumed. Then there was Gerty, his loyalty to Gerty.

What was Florence doing with this man? Papa wondered. How truthful had she been? In the morning she couldn't get out of bed. When she finally stepped outside Papa called her to help him in his garden.

But she didn't follow him.

She sat on the ground in her circular herb garden, watching the passing hours on the sundial, already feeling the empty pit in her stomach, but knowing it was over with Edifice. What a stupid person she was. She wondered if she could find where Papa hid his money. Then she would get on a train back to Chicago. She didn't even care if she lived on the streets. Her mind flittered and wandered. Edifice, her anger at his leaving her and also her humiliation was there at every turn. At lunch she braced herself for more anger from going against the new bridge. But she found

Noncie saying Papa, - I'm so happy. A new bridge.-

-Yes. I'm glad, - Papa said.

Florence just sat. Couldn't eat. Couldn't look at them.

As Papa threw scraps to the three dogs, all their noses in his lap, he said. -There is no way to tell what's going to happen when people are involved.-

-I think a whole revolution of good will take place,- Noncie said. –What are you looking so sad for, Florence? Just because you didn't get your way?-

Florence looked up at her. - I care about history.-

-It's him you're upset about. He didn't come near you, did he? He's not worth anything and not worthy of you. - Noncie took her sister's hand but Florence jerked it away.

Florence left the kitchen and even though it was early afternoon she crawled into bed. She was nauseated. So much so she didn't feel an intense craving for vodka. Any minute she thought she was going to throw up. What had she eaten to bother her so? Or was it just am abyss of emotions?

Two days went by, maybe three. No sign of Edifice and couldn't face him ever again. And she kept feeling sicker.

She threw up each morning. She made it out to her herb garden to do her vomiting and cover it over with dirt. Then tiredness attacked her and she lay in the grass, a black shade covering her mind. So Edifice only cared about his reputation. What a false, fake, phony, divisive, creep.

The table was silent the next day at breakfast. Florence played with her food. She couldn't stand the smell of brewing coffee or the smell of Papa's smoke, lingering and seeping from the curtains and rugs. On the third day, as breakfast ended there was a knock at the door, fierce-like. Papa jumped to open it.

-Why Mr. McHuron.- A light rain was dribbling off his cap and had tightened the look of his beard. He stepped inside and went straight to Florence, not even saying hello to Noncie. -Where have you been? It isn't right, you disappearing without one word. I thought at first you might have had an accident or something terrible had happened and the postmistress didn't know either. What are you doing to me?-

-What are you doing to me? You left the meeting just like I was nobody,- she said.

-What are you talking about? I was having a fight, a verbal fight with Dumont Jones, who wants the bridge torn down and then I couldn't find you, or your father or sister anywhere. I thought you'd come to me the next day.-

-I think you know,- Noncie said, -She won't be seeing you anymore.-

He held onto Florence's chair. -Would you be that cruel?-

-I think you better leave,- Papa said.

-You don't...love me?-

Florence looked at his swollen eyes. She stood up. Noncie grabbed her back. Edifice pulled her away and then Papa said sternly to Edifice, -Goddamn, let go of her and get the hell out.-

The world stopped. The sisters looked at him with astonishment. Papa pretended he hadn't sworn. All confused he quickly said, -Come sit. We can talk about this. Here have a cup of coffee, -like this was a social call. -Let's talk this over. Make a little sense...-

-I'm going with him,- Florence said. She gave Edifice a gentle shove toward the door. They opened it and went down the step, leaving without looking back. Florence covered her ears so she couldn't hear Noncie shouting, begging.

In the truck he said, -Did, you really think I had left you or are there other reasons?- His voice was down, afraid to ask.

-Faith,- she said, -I'm low on faith. I guess we are both low on faith.-

-I guess.-

As they drove quickly to the dirt and grass lane leading to the cabin he said, -Did you see that?-

-See what?-

-When we first came across the bridge, there was a strange Ford parked at my house. That's when I drove like a bat out of hell. Could be the sheriff.- But Florence didn't care right then. She worried the whole way about throwing up. She didn't want to tell him she was feeling sick, afraid she had something dire, cancer, a bleeding ulcer.

-Oh, wait, I realize I know the car,- he said. -The meat locker guy who comes from Manchester twice a year to pick up Gerty's carcasses for her cold locker. She doesn't drive so Peabody drives her to town to get the meat out and she gives Peabody meat for taking her.-

-Thank God,- Florence said. –But shouldn't we move the still some place they can't find it? Like move it near our cabin. –

The word *our* struck him like heat on frostbite.

CHAPTER **39**

*T*hey ran up the hill. Nausea had somewhat subsided. They tore at
the equipment. They disassembled the reflux columns, the gallon
pots, the tubing and the coils. Some had been soldered together so he had
to take the whole awkward load. He wheelbarrowed them down, making
a bunch of trips.

When they finished, the still shack was empty except for the stove, his
Harvard chair, miscellaneous books, a rusted boot scraper and items he
would get later. He shut and padlocked the door.

-I'll get the woodstove at night.-

-How?-

-I'll drag it down, like I did up the hill.-

He decided to rebuild the still shack behind the cabin, conceal it in
the thick of spruce trees. When they finished juggling the equipment
across the brook they lay down on the grass and she erupted into a hail of
giggles.

-What ?- he asked.

- Keystone cops. Nothing about this is real.-

-First we'll build the outhouse.-

-I thought of a design.- Florence said, - A roof to go from the cabin to
the outhouse in winter.-

But she also thought of the chill breezes rising up from under the outhouse seat and hitting her behind, oh my, she thought, oh my, a roof
won't take care of that.

-A roof,- he said amused.

-I always loved birds, though I don't know a lot of names. The wings
in flight is what I love and I thought, but I need a piece of paper to show
you.- Edifice produced a pad. She drew a pitched roof made in a pattern

of bird wings spread as if about to fly. - Made of metal, in a design of over-lapping scalloped feathers.

-I love the idea.-

-But where do we get the metal?-

-My house, has a metal roof over the breezeway. Or I might take some from the roof of the chicken coop.-

They worked for the next week, or tried to. She was back now sipping along with him but only sipping. Her stomach still bothered her.

It took many days building the roof, cutting the metal with metal cutters that were difficult for her stiff hands. She soldered the joints instead. But she had to take long naps in the afternoon, not just from the booze but something was definitely wrong with her.

She ate less and less. He commented on the circles under her eyes, - Not enough sleep?- But she didn't answer and each day she returned to her home sooner than before.

Should she see Peabody? That thought gave her apoplexy.

The roof finished he said, -Look, a monster bird has landed.-

She clapped her hands.

He brought them the Bennington jug full of vodka but when she took a sip she told him -I don't feel well.-

He frowned and felt her head, ran his hand down her cheek. Her image changed in the dispersion of light that had risen into high noon. Shadowless light flattened her round cherubic face as if she were melting, as if slipping into a mirage. Then a cloud moved over the sun allowing her features to emerge again. -You are beautiful.-

He necklaced her long neck with his thick short fingers, lacing her so gently she was hardly aware. -How long have you felt sick?- he asked.

-A while.-

-Why haven't you told me, like you mean for days?-

-Weeks.-

-Weeks?- he hollered.

-Yes.-

-Florence, why haven't you told me?

-I should go see Dr. Peabody,- she said in a hollow voice as if not attached to her.

Late afternoon she drove the truck alone to Peabody. When she kissed Edifice goodbye swirling emotions rushed at her. She had an idea what was wrong.

-Let me drive you, please.-

-I'm fine.-

She parked the truck in the village and climbed the hill by the church and passed the house with the turret tilting like the tower of Pisa. As she stepped out three children stared at her, with what she felt was rebuke in their clear eyes. Peabody's house seemed more starched than she remembered. The white clapboards made shadows of midnight blue, like shadows on pristine snow.

Would Peabody even give her one? Was there no hope for her repeating her life's worst horror in an endless belt? Perhaps she would die this time. After all look at what the skeletal, pinched mouth doctor did to Edifice, just cut off his finger and threw it into the garbage pail.

The scrubbed steps squeaked as she climbed to the porch. Two black rocking chairs moved in syncopated rhythms from a budding breeze that curled and flipped the quaking-aspen leaves in a portent of more rain.

She read the office hours, 2 -4 p.m. It was seven after four. She tried the door. Since it was unlocked she entered and saw no one else in the waiting room. She sat on one of the four straight chairs. The horsehair sofa was too scratchy. The room was too hot, yet the oil stove in the center of the room was burning oily fumes. The design on the linoleum floor was worn into an undefined brown that was neither muskrat nor tree bark, reminded her of mud season. The tan walls had not one picture hanging. Nothing was inviting.

Florence sat and waited, hearing noise from the door to the examining room. So obviously Peabody was still in business, and also the front door was unlocked. Florence waited. After a bit she stood up and paced the floor. She thought of leaving, I don't have to make a decision today. Her head began to ache, though her stomach was okay at the moment. Unable to endure it any longer she decided to go to the door of the examining room and perhaps knock. Probably Peabody didn't know anyone was in the waiting room. As she came toward the door she heard strange groans. Was she cutting off a hand, or a leg. The door was ajar. She peeked in. What she saw didn't register until the whole length of a body on the examining table became clear. A woman, her face turned to the side so that Florence couldn't tell who it was lying with her legs spread, feet in the stirrups. She was exposed from the waist down, her skirt flung up and her black pubic hair sticking wildly straight up.

Sitting on the stool underneath her was Dr. Peabody. Her hair, usually in a tight topknot, was flowing with shining abandon over her shoulders. Her head was moving. No, her face. Her mouth moving up and down. Where? Right there in the V. The V of the woman in the stirrups.

Sounds filled the room like a bird screeching. Florence stood paralyzed. It was then that Peabody must have felt someone there, lifted her head and saw Florence. She bellowed, -Get out.-

Screams. Frantic Scurrying, clothes grabbed wildly. -Get out, out. Out-Peabody hollered at Florence. But Florence was too stunned to move. The woman. My God, it was Gerty McHuron who frantically fled out another door to another part of the house, slamming doors.

Peabody, so used to the unspeakable, now was violently shuddering. Could not pull herself together to speak immediately -What are you doing here?-

Florence was mute.

Peabody stamped her feet. Her hands quivered. Dread hurtled across her bony face. Her lips still moist from her activity, hung loose.

-How dare you come in here? This is a private room. Can't you read office hours? Are you nuts?- .

-The front door was unlocked.-

-All front doors are unlocked. Nobody trespasses. You some low down...- she paused to gather herself, realizing that wasn't the right tact. She croaked out, -What do you want?-

-I came,- She stuttered.,

-What for?-

-I think I'm pregnant.-

-What are you telling me for?-

-You're a doctor,- Florence whispered. They stayed facing each other, that moment of taking in the impossible. Florence was beginning to understand, as if a foreign language had at last clicked. She began to breathe slowly. She, Florence had the upper hand.

-Get up on the table.-

Peabody was holding onto the examining table in order to steady her feet. Her hands were shaking worse. Her knees rubbed together. Her body slumped. Her mushroom colored eyelids twitched.

-Don't you worry I'll take care of it. And we keep everything to ourselves. Everything you saw. To ourselves. Isn't that correct? Get up on the table.- She said again.

-Wait a minute here,- Florence demanded, what do you mean take care of it?-

-Everything. Anything- Peabody continued shaking.

-What do you mean that you'll take care of everything?.- Florence wanted her to say the word, put her over a barrel, tighten the rope.

-You know.-

-No, I don't know, I have to hear.-

-I'll get rid of it.-

-Say the word.- Florence folded her arms over her chest.

-Abortion.-

-You'll go against the law?-

-Yes. Yes. I'll help you out if....-

Florence's mind ripped apart, couldn't handle that word or the specifics. But she fathomed that the whole situation between them couldn't be better, like discovering a bank robber and the robber offering half his loot to keep her mouth shut.

-Get up on the table,- Peabody said. -You want me to take care of it right now.-

She looked at Florence's belly with the dark line that ran down to her public hair and her swollen breasts, her slightly swollen belly. -You are.-

Florence felt faint, her heart skipping the way stones thrown can hiccup along a lake. -I have something else to ask you.-

-Ask. Ask.-

-It's Gerty you have to get to promise something.-

-Yes. What? Anything-

-No calling the sheriff against Edifice for any reason, then I won't tell what I have seen you doing here.-

Gerty will not call the sheriff, for any reason. Don't worry. Absolutely not.-

-And you do what I want or need?-

-Of course. Yes.-

-Okay,- Florence said. -I'm going now.-

-Don't you want?-

-No. I wanted to know for sure that I was pregnant.-

-I'm available.-

-Just not after hours,- Florence put in as she went out the front door and past the ghost chairs swinging on the porch. She heard the door-bolt clank into place. She stepped carefully, as though she might pass out right down on the steps. She held tightly to the railing and walked toward the truck, past Lorene Brown hurrying in the drizzle and two women whose names she didn't know but who smiled with that smile that indicated they were minding their own business as Florence stepped up into McHuron's truck.

On the grassy lane to the cabin she had to stop and vomit again, jumping out of the cab just in time.

Edifice was waiting for her, pacing on the lane. –Florence,- he said,- But waited anxiously for her to tell him. He helped her across on the pulley. Rain was heavily pouring. Inside the cabin, ,before they spoke he took off her shirt and wiped her face and wet hair with a towel and put another shirt over her head. Finally he said, taking both her hands, -Tell me.-

-I'm trying to think how to begin. She didn't have office hours.-

-So you never went.-

-Yes, I did go.-

-And?-

She started from the beginning with all the details, needing to relive it, to believe what she saw...climbing the steps, finding the front door unlocked, the waiting room too hot, the examining room door ajar and the strange unearthly groans, peeking and.. and seeing those long skinny legs in the stirrups and Peabody's head bobbing, slurping, and with rotating movements, at first slow, then faster and faster, the sound like a hungry sea gull. Gerty McHuron.

When she finished they locked eyes.

-The truth?- He asked rhetorically. -How could it take this long for me to discover who I was living with?-

-Now we don't have to be afraid of her. I made her promise that Gerty would never call the law against you for any reason and we wouldn't tell on them. That way she wouldn't have to leave town.

He shook his head over and over. –My God. What a secret she lived. Wait. So you never found out what was wrong with you.-

- I'm pregnant.-

-Pregnant! We didn't think. We weren't thinking. Booze takes away our thinking. You mean? I can't take it in. I never thought about...my God, Florence.- He held her. -That's so wonderful. I am so happy. A baby from you and me, Florence Logan, ours- He kissed her lips with the slightest pressure of tenderness almost beyond his own control and she kissed him back with everything...everything she felt.

-You'll need calcium. I know Landsman will give us cheese. Oh my love. -

-Can't you divorce Gerty?-

He covered his eyes. He shook his head. -If I did she would find a way to destroy us.-

He held her at arms length to look at her.

-How?-

-The day I lifted the gun. If she saw me she might tell the sheriff, after all. She might think it was worth it and I'd go to jail. She has foul malice in her heart. -

-She wouldn't dare. I'd be left to tell on her and Peabody.-

-That's true the village would boycott Peabody. And she couldn't just move. Takes a long time to build up a practice and people would be suspicious, wouldn't trust her, gossip travels a long distance.-

They sat together, holding hands and watching the rising mist on the swollen river and the shiny black woods on either side. The rain washed the air and the leaves, and crushed the hay-scented ferns just enough to release their sweetness, just before the sun appeared. –A baby!- he said.

$\mathcal{E}$ difice drove Florence home to spend the night. As she opened the kitchen door she fought with herself: to tell them, not to tell them.

Noncie said, -Hi,- in such a cheerful voice that Florence felt momentarily exonerated from any antagonism her sister might be feeling.

-Supper is almost ready. I found out today that the bridge would be built in a month or two.-

-That right?- Papa came in with his basket full of beans and potatoes.

-I'm glad for you.- But decided not to say, *but sorry for the covered bridge.*

-Papa could you not light your pipe?-

-Why?-

-I've become allergic.-

He narrowed his eyes at her.

Florence plunged -I'm going to live with him permanently.-

-What are you saying? Noncie said.

No,- Papa said.

-With his wife and him? Why would you do such a thing?-

-No, Noncie, not with his wife.- She paused. -At the place he's—-we're building.-

-If you are not seen with us then people will deduce even worse about you.- Noncie said.

-That we are lovers? Like they don't know?-

Noncie swallowed. –So you're going to live with him in adultery.-

-Doesn't reflect on you, Noncie. We are separate people. And it's none of yours or the villagers business.-

-We live in society,- Papa said, -Disgusting and... -

Florence sat down. She couldn't tell them about the baby. They ate supper hardly talking and just before chocolate pudding, Florence said, -

By the way, Noncie, you can have all my makeup since I don't need it anymore.-

Noncie wanted to say, *oh please don't. I want you to get back to fixing
yourself. I want you to come home and live with us.* She couldn't bring herself to thank her, hoping Florence would change her mind. She said
instead, -We will be having a bridge christening. I sent an invitation to
Persons. I want you to come.-

- Good,- Florence said. -Sure.- She leaned over to pet the dogs. -I'll
come visit at least once a week.-

-And stay for supper,- Papa said.

-Yes,- Noncie reiterated. She made her a cup of tea and tried to erase
her shock, sadness and deep despair that Florence was a degenerate
through and through. What was going to happen to her?

*I*n the next months Florence and Edifice worked long hours to finish the cabin, racing against the cold. Edifice tacked up old newspapers for insulation. Didn't have enough for the south wall so he doubled the boards on that side, but there were small leaks of air. There would always be small leaks of air.

Florence, being over her morning sickness, drank just a little at lunch and when the late September day was warm enough, she and Edifice laid outside to nap. He told her the names of plants and trees that were turning bright sienna and fire red. He knew naming other things was to ignore the nameless phantom in their lives. The word baby didn't come up, nor the word abortion.

-I'll tell you the rivers.-

She shut her eyes and his naming the rivers for a while annulled her anxiety.

-The West River, up north, east to west winds about and grows into waterfalls around Tillsbury. Chester River goes north and south and meets up with the Black alongside the Under Mountain Road. Cobb's brook. Harry's Brook runs into it. Nobody knows who Harry was. The Yellow River runs into the Green River, but nothing runs into the Battenkill. It just begins all by itself and knows its way to the Hudson River. I'll show you the Battenkill someday. It is deep and cool where trout live.-

Before she fell asleep again she braved the subject, -We will have to talk about *it.*

Dr. Peabody stopped me on the street to tell me, even this late she would take care of it.- Florence rolled against him as if to hide her words.

He sat up. -What did you say?-

-I didn't answer. But we have to think what we are going to do.-

-I know. - And she felt her heart beating fast. But they didn't go farther.

Later in the moonlight he glanced at her puffed cheeks and pouty bottom lip, her shut lids and thought of the distance that sleep made between them, but cuddling against her belly he thought of what this meant, the most intimate link between them, more than a link, a creation melting them together like an eclipse, sun and moon, but could be destroyed by their decisions. What should they do?

Once a week Florence went home for dinner. That night so did Edifice to salvage more lumber, slate and a door for the front of the cabin. Then the cabin would be just about finished.

In the late October dusk, when only somber oak leaves were left clinging and glistening from new frost, Edifice walked into the kitchen of his old house. Ever since Florence had caught her and Peabody in *flangrante delicto*, Gerty ran to another room when she heard the truck, leaving her plate of half eaten food.

But this time she stayed. -Hey, Edifice,- her voice was high and struggling to be pleasant.

-What?-

-You never eat at home anymore. I made you a vegetable stew.-

-From whose garden? Yours or Isabelle Peabody's?-

She rose. Her skinny shoulders and big breasts and ax-cropped hair spiking at him. Her shoulders sagged with the jab. He waited before he ate. She turned around, said nothing as he swallowed the hot stew with carrots and new potatoes and a bit of cabbage. The string beans, gone-by, were tough but he was hungry.

She said, -We're even?-

-It depends.-

-On what?-

-Maybe if you answer some questions about your disgusting behavior...maybe.-

-Who are you to be coughing up scruples when you are as daggerdly as they come.- She thought better and changed her tone. -I will tell you nothing about my life.-

-Oh, I bet you will. -

She was silent.

-Did you kill the Logan dog?-

-Any decent person would have.-

-Why?-

-Bringing dogs here, chasing away deer.-

His sarcastic laugh erupted. -It is their land.-

-Everybody hunts everywhere and you know that.-

-Like everybody leaves their doors unlocked.-

She started to leave the room.

-I'm not finished. When did you know you were a lesbian?- It was easy to read her face. Those bronze woodchuck eyes and that mouth drawn into a line, teeth clamping down. On the other hand she looked excited at the prospect of telling.

-My father found me in the hayloft, naked as a jaybird, with Diana Cross. She was naked as a jaybird too and we were going at each other with...-

-Okay, I get it.-

-No, you don't get it. You killed my old man who was going to kill me because he found out what I was. So for that reason you made me free to love *her*. What do you think of that?-

She knew all along that he had killed her father. -To love Peabody? That's all you thought I did for you. I saved your life.-

-True, but you did one even better, you married me and that gave me the right to love Isabelle undetected.-

-Yeah, well, you go live with Isabelle, that's it. Get out. And if I die Florence Logan inherits the house.-

She leaned against the table. -Please, you know I can't live with Isabelle.-

He put on his lumber cap and wiped his beard. -You'd both be run out of town.-

-I'd risk telling about your still, yes I would. I would, if you took the house from me.-

-Is that right?- He turned his back.

As he walked toward the door, she called out, -I'll give you food. Isabelle will give you life long free medicine. She'll get rid of the bastard that will be a terrible humiliation to your girl friend and to that fancy family of hers.-

He rattled his truck motor on. He was satisfied. He had gotten to her, with no intention of ousting her from the wreck of a house, but slowly tear out most of the house around her, with no guilt, given how she had torn out his guts for a lifetime.

CHAPTER 42

W hat's happening with the bridge.? I... Papa asked Noncie.
-Soon,- she reassured him.

He was thinking about jumping off. One of the town people had given him that brilliant plan. Yet shouldn't suicide be your very own style, making some sort of statement, so he rejected the idea for the moment.

He realized how he was beginning to change from commanding the girls' attention with his antics to darker, committed reasons. His own commitment. Maybe that's why suicide was called committing suicide, your own private final commitment.

He smiled at himself for the revelation, feeling sunny now. He wasn't serious about death for the moment. Yet death would bring the only way he could be with his eternal love, Clara, under the same blanket of earth.

Now the worst was when he thought of Olivia, the memory of his twisted, evil, dead wife, polluting the pure memory of Clara.

When he fiddled with the idea of his suicide he thought of the gun in the garage that Persons tried out on Hugh, but how would you point the long muzzle at yourself? Or there was jumping out the attic window above the terrace but what if you didn't die, just mangled your bones? He had heard that a village woman, leaning way out her upstairs window to shake a rug, shook herself right out with it onto a stone walk and to her death.

The barn was too open to fill with monoxide. Maybe wander in the dark and cold the way he read that Alaskans did when they were too old to be useful, or he could copy the woman he read about in the newspaper who drank so much water that it leaked into her lungs and drowned her.

Yet he had to admit, when it had been warm enough this summer his body had been sweetened in his garden episodes and he had felt as lose as the soil, happily cozy with himself. Made him feel close to others. And digging in the soil was a godly pleasure. Anyway he would need to stay with his daughters, to provide and protect them. That is if he knew how.

Because of the slick ruts from last week's rain Edifice drove slowly so his worn tires wouldn't get stuck in the deep ditch on either side. It was almost dark with a fall chill, trees molting, leaves sticking together, slowly composting, filling the air with a luscious earthy smell. What started her on loving women? She had pounded down his years, driven him to drink. He wanted to destroy her.

He had never been adept at knowing the insides of people and came to the conclusion people mostly desired to be hidden, or not know other peoples upsets, like his friend Landman. Soon as he mentioned something emotional he squirmed. The village in general was like a family but sometimes a smoldering resentment could volcano as it did at town meeting and as it certainly would if they knew about Peabody and Gerty.

A few years back Landman had asked Edifice, -How are you?-

-Good and depressed,- Edifice admitted.

Oh yeah, the weather is bad. My Sally got the sciatica right here.- He slapped his lower back.

-My depression is because of my wife.-

-I see.- Landsman chewed at his lip and took off his cap, rubbed his large head and looked up the hill.

-I been wondering about Brown's cows. They look thin to me.-

-It's my wife,- Edifice persisted. -And my life with her.-

-What ill has struck her?- Landman looked concerned.

-We got problems. She never loved me. She wouldn't let me in her bed.-

Landman moved his large shoulders right and left and tucked his Adam's apple under his red chin.

He touched Edifice's shoulder and shuffled his feet as if in a pantomime. –I wouldn't know about that.- Edifice knew what he meant, *I don't want to know about that.*

-Going to get a bit of snow, - Edifice said to relieve his friend.

-Wait here.- Landman disappeared inside the wide barn doors of the cheese factory. But reappeared quickly and handed Edifice a large wedge of cheese.

The next day he and Florence walked up the chilly slope behind the cabin. The tall grass was frosted into brittle rustling spikes. Cinnamon, hay scented, maidenhair and tall plumes of ostrich ferns curling up, as they submitted to dying, yet were waiting for the quilt of snow to save them for next year.

-I want to plant ferns around the foundation of our place,- he said. -It's a tradition in these parts.- She held his face so she could concentrate on his eyes, which seemed to enlarge into pools and lakes, and oceans, now her entire conscious world.

Florence stayed at the cabin most of the time. Why did she feel so tired? She needed to stop and have a sip. She found her small collapsible cup, filled it and carried it about sipping. This sipping was new. They had not given up their afternoon nap which really meant lips together, roaming hands, hips together, and toes mingling.

She set the cup of milk down to watch him pick up old newspapers, which had been stacked in his barn, and tack them between the cabin uprights for more insulation. She stood. -I have an idea. Why don't I bring some of my winter skirts I don't want anymore and we can cut them up and tack them in also and I have some coats that are too citified and I could sneak a couple of blankets.-

He eyed her with merriment. She was tipsy. -I'll keep it in mind,- He said.

When he went off to scavenge she was alone. But she didn't care. Sometimes she waited for hours stoking the wood stove, reading and remembering Whittier's poem, "Snow Bound"...which she had memorized in the eighth grade. *"The sun that brief December day/ rose cheerless over hills of gray. And darkly circled, gave at noon/ a sadder light than waning moon. /Slow tracing down the thickening sky/ its mute and ominous prophecy, /a portent seeming less than threat.../ the coming of the snow storm told."*

To Florence the poem seemed exciting because of the anticipation of what was certain but unknown....like her engulfed body now. When alone she talked to her belly and at other times she sang, in a sweet voice, songs from her childhood Nanny. Yet like the snow storm what would be the out come? *Omnious prophecy.*

One sunny day as a surprise for Edifice she painted the floor a tangy Dutch blue she had brought from home. But she left unpainted spots for stepping-stones until the floor dried. Then she decided to paint lambent clouds over the bare spots, whisking the paint capriciously.

Edifice was enchanted. With a whiff of shyness he asked if they could make love on the floor. She gave him her Mona Lisa smile.

Afterwards he said, -I'm on cloud nine.-

She thought quickly. -That's why I painted eight so we could make our own cloud nine.-

Noncie was glad and angry both that some nights Florence came home, hoping she would see the light give the awful man up and move back with them permanently. And look how fat she had grown, wearing unbelievable outfits to hide the fact. Slovenly, backwoods, down-at-the-heels white trash wearing Edifice's old hunting coat, hanging off her small shoulders. And above her fat waist was a clothesline for a belt. No matter how poor not a single villager looked like that. She must be enjoying shaming her family.

She sighed at remembering how Florence once dressed, the way she slung a scarf, a ribbon around her throat, earrings of pink and black pearls and at the waist a wide rattlesnake skin belt. Once Florence had pride over every piece of fine clothing, which she smoothed out at night and hung on silk-padded hangers.

Into the house Florence clomped in her mukluks and Papa had to ask her to take them off. Noncie wondered if she went to bed in her clothes. Her once sweet smelling perfumed sister now smelled like the outdoors, or a wood-burning fire. Yet at times Noncie saw her as a woman ablaze, filled with the spirit of mystery and such daring she envied her.

And all these months no word from Hugh. And she couldn't get him out of her mind. She still hoped.

But at least now she felt she wasn't wasting her life. Helping the village she had grown fond of. The bridge. It came to her she would plan a dedication, sending out notices of a party that she would get Papa to pay for. The bridge was her hope come true. This was almost as good as producing a namesake. Of course not, of course not, but she tried to believe that. Right now she wanted to believe that. Perhaps she would even be remembered by the town naming the bridge the Noncie Logan Bridge. That week a letter came saying they would start the bridge right after Thanksgiving.

Some people stopped her and said how grateful they were. She would send the first invitation to Hugh and Persons.

In headlong energy Edifice tore out the only bathtub in the dying mansion. Gerty stood by and watched, her arms folded over her chest. He thumped the tub down the steps and onto a dolly and out through the woodshed and levered it on a board up to the truck bed. She followed him and said, -Where do I take a bath now?-

-How about across the bridge in the sparkling white house?-

-You'll be sorry.-

But he was full of himself with his new wave of power.

-Look,- he shouted to Florence who had heard his truck. She had had no idea he was bringing a tub. -Got any notion on how to get it over there?-

Her giggle rose into hilarity and he laughed too, scratching his beard and rolling his head from side to side. He had pulled the tub in the dolly to the brook's edge. He pulled himself across the brook on the pulley and they stood side by side.

-The brook's low,- she said.

-Yes, but it's too heavy to drag,- he answered.

-Maybe we could lever it over and over.-

-Too risky. Might chip.-

-So, we chip it,- she answered.

-I want it perfect for you.-

-Wait, maybe we could put boards down and slide and push it across the boards,-

she said.

-Good idea.-

-We better rope the tub from tree to tree so it won't slide off.-

They tied the ropes to the trees, untied them, and rested on the bank, discouraged.

-I have an idea,- Florence said. -We leave the bathtub on that side and build a house around it.-

-Fine except for winter. No, I'm determined to get the tub across.- They tied the tub again from tree to tree, pushing it along the boards for a few feet. But they succeeded in shoving the monster up and over the edge of the opposite bank.

-Now what?- she asked, out of breath.

He inched the tub onto the dolly again and dragged it on up to a quiet place right next to the still.

-We can use the still stove to heat water, - he said. -You can design a shed over the tub.-

-I want a bath right now,- she screeched.

As she lay in the tub in the chill afternoon he poured water over her that he had warmed on the stove. He couldn't concentrate on anything but her beauty, this woman who had dropped from heaven to him.

Florence was lying the length of the tub. She scrunched all the way down, with just her head propped up, her silky hair, almost to her shoulders now, drifted in the water. Her slightly swollen pearly belly peeked out of the water like a floating buoy.

He took the soap in his palm and rubbed her calloused feet and her short curvaceous legs, shutting his eyes to feel more clearly the vivid sensation. Difficult to control himself from jumping in the tub on top of her.

As he dried her she hummed a lullaby from her childhood. She felt a twinge of wanting to be home to Papa and Noncie.

That week they gathered galvanized pieces from the dump and built another shed to enclose the tub. When she was resting next to the wood-stove in their cabin she finally brought up the subject. -Let's leave everything to Peabody. She told me when I went to a check-up she will take care of it when the time comes, a fair trade, she says.-

-Come on, what does she mean?-

-Whatever we want done about or with the baby. We can figure that out later.-

-What's there to figure. It's our baby.-

-Yes, - she said with a sigh. She knew he couldn't interpret the sigh, well neither could she.

He thought again this is our combination. This is everything we are made of. Our life reincarnated. This is more than our creation, this makes us one. Why did she sigh? Has she given up, given into Peabody?

She said, -I can't imagine what winter is going to be like. I'm already cold.-

He thought, she won't stay with me.

CHAPTER 43

*A*fter Noncie had received the letter as to when the construction of the bridge would happen she was in such a good mood Noncie asked Florence will you come to Thanksgiving dinner?

-Not without Edifice,- she answered.

-Yes, Edifice, of course.-

-Okay, We'll see.- She was so glad to be home.

She petted the three dogs, cooing to them. The dogs rolled their tongues over her hand and whined.

Edifice didn't run into Gerty when he returned to plunder, but a meanness in him wanted her to see. He found the crowbar hanging on the wall and the sledge hammer and began at the outside wall to the kitchen for the tub shed but wondered if he could do all that by hard winter.

With care he cleaned the boards of clinging mice matter, dust and nails until the maple was smooth. His father had built with the best, not cheap spruce. He laid the boards into the truck bed. The whole of nature, wind and weather, would enter his old kitchen now. For only a moment his burning anger gave him pause. Was this just his way of getting her out of his house? But wasn't taking that wall justified? As he carried the last board he saw her standing in the exposed kitchen, her hands flaccid at her sides, her pale face, looking human, dusky-eyed and sad. He turned away, jumped in his truck and sped down the drive.

He stopped. He parked. Stared out at nothing. He turned around and drove back. He walked around back. He called out to Gerty. She came to the edge of the kitchen, her face red, perhaps with tears. -If you get Peabody to buy you new siding I'll put it up. And a tub too.- Then he sped off again.

CHAPTER **44**

On Thanksgiving when they walked in Noncie was guardedly pleased. Florence looked cleaned up, her hair brushed, though her face had that telltale blush of alcohol.

Yet couldn't the nippy air be the cause? But heavens, she looked so over weight in her tight dress.

Edifice shyly stepped inside. In his arms lay stove-wood he had brought as a present. He went back outside.

-He isn't...?- Papa started.

-Yes,- Florence answered. –He's coming back.-

Hanging from his hand was a dead, fully feathered pheasant.

-He didn't shoot it,- Florence said. He found it dead on the road. It's a present for you and Papa.-

-It's dripping blood on the floor,- Noncie said.

-Won't last. I'll hang it in the shed for you.- He rushed out the door.

-It's a special prize,- Florence explained. She pulled a rag from the cupboard to wipe the blood from the floor. Noncie noticed that Florence had trouble bending over because of her fat stomach.

Papa shook his head, though he didn't know why, other than uncertainty about everything. He lit his pipe as if to put up a smoke screen between him and the horizon.

Florence was over the queasiness from smoke and liked smelling his pipe. Home.

-Would you mind stirring the gravy?- Noncie asked Florence. She had learned to make it thick and smooth. On the counter lay three cookbooks open to gravy recipes.

Papa escorted Edifice into the living room.

-How you doing?- Papa asked, noticing his trimmed beard.

-Fine, just fine-

-Glad to hear it.- He paused. -Snow is coming soon, right?-

-Right.-

Papa poured Edifice cider. They sat in awkwardness. Then Papa said, -I wonder, I mean could you tell me why you love Florence?-

-What?-

-I mean what do you see in her?-

Edifice clipped out, -She's your daughter and you don't know?-

-I meant I just wanted to hear from you.-

Edifice tried to dispel his nervousness. What was he after? He paused to think. He hoped to choose the right words. -I guess you might say it's mostly her essence.-

-You mean like wine?- Papa actually blushed for mentioning alcohol.

Edifice twisted in his chair. What he couldn't say was that his love for her was nearly unbearable, like scorching heat.

-Essence.- Papa was amazed. -That's quite beautiful.-

He was beginning to have a new image of this man. But not sure what kind of an imagine.

And Edifice sort of liked this old stuffed shirt, no, liked him a lot after he had said, "quite beautiful."

They sat on the couch together. Papa passed him cheese and beaten biscuits.

-You going to marry my daughter?-

-No. I'm afraid not.-

-Because you are already married,- Papa said.

-Yes.- But the other reason was he and Florence were allergic to marriage. Tried that once. Yet why hadn't he said, maybe someday?

-Well, well,- Papa said, wondering why not, having had a good look at Gerty, a fright of a woman. -The thing is, I don't want harm to come to my Flossy, you understand?- He catarrhed near Edifice's ear.

-Harm?- Edifice asked. (But rushing through him was what was growing in Florence.)

-Well?- Papa asked. But Florence appeared. -Everything is ready.-

Edifice stood quickly and followed her into the dining room so Papa wouldn't ask him more. Papa felt *the ancient terrible letter* in his pocket and wondered if he had the nerve to read to them after dinner. But he wanted them to know before he died.

Florence carried in the huge burnished turkey that the grocery biddy actually sold them, though it had crossed Noncie's mind there might be something wrong with it. Noncie and Papa sat at the ends of the long table, and Florence and Edifice on either side. The sun poured in through the long windows, tinting the edges of the crewel curtains to a pale orange and splashing delicious yellow onto the white plaster walls. But even with all the bright light Noncie lit ten candles in the glass candelabra for the festivity.

Instead of a tablecloth, oval lace place mats lay under the warmed blue and white Wedgwood china. She looked over at Florence. She felt kindly toward her, almost like a back-in-the-fold feeling. Papa carved with grace and skill, laying the pieces in overlapping circular patterns on the ironstone platter.

Edifice said to him, -I haven't had turkey that good in ages.-

-I'm sorry the vegetable is poor man's cabbage,- Noncie said and then thought she shouldn't have said, poor man's.

But Edifice said, -The cabbage tastes wonderful with, what did you put on it, wine vinegar?-

-Yes.- She smiled.

-And see how the mashed potatoes are in the shape of a volcano with butter running down the sides,- Florence said, -that's what our cook Agnes used to do for us when we were little.-

-Nice,- Edifice said, wondering if he would ever feel easy in this family. Florence couldn't keep her mind off whether or not she should tell them she was pregnant. She sat clumsily in a chair and agitated. She fidgeted with her tight dress. Gerty was right. They would be doubly humiliated.

-Good dinner,- She choked out.

Noncie thanked her. -I've learned a lot of things I never thought I would.- She rose to pour water into the glistening amber goblets. As she poured, the water sparkled, mirroring the candlelight and making her dizzy. She sat down.

Yes, Papa decided to read the letter. And it was fine that Edifice was here. He might as well know the family history.

In the living room having their after-dinner demitasses he pulled the frail letter from his pocket, and clearing his throat, asked them to listen.

Florence felt drowsy. She had been leaning against Edifice, but that woke her up.

-A letter?- Noncie asked as she sat herself into the armchair by the fire.

-But first I have to explain. This is a letter from before I was married, back in Kentucky. I was in love with two women. Yes, two. One was your mother, Olivia, the other was Clara Montclair. I was in a terrible quandary, couldn't sleep, couldn't decide which to ask to marry. For almost three years I courted them both. They each knew that I was dating the other. I wasn't being secretive. Then one day I realized I was head-over-heels in love with only Clara Montclair, and I knew she was with me.

-We were having a picnic. Mosquitoes were biting us and wherever they bit her I kissed the spot. "Come mosquitoes,"- she cried out, "bite me more." -She was effervescent and transparent. Clear, like her name. She did not know how to lie or be divisive. She was remarkable in her wonder of the world, simple wonder of nature and with empathy toward mankind. The feelings of others became as real to her as objects she could touch.- Papa paused to wipe a tear. His daughters and Edifice sat rapped and silent.

-The next day after the picnic I was going to ask Clara to marry me. But that day I received this letter.- Papa unfolded the letter:

> *Dear Coleridge,*
> *I'm sorry to tell you that I can't see you anymore because I have fallen in love with a man up in Louisville. I have had a very nice time with you. I thank you so much for that. Please don't write me or come and see me since he is a very jealous man. I hope you marry Olivia. She is a wonderful woman.*
> *With affection,*
> *Clara.*

-We had never exchanged letters before so I didn't know her handwriting. Trying to accept, trying to pull myself out of the tragedy of a broken heart, trying to live without being totally destroyed, I proposed to your mother some months later. I tried to dismiss Clara from my mind, but the hurt screwed into my heart deeper and deeper. I didn't see her. She lived in the town next to us. How could my Clara have been that divisive? How long had she known this other man?...and on and on my mind spun. And how often throughout my life something would remind me of her... a lift of a hand, a young girl with dark-cedar hair, a lucid smile, a figure running into a doorway, and even mosquitoes.

-Then when your mother and I came back from our honeymoon to San Francisco I heard that Clara had died, died, on our wedding day.-

-On your wedding day?- Noncie gasped. -Clara had been doing laundry, though I knew it couldn't be true, the laundry part, with all the maids they had or the accident part. She had taken her life, mixing ammonia and Clorox and drinking it. A maid found her on the stone floor lying among the dirty laundry. Her eyes staring up, wide open. She left no note and....-

Noncie clutched her forehead and Florence put her hand on Noncie's arm. Edifice looked down on the floor.

-The man had broken off with her?- Florence asked.

-She was not engaged. There was no man at all. And for seventeen years I lived without knowing the truth. We had moved to Chicago and you were eleven, and Noncie, you were sixteen. On our seventeenth anniversary, your mother's and mine we were sitting by the fire that night drinking sherry. I was never happy with her, but I accepted my life, tried to be a pleasant husband.

-She was looking at me with glowing eyes and said, Coleridge, I have something to tell you. It's about a letter. -

-What letter?- I asked her.

-The one from Clara.-

-I don't understand what you mean.-

-The one supposedly from Clara. I wrote it. It was not from Clara.The letter saying she was in love with another man and don't contact her again and to marry Olivia but aren't you glad I wanted you that badly? She came toward me to kiss me. I pushed her violently away. But your mother went on, confessing more. She had also written Clara a letter from me saying Olivia and I were marrying. And she shouldn't contact either one of us anymore, since she, Olivia, was very jealous.- Papa sat still, letting the letter fall on the table. The room was quiet.

-I can't..- Noncie said. -I just can't.-

-And Mother thought you'd go on loving her?- Florence cried out.

-Why did you stay with her?- Noncie asked.

-Two opposite reasons. One, so you would have a mother. But my other reason was not noble.- He paused.

-Tell us.- Florence said, -We wouldn't think less of you after what she did. She was a murderer.- Florence had never felt close to her mother. She had sensed something hidden.

Noncie sighed, not letting the full impact reach her yet.

-I wanted her to face my rejection of her every single day. Live a life of misery in my house, which I thought could be only half the misery I felt. I went to all social engagements alone, isolating her. I slept in the guest room. As you know I went to my study after supper. Never took her on vacations with the three of us.-

Edifice looked from face to face.

Noncie got up, yelling, -Horrible,- as she ran to the kitchen to compose herself. She leaned against the sink and splashed water on her face. Unlike Florence she had loved her mother.

lorence followed her. Florence put her arms around her. -We had an okay childhood, just think of that.-

Noncie held onto Florence until she was okay.

Papa tried to pull himself and them from gloom, particularly since he now felt relieved that he had told them. –Let's have more coffee,- He called to them.

Edifice thought the old man and he were brothers with their horrifying wives, yet the difference was he had Florence and his poor Clara was buried.

When they were saying goodbye Florence said, -I'll visit next week.-

This certainly was not the time to tell them about their baby.

He had detected, -You didn't like your mother,- Edifice asked on their way home.

-I wasn't altogether surprised at the evil person she was. From the time I was little when she came near me a kind of animal raising of hairs came at the back of her neck. She tried hard to win me. I avoided her eyes, her hugs and kisses and squirmed away. But when she died of a sudden heart attack when I was fifteen I began also to think of her as pathetic.-

The next day she returned to hang around Noncie and talk about their childhood, talk about the happy memories for Noncie's sake.

CHAPTER 45

*F*lorence took only a few possessions. How strange she felt now about organdy curtains with lavender ribbons as tiebacks, the wooden shoe box overflowing with heels and street shoes, the mahogany bureau with brass chrysanthemum knobs.

She had traced old sleeping Borie on burlap and hooked a rug of his white body on a viridian background. She cradled the rug in her arms to remember his woolly fur against her neck. She would lay it beside their bed in the cabin. She took the picture of the Great Wall of China she had always wanted to visit and a Winslow Homer watercolor of the sea.

Leave her clothes for now. As she ran the hangers along the rod they seemed to belong to a silly lady, from long ago. In fact the whole room was someone else's, a young girl's fantasy. A room of sweet nothing.

Papa and Noncie rushed to the bridge to watch the spewing backhoes and the workers in hip boots digging a drainage ditch to dry the holes enough to pour the concrete pilings. Papa told Noncie what a thrill he had when his flourmill had been built. What a rush it was to see a structure appear from the ground up. A growing thing, sprouting and branching into life.

Noncie rubbed her cold hands and pulled her sable hat down tighter over her disobedient curls. She had given up her fur coat, feeling them out of place. Her pale skin glowed rosy in the cold. Her straight back and even features gave her boots and jodhpurs authority. The workmen gazed at the stunning woman. All she needed, Papa thought, was a small leather-riding crop in order to give little flirtatious snaps at them.

Hugh flashed unwanted into Noncie's mind. She wondered, once again, if she would visit Hugh. On the other hand, just visiting would make her heart ache or maybe it would bring him back to her. But he would soon know about her eyes. Her sight so dark in the middle she soon could not drive.

She turned back to the bridge workers, in awe of what they could do. Mysterious how bridges got built and she did not want to miss any of its birth.

Chapter **46**

*I*n early December, when the bridge was almost finished, Papa had been at the Post Office for quite a while leaning against the windowsill, waiting for the mail to be sorted and reading the Rutland Herald. Just the local news...didn't want to read about the Depression and sorrowful times around the country. Just plain everyday local fires, floods or juicy murders now and then suited him. By God, maybe he was becoming local. Stories close by seemed more pertinent.

But the newspaper was also a ruse to be close by watching *her* sort the mail with deftly sudden fingers, hear her high-pitched voice on the verge of making fun of someone after they left. He liked to peer at her strong face and puddle-gray eyes and yellow hair and thick eyebrows that almost ran together in a perfect semicircle. Feeling more entitled to be near her, as if they had a secret together, because he got the drift, the innuendoes in her tiny spears of gossip.

Sloan Singer blustered through the door, -A bit of the river overflowed last night and washed down some haystacks from Neil Bridgewater's. The hay stopped at my bend and I'll spread it to protect my corn field.- He chuckled.

-You old coot,- the postmistress said.

-It is getting rough around here,- said a man with a low forehead Papa had never seen before.

-Yeah, what you talking about?- The postmistress counted her change.

-Not everybody is for the new bridge.- He had turned to include Papa. Papa didn't answer.

-Your daughter come in here and started the dumb idea?-

Papa mouthed silently, You goddamned-son-of-a-bitch.

The postmistress rolled her eyes. She understood his words. She leaned over the counter to better observe the show.

With his hand on the door the man said, -Bridges are supposed to unite sides of the village. This one is tearing them apart.-

The man opened the door, as if to run.

-Fuck you,- Papa mouthed straight at him.

The man left with an uncompromising swagger.

-Good for you,- the postmistress said to Papa. -He's a crab and as lazy as granite rock.-

-You saw me swear didn't you?- Papa moved up to her. For that moments they were alone.

As if saying some melodic love poem, she said in a whisper to Papa, -He doesn't live here. He comes to visit his old father Graham Hill, on the Under Mountain Road, and not that often, just to get money out of him. Don't heed him.- She winked at Papa.

He was so taken off his pins he couldn't get his own lid to wink back. Both of the goddamned flapping pieces of flesh shut at once.

As he drove home he realized again what a silly, desperate man he had become. What was he to do? His festering boredom was worse than death. Even the men he had chewed tobacco with had gone in for the winter. Now that his garden was put to sleep and he had helped Noncie can the beans and put the carrots and turnips and potatoes down in the root cellar he had little to think about. He did read, but his mind often escaped whole paragraphs and his thoughts digressed into yawning.

Near Christmas Florence's slacks were resting below her round belly. She had to sneak some suspenders from Papa. Every time she sat rolling waves of baby kicks attacked her. This was real. This was something taking over, a dybbuk and she needed an exorcism. She had walked around the question for weeks, turned her back on it and rehearsed what to say. Finally it came out.

-Edifice, what exactly are our plans?-

-I don't know. It's too late to stop the baby.- He added, -I'm glad.- But was afraid to ask her if she were. And he worried all the time how they could possibly raise a baby, a baby they had separately dreamed of having their whole lives.

-How do we pay for baby clothes? Who else but Papa can we sell wood to?-

He was silent.

-And food?-

Gerty had fed him from her garden, and a few chickens. The conversation ended as it always did on the undefined, the horizon lost and the sneaking shade of Dr. Peabody.

-I'll be there at the birth, no matter what. You just have Edifice get me when those contractions start. I'll take care of the baby, you know that. Have no qualms.- She said this with her skinny mouth pinched so hard the blood rushed to them when she let them go.

Florence didn't dwell on what she said. At the moment she hated the idea of dwelling on anything. Then the idea of Peabody taking care of the baby flashed at her, *get rid of it?*

-Are you going to tell Papa and Noncie you're pregnant?- Edifice asked Florence as he handed her a piece bread he had taken from Gerty.

She ate it with relish –We'll see.-

But she didn't go home any nights now. And hadn't seen them for two weeks or more. Their cabin was warm enough, but she was hungry sometimes and wondered what they were eating back home. Edifice trapped a rabbit once in a while or picked a quail off a limb and she made biscuits in the small wood stove. Every week he went home and got two big jugs of milk that Gerty gave him and each time saying it's from Isabelle and me. He took them without a word.

Eight days before Christmas was the day of the bridge dedication. The bridge had been plowed. The covered bridge still beside it was also plowed. The snow banks now lined the streets so high they walled in the houses except for a small path to the back doors.

Lement Brown was the new chairman of the Select Board. He stood shivering in his hunting jacket, leaving his bald head exposed, as if this were more fitting for his important role. Noncie held her gloved hands together, hoping, hoping the bridge would be dedicated to her. When the concrete was soft she told Florence she had sneaked to place her handprint in the column near the floor of the bridge, like the movie stars on the sidewalk in Hollywood. Florence smiled. -Did you sign it?- Noncie said she wished she had thought of that. But in dedicating it to her there would be a plaque.

Today some who didn't welcome the new bridge stood by the old yelling angry words. Lement gave a short speech about a new era and the hopes of the future. Some cheered, some booed. -We also want to thank Miss Noncie Logan for her idea and fulfillment that the bridge was built.-

But that was it. She waited but no dedication, no plaque with her name, or naming the bridge the Logan bridge. People would soon forget her.

Someone grabbed her hand. She turned to see a boy, a teenager. She started to remove her hand when she recognized Persons. He had grown at least an inch and his smile was broader than she remembered.

-Persons, Persons,- she stuttered, trying to remove her mind from her disappointment. -How did you get here?- She squeezed his hand.

-Hugh brung me. He taught me to play the ukulele.-

-Hugh?-

Persons waved wildly at Hugh. The sun was in her eyes and she couldn't make him out, until he was very close.

-Howdy,- he said, in his easy confident way and she tilted her head so the sun was out of her eyes. -Hugh, my goodness gracious.-

-I heard about the bridge and how you started the whole project. I thought Persons would like to see you. He's living with me now.-

-Is that right?- She must pull herself together better than this. But her wanting him came roaring back.

-Actually, I adopted him.-

-Wonderful... I have missed...him.-

They looked at each other.

To break the spell he said, -By the way, is that your sister over there? I wasn't sure.-

-I don't think she's here,- Noncie lied. -She doesn't live with us any-more.-

-Yes, she is here,- Persons said. -I said, hi, to her. I like her a lot.-

-I see she's pregnant,- Hugh said.

Noncie felt faint -Oh no, not true.-

-I guess it's just a little weight she's put on.-

-Papa's over there.- She gave Persons a little shove. -He'd like to see you.-

Alone with Hugh she said, –We miss seeing you,- *pause*. -And Per-sons.-

-How is your father?- He asked.

-Fine. He had a beautiful garden and I helped can the food. And my garden, I never visualized the lushness, all because of you. It's all so new and wonderful, this country life.-

-I'll go say hello to him.-

-Wait.-

-Yes?-

-I'd like to come over to the Home and see Persons once in a while. I mean and bring Papa. We came that once.-

-I was so sorry to miss you.-

He started to leave but turned back, and looked directly at her. He took both her hands. -I'm sorry about everything. I'm sorry the way things turned out...my fault. I wanted to very much...I was just unable.-

He did not let her hands go. He kept his eyes searching hers. -I was unable. The dictates of the Children's' Home and with my promise to my wife. My promise to keep the Home running. Be their father. Do you understand?-

She couldn't answer.

-I didn't want things...I wanted us to go on...I wished we could have... please come see us.- Moisture filled his eyes as he turned away.

She waited for her desperate feelings to congeal. Why couldn't he? Come see him. As if that would help. She *must* forget him. And she was afraid of hating Florence again. Most likely the cause was Florence, his not wanting her near him or his boys ever again. She didn't believe it was over guilt for loving someone other than his wife. She had died too long ago. Yes, the cause was Florence, Florence ruining her life.

The sun had flashed her into blindness. Even so she could see him wave, a sad wave from his car as it climbed up the church hill and was gone.

That night Papa gave a party in the town hall. At the party almost all the village seemed to have gathered, even though some were against the bridge. Many graciously thanked Noncie for getting the bridge built but she could hardly listen, hardly care. Hugh had driven off.

Florence and Edifice attended the party even though they were very upset by the sight of the monster with thick squat ballasts and clunky railing, the wide plain unforgiving floor. To Edifice the frailty of the covered bridge was like a beloved sick pet that to destroy would be unthinkable but the wrecking ball would take it next week.

Lement stood up again and with a knife clinked his glass and quieted the hall. -I have one more item of interest. A lot of you have talked to me about also keeping the covered bridge as a walking bridge, like a historic remembrance. So unless there is a huge objection we will and we will shore it up. Edifice called out, -hurrah.- Florence squeezed his hand.

Lement went on, -And again I want to thank Miss Logan for starting the idea for a new bridge.-

It seemed as if the whole room clapped for Noncie.

CHAPTER **47**

*F*ive days before Christmas, Edifice said, -One can't really be intimate unless you tell all the nightmares in your heart.- Florence
looked at him carefully. She didn't know how to answer him. She could
only concentrate on wanting the baby out. She could hardly move.

She had been reading an old medical book she found in her attic at
home. *How to bring labor on.* Eating peppermint, sniffing hot peppers
flakes up your nose so you would sneeze with such force that the baby
pops out. Where would you find hot peppers? Besides, she felt lazy, too
lazy to do anything. She leaned back in Edifice's captain's chair. He had
brought her a rocker from his house, but that hurt her back now.

-What did you mean, telling the nightmares? - She finally asked. She
pulled her soft afghan over her shoulders. -Come here.- He leaned over
and she kissed him.

From the corner where he had stacked split wood he took a piece and
laid it on the fire. He poured them a glass of vodka.

She knew what he was thinking. -I don't want some stranger raising it,
- She said, -or put it in an orphanage. But how can we keep it? How can
we feed it? How can we raise it?-

-I don't know but I want you to decide what we should do.-

-That's not fair.- She said with anger.

-I'm a coward, that's what you're thinking.-

-I think we might let Peabody decide.-

*Peabody, he thought! How could they let her? And what did that really
mean? Was she going to cause the death of their souls?* But nothing more was
said that night.

They cuddled down on the great walnut bed that his mother and
father had slept in. They woke in the dark of morning and he lit the oil

lamp which cast a soft blush on the whole room. She had cleaned the lamp chimney to a sparkle. She would think about trouble some other time. She was hungry. They ate toast and raspberry jam from wild raspberries they had gathered.

CHAPTER 48

*P*apa said, -Shall we invite Florence and Edifice to Christmas dinner? I'll leave a message at the post office. -

-They probably won't show up. We haven't seen her for three weeks,-
Noncie said. -God knows how she must be living. She looks awful.-

-Like the first settlers,- he said, trying to make his daughter seem less
hopeless and more romantic.

-It might be the last chance she'll get to see us.-

Despair met him headlong. -We'll give them the leftovers to take
home.-

What was that, Noncie dropped the stirring spoon twice on the floor.
She cocked her head like a listening bird.

-Your eyes getting worse?-

-Certainly not.- She slammed the spoon back in the turnip pot.

Papa read the Bible to himself, the story of Joseph and the coat of
many colors. The betrayal by the brothers. Seemed significant thinking of
what they were going to do to his youngest daughter.

They waited past the time Florence and Edifice were supposed to
arrive.

-We should wait another half hour,- Papa said .

The kitchen door opened and Noncie jumped.

-Hi.-

They greeted Florence as she pulled off her snowy boots, shook her
hunter's cap on the hearth of the wood stove and undid the clothesline
rope around her coat. Papa helped her hang her coat on the rack.

-How are you?- Papa was also shocked at how she looked.

-Fine.-

Noncie couldn't believe what was she wearing, some long flannel thing, maybe a nightgown, and a man's flannel shirt to Christmas dinner? Yet there was something rosy and alive in her face.

-Edifice coming in?-

-Loading up the woodshed for you.-

Papa called out to him, -Why don't you do that after dinner? -

Noncie pulled the roast from the oven and stirred the mashed potatoes and buttered the yellow turnips. -Just in time. Dinner is ready.- She led them in.

-The table is beautiful,- Florence said. -I remember this red silk runner.-

Very tall white candles sat at each end. The gold-rimmed dinner plates had been their father's wedding present.

-We have a little spruce tree in the truck Edifice cut for you. We can get it after dinner and set it up in the living room and all of us decorate it, like always,- Florence said.

-Oh, and I brought a bunch of ornaments from my childhood,- Edifice said.

-Thank you.- Noncie glanced at Papa.

Papa carved and the platter filled quickly with blood from the rare roast beef.

Florence said. -What a feast. I'm really hungry.-

-Look at that,- Edifice said.

Noncie looked at her...*really hungry?* She was so fat.

-Too bad Christmas isn't every day,- Florence said.

Just before dessert Papa rose, went into his study to find what he had hidden. He came back with a bottle.

-Champagne?- Florence was knocked for a loop.

-I brought it from Chicago for our first Christmas.- The cork flew hitting the ceiling, the sound of joy. Joy, Florence thought, as some of the bubbling wine splashed on her. Joy, pure and simple. Translucent sweet amber and her father was pouring her some. She drank slowly, the taste sparkled in her throat. Helped her be brave. She stood up.

-I have an announcement.-

-All ears,- Papa said.

-I'm six months pregnant.-

Silence.

Papa coughed loudly.

Noncie said, -I wondered why you looked so...she stopped herself...particularly rosie.-

Edifice at first was going to lower his head but held it high. He held his head high and steady even when the dog Babcock found his leg and vigorously humped him.

Papa said, -Well, I'll be.-

Florence said, -Edifice has the cabin done.-

-I'll light a fire in the living room and...- Papa needed to rise from shell-shock.

Noncie, unwilling to digest the news, said, -Let's have demitasses there and I made little meringues with chocolate sauce.-

Florence had known they weren't going to express what they thought. Anyway she didn't want to know what they thought. But obviously the news wasn't like telling them she'd been crowned princess or something.

-Are you coming? Noncie!- Papa called, needing support.

Florence sat a moment more, and then went to find her. As she passed by the study she glimpsed sealed boxes stacked high.

She swung back, - Papa what are the boxes? –

-I'll tell you in a bit.-

Noncie set meringues on the coffee table. –We've decided to move back to Chicago.-

-Noncie, you could have eased into that,- Papa scolded. -Noncie feels she has done all she can here. And you, you have your own life,- Papa said. -You hardly come home anymore. We would leave you the house but we must sell it to get enough to live on.-

-We'll write you all the time,- Noncie said.

-And if you get a phone. Maybe someday you will visit.-

Florence didn't move. Then she held onto the sofa arm. –Goodbye then.- She rose and reeled back to the kitchen, tore her coat from the hook, stepped into her boots, Edifice following.

Papa ran to stop her.

-Was this your idea?- Florence turned on him.

-No, it was Noncie's. She needs to have a purpose. She thought the city...-

Noncie called out, -Not my idea, his.-

-It was hers.-

-I don't care who in hell idea it was. You both hate me. Is that it?-

Noncie was next to her -You know we love you. I don't even think it was altogether your fault that Hugh is not interested in me.-

-Not altogether my fault? But you are goddamned ashamed of me more than ever. That's why you're leaving. You could bloody well find other causes here. The world is steaming with causes. I'm pregnant and a drunk. But what kind of a family do I have? No loyalty. And you Papa, my own father. I never want to see you again. I need you. I wanted you to be here. No matter what I have done you are doing worse to me, deserting me and at this time.-

-It's just that you deserted us. You don't care about us when we settled here only to get you cured,- Noncie said. -Now we hardly see you.-

-Goddamn.-

-No swearing, - Papa said, knowing that was totally inappropriate at this moment.

Edifice had cautiously made his way next to Florence.

-How could you? Were you just going to leave and not tell me; what kind of people are you? I never knew you, did I? *Did I?*-

Papa threw his arms around her as she sobbed.

Noncie stroked her head and said, -Of course we were going to tell you and we weren't going for weeks.-

Laying her face for the first time in years against her father's shoulder Florence marveled at how much she wanted him, them. She choked out -There is more than me in this village. There are people in other villages, people to be part of, people to help.-

She lifted herself away from her father and snatched up a dishtowel to wipe her tears. She opened the refrigerator and took out a bottle of milk, put it to her lips and gulped. Something in Papa adored her crudeness. How could he leave his Flossy? And he knew how he and Noncie both were dependent on her. She was their *raison-d' etre*. The trouble was, not any longer. -We won't leave now. Maybe never.-

Florence sighed. Every fear she had was packed in cement and lying in her throat.

After Florence and Edifice had gone, in an embarrassed silence full of shame they unpacked a few essential boxes. Papa poked the fire and brought out his last hidden bottle of champagne. He sat in the wing chair and she opposite, lying the length of the sofa and kicking her shoes to the floor.

He said, -I don't want to leave her now. Maybe not at all. And don't you really think you can nudge more improvements out of the village?-

-Why should she have a baby? They won't be able to care for it. Why should she be pregnant and not me?-

-Yes,- Papa said, feeling the same.

She was turning rosy from the firelight and the champagne, her long lime silk dress tucked around her ankles, her head thrown back against the pillow, her freckled hands, pale as if struck by moonlight, lay over her belly. Beautiful Noncie, he thought.

-It's more than about me trying to nudge improvements. I see the world differently now, with deeper unease and frustration as my eyes slow down. The center gone I see only edges of the world. The city would be better.

She paused to tell him greater truths. -I've always been afraid to go into uncombed woods, raw, sumptuous abundance, an abundance I am not a part of and Florence is. I wish I appreciated the untamed. I wasn't willing to scrape my knees through the bramble, ford icy streams, climb mountains, in other words, make my own path. I am afraid of unmarked paths. I should have taken advantage, been lenient about a man to love, and unafraid. Here when I found one...-

She stopped. -I want to fuss and fix, not interpret. I wish I had been an artist in order to praise what was natural, seek out nuggets of the wild and display them with the hope that others would see their beauty. Instead I see beauty only in four walls or in vases. My love of what is beautiful has been superficial compared to the complexity of the world. I craved to take chances without moving to fulfill. I'm ordinary and Florence isn't, Papa.-

-You are anything but ordinary. I'm sorry you have regrets. But the fact is you are noble. Look what you have done for this village and tried to do for Florence.-

He lit his pipe and put his feet up on a needlepoint footstool. The smell of the pipe was powerfully narcotic, or was it the champagne? His eyelids faltered.

-I wanted to have a baby so badly,- she said.

-I know.-

-We are both cowards, you for giving up hunting down Florence and tearing her from that despicable Irving and me for never leaving home. In a way that was your fault.- She wasn't angry. She didn't move from her tranquil slump into the couch pillows. -I'm not blaming you, Papa. You know how I feel about you.-

-My fault?-

-Every night when I was little, you should have known how it might affect me; you read me the same story at bedtime for nearly a year.-

-What story?-

-You don't remember?-

-No, how old were you?-

-Around ten.-

-You must have wanted the same story over and over.-

-Yes, but it frightened me.-

-Oh, for heaven's sake, what story?-

-Europa and the Bull. How she rode on his back to roam the world and never see her father again.- She took another sip of the champagne. -I couldn't bear that we might be separated, that your whole life you would hunt for me. Down deep I guess I felt marriage would make me lose you, and you me. Only recently I realized how I really felt about men, gentle and courtly, and like the bull, persuasive, kneeling for Europa to mount, then turn out differently. And Florence and Irving made me sure of that.-

-For Heaven's sake. You never know what can affect children.-

-I'm trying now to get rid of those feelings about men and I think if we go back to Chicago I might have another chance. You know, with more men to choose from.-

Silence surrounded them. Noncie looked over at her father and thought he looked like Hugh, tall at his age and straight and his auburn hair with not a fleck of gray. His freckled hands were as smooth as a young man's, his lips as large and sensuous as a movie idol. She was able to say to him, -Papa you are handsome.-

That night as Noncie slipped into bed she thought with bitterness how totally unfit her sister would be as a mother, and she had no real hopes of ever being one.

Papa heard her sobbing. He wanted to go console her but she would be ashamed that her sobs had been that loud even with their doors shut.

Chapter 49

*T*wo days later Papa drove to the village alone. He hung around the post office waiting to speak to Edifice McHuron. He looked out the window up and down. The postmistress was too busy mailing late Christmas packages to talk, so he moseyed outside and spotted Edifice's reddish beard, his wool cap pulled down nearly to his eyes and his powerful torso swinging back and forth as he trudged to Miss Webster's grocery. Papa couldn't walk fast in the snow but he called out and Edifice, thank God, heard him. He crossed the street to Papa.

-Edifice, I got a bunch of extra dollars in my pocket. I want to give them to you. Don't be offended.-

-That's nice of you but I got to ask her. She can be stubborn.-

-What kind of a goddamned man are you? You make her take the money.-

Edifice walked away. Papa caught up to him. -I know you are correct about my daughter.

She's got that stubborn streak from me. But please. Now and then let me help.-

He looked Coleridge Logan in the eye. -That is thoughtful. Maybe if you asked her. She's in the truck at the end of the street. -

Papa knocked on the window. Florence rolled it down a quarter of the way.

-Papa,- she said cheerfully.

-Don't take offense or anything but I want to give you some money from time to time.-

-Money?-

-Food money.-

-No thank you,- she said. -We can take care of ourselves.-

-Please, Florence. Don't be full of pride. After all I support Noncie.-

-Papa, I've got to get along in this life. Edifice and I got to get along. We don't see no way out except to be independent.-

Don't see no way out. Has she sunk that low that her grammar has deteriorated?

-I means it, Papa.-

-But he doesn't even hunt.-

-You're right he don't shoot nothing, but he traps, rabbits even squirrels. I make soup out of the tail, thin soup but not bad.-

He shivered. -Florence, please come to me if you need help. Please. I thought you said you needed us.-

-Not that kind of need, Papa. It ain't physical but spiritual.- She gave him a little smile and rolled up the window.

What was happening to her? Edifice didn't use bad grammar. She was giving him a message? She was ensconced in this life here. But not everybody here had bad grammar. And *squirrel soup*!

Florence had amused herself with him. But when she saw Papa's bent body she got out of the truck and ran to him, -Papa, I will come by if I need you. And I'll come see you often, you know that. And we'll stay to supper. And I was teasing you with the grammar, you know that, and squirrel soup. It's really skunk soup-

He kissed her and chortled all the way to his car.

-Nope, I wasn't successful,- He told Noncie the next day at breakfast.

-We got to cut her loose. I still think we should pack up and go.-

Then we'll have nothing, Papa thought. -See the bright side.-

Noncie pursed her lips. She served him pancakes with warm maple syrup.

He tried to wink at her but his wink was still unsuccessful.

-Remember the time,- he said, -when you were four or so and our cook brought you a bowl of oatmeal, full to the rim? And we had that important guest with us.-

-I don't remember.-

-That industrial giant, what's his name, who came from France to buy my formula for bleaching flour.-

-I'm supposed to remember when I was four?-

-You were all dressed up, ready to go to the park with Nanny. The industrialist had spent the night. He was dressed in his white shirt and seersucker suit. If it had been dinner we would not have allowed you to sit with us but since it was breakfast and...just as you took a mouth full of oatmeal you sneezed. A cannon of oatmeal bombed onto the man's shirt.-

-Oh Papa, did that ruin the deal?-

-Nope. Turns out he thought you were cute as a button. He bought my bleaching flour formula and picked you up in his arms and danced with you all around the room and...-

The picture of the man in his white shirt tickled her throat into a single laugh.

CHAPTER **50**

*T*he first week in January Edifice drove to his tilting home to pack up his best books. He hoped not to see Gerty. But her head reeled around the corner of the library room. He said nothing, filling the boxes he'd picked up from grocery store, where Miss Webster hoarded them until she had no more room.

Gerty followed him to where the bed linens were kept in a trunk and he took an armful. That's when she spoke in an unfamiliar welcoming tone.

-How about a cup of tea? -

-Tea? Since when do you offer me tea? -

-I know this isn't your usual drink but...-

He didn't answer. The sky looked like more snow; so he loaded the boxes in the front seat of his cab. He returned to the kitchen, which smelled of spruce logs he had cut last year. She sat opposite him.

-Tea?- she asked again.

Though he thought it was unworthy of him he reached for her cup and drank. Her face changed back to the taught bony look.

-I don't need to poison you. You're doing that yourself.-

-So, what's the sweetness and light?-

-I'm a civil woman.-

-No comment.-

-Bitterness does not become you.-

-How would you know what becomes me?- He rose to leave.

-One minute, please.-

He stopped. –What do you want.-

-What I know is-...she paused to take on a lighter, younger tone. He didn't dare believe, a flirtatious tone. -You have generosity,- she said.

-You got somebody else who better damned well be generous to you.-

-That person can't give me what you can. -

He stiffened. -What kind of insinuation is that? -

She switched quickly to stand in front of him. -Please, I beg you don't throw me out of here, and Isabelle will do anything you want concerning the baby. -

He decided to scare her. -Come spring we're moving in. You be thinking of quarters across the river. -

Terror scored on her face. She held onto the chair. -You know I can't do that. And if you throw me out, I'll tell about your hooch and you'll be looking at a new, not so friendly, dwelling. yourself-

-This is a tiresome conversation I don't have the time for anymore. I'm a working man.-

-I've been thinking, she said. -Nobody's going to believe you if you mention Isabelle and me-

-I beg your pardon. You wouldn't take the chance on such a scandal. Was it the light or did the blood rush away from her cheeks? -What's more, there better be a two-gallon can of fresh milk Tuesday and Saturday from now on.-

-Just let me live here.-

He didn't answer to keep the spikes in. He leapt out the door. Let her keep on being tortured with the fear he might oust her, which she deserved, but he never would.

Florence had another month to go. It was the ides of March. She had to keep her strength up and tried to pull herself out of a growing depression. She was sure she was going to die in childbirth. Edifice was snowshoeing the way ahead of her to make the trail easier. He was taking her to see a thicket of white birches, to see what he called the glory of light.

Inside the thicket they stopped to look up at the huge white trees encircling them.

-Oh Edifice, a temple.-

A quick and recent rain had frozen a glistening coat, in perfect detail, out to

the smallest fragile branches. But as they stood in awe the sun quickly melted away the glow. Like her own flitting life. But at this moment tranquility came over her. -Thank you.-

When she sat by the stove she was restless. She hadn't seen her sister or Papa in two weeks. She didn't ask Edifice about the groceries he brought now and then, though she wondered if they came from Papa.

-Will you take me to my home?-

-Your home?- he said, -Is that your home?-

She smiled at him -You know I mean my former home.-

196

-Yes. I'm going to my former home too. I'm tearing down the barn. The bad parts we'll burn in the stove. The good parts I'm going to build us a small barn come spring.

When Florence arrived home Papa was asleep in his chair. Noncie was startled up from the couch. -I'll be,- Papa said. Babcock, hearing her voice, rushed from another room and the other two dogs followed, crying out. -You have come to visit?- Noncie asked.

-Yep.-

Over tea they all talked about what they were doing from day to day, erasing the smudges of gray and pretending the picture was bright. Papa tried not to show his underlying *what's it all about* mood. But the only thing really in all their minds was the waiting, the waiting and waiting, as if hearing sirens in the distance and seeing ominous lights without knowing what it was.

Two hours later Edifice knocked on the door. Papa responded, feeling again an inexplicable fellowship...*the travails of men in the world of women.* He said kindly, -Come in.-

As Florence put her arms in her coat she turned to Noncie and then to Papa, -Could I borrow Tanya for a bit? In fact could I take a different dog each week?- But as she said this she realized it was taking one more thing, from them....mostly Noncie. -Never mind.-

-I'd like you to take Tanya,- Noncie said.

Papa said, -It's something we can do for you and...- He thought she knew nothing of his gift of groceries.

Florence called to Tanya and the slim wire-haired followed happily at Florence's heels and into the truck.

-That was nice of you about the dog,- Papa said. Then as if they might stay he said, -Let's talk about what seeds we want to order for the spring.-

She thought, ridiculous but to keep her mind busy she slid the Burpee catalogue onto the coffee table and sighed.

-What does that sigh mean?- She stood up screaming, -I can't stand it. Why won't she have that baby and let us go?-

-You're right, darn thoughtless of Florence not to give birth whenever we want her to.- Papa thought how far away Florence seemed, dwelling in the forest somewhere with no phone and probably in a stupor. And maybe down deep the bearded hulk was as evil as Irving. Papa revised that...goddamned bullshit. But he could not evade fear for his daughter. How could they take care of a child?

They picked this and that from the catalogue, as if they had a future here.

Florence sat, her bare toes curling at the stove, and watched the heaving waves rise and fall in her belly. They weren't any closer to facing the fact of a child. She couldn't drink alcohol for the last month, made her feel sick but the pang remained. She wanted the creature out of her. Out, out, out. So uncomfortable. She waddled, needed help getting up. She peed all night long. The worry. Edifice drank for both of them, taking long naps next to her.

She was afraid that she wouldn't be able to wake him when the time came to get Peabody. What if? What if? What would Peabody do to help them? That look in her eye, cold as winter. Yes she certainly might want to get rid of Gerty's embarrassment. Edifice was not talking about the baby anymore either.

Yet they were lovers, snuggling in bed, consumed with each other through their bodies, making a fortress against fate. Talking softly. If she woke he read Shakespeare sonnets to her.

-I can hardly stand a minute more of this. This foreign object, this squirming snake of a being. I feel my privacy slashed. Yet it is ours, yours and mine. Ours to love. We would be no good parents. How can we keep it?- A sudden sobbing hysteria attacked her. He held her tighter, feeling the awkward boulder and the life kicking against her. Yet his attempt stopped her from shaking and crying.

-We are strong people,- he said, but not feeling at all strong.

-I'm going to die, aren't I, or the baby?-

-No, you are not.- He rose and poured her a glass of milk. -I won't allow that.-

But she spooked him. In the night next to her now with her constant fidgeting he planned his death, if she should die. Easy to do. He would simply drink himself to death.

The pallid dawn filmed the east window like a shimmering ghost. Florence slipped out of bed to pee. She was naked. In the light he could see her glossy belly, with the wisp of pubic hair looking like grass that was trying to survive under a huge boulder. When she rolled under the covers, shivering from all that was left of the stove's embers, he moved toward her and with his right hand caressed her belly. He marveled...-a floating planet.-

That day she didn't eat. His eyes followed her pacing as he sat at the mahogany table. Any friskiness had gone out of her; the playful, inventive brightness was drained. He was speechless. He wanted her help, to help him get through this. He knew it was still a decision that she insisted they make together, and what if they couldn't?

They could have the baby alone without any doctor. But then he knew he would get Peabody. He was too afraid of some tragedy. No, he would not decide. She must decide what should happen to their baby. It was out of his hands. He knew himself. That's the way he was, let life happen to him. That one split second of lifting his gun had cured him of decisions for the rest of his life. But he also knew he must be strong for Florence.

He stayed in the cabin with her that day. He had fitted a basket with linens to make a bassinet. She didn't stop him. He tore sheets into diapers and once over at Chester he had bought baby bottles, and a brand new item, formulas. She said nothing about what he was doing. He pictured the baby. He pictured a girl looking like Florence. Rocking her to sleep.

He kissed Florence, nearly toppling them both. Her dog came in between them, feeling left out. -Look at this home of ours,- she said. Her spirits had lifted to euphoria for no particular reason, or maybe there was a reason.

-Over there you built us a closet, like an elegant corner cupboard. Good enough for a museum. Look at the paneling on these walls you paneled in cherry. Almost no breeze comes through.-

He was made happy by her enthusiasm.

-And your blue floor with clouds,- he said. - Someday I'll make a counter by the sink.- The sink had running water now, dripping all winter so it wouldn't freeze. The kitchen part sat on the west wall next to the closet. And there was a nice oval oak table and two chairs. On the floor nearby sat the vodka jugs. Hanging in the basket overhead were onions and potatoes. They wouldn't need an icebox until summer. Anything needing refrigeration was kept in a box outside the door under the bird-winged roof now.

In this sunny mood she sat on his lap and toyed with his beard and they petted Tonya so she wouldn't whine for attention. She began to braid the sides of his beard and he took her hair in his fingers, and braided the wisps on either side of her ears. They were contented for the first time in months.

A new snowstorm rustled and blew through the thick woods, making the clapboards groan in protest. Giant howling wind roared off the mountains like an injured beast. The icy sheen of spring snow was being made fresh and deep. She began to pace the floor.

The snow dumped huge quantities against the door and up to the edges of the windows. A blizzard. Edifice glanced at Florence. She had finished Anna Karenina and sighed over her fate. And she was lying there not sleeping, but calm. He recognized that peaceful lying-in-the-sun look. But this peaceful state of Florence's was also upsetting. Her eyes looked too black, too lost in the woods.

A smashing, thunderous noise hit the door. Edifice ran to open it to see but it was blocked. From the window he saw a huge tree branch had fallen against it. This might entomb them for days. He didn't know if he could move it at all.

Even if he jumped out a window the snow was over his head where it drifted against the cabin. He must clear the door for Peabody. Damn, the snowshoes were in the truck. The river was solid ice now, so he could get to the truck if he could move the branch. He turned to Florence. Her hands were over her eyes, pressing them. And he had to be the man, take complete charge when he wanted to curl up by the stove. They still had some milk left. They had a bucket to pee in. There was wood enough for two days. All that flashed in his mind, but it didn't help him.

She was thinking. She was looking and thinking. She said. –Can't you just step over it?-

-No, but I think I can chop it.- With the one tool he had inside, a hatchet, he opened the door a few inches, gusting in freezing air in. Florence pulled the covers over her head. So this is how they would die, entombed in their lonely cabin. He hacked at the log, his hands turning white with the cold, but he was able remove one piece just enough to walk through.

He trudged out and shoveled again as the wind and snow subsided. An hour later, pitch dark, early evening, she wondered, was the feeling real? Then she felt the muscle of her belly contract so hard she gasped out at Edifice. –Oh my God.-

Was it just practice? She crossed her fingers of both hands, in hopes it wasn't. But her stomach clamped her so hard again twenty minutes later. She stopped crossing her fingers and said, -Go.   Go get her.-

The way she said, *her*, was as if calling for the priest for last rites. Grabbed his coat, grabbed his hat, gloves, boots. –I'll race. Hold tight, Darling.- The key to the truck? Where was it? In the truck. He grabbed the flashlight and took one last look at her frightened eyes.

Across the brook and into the truck through the drifting snow, the sky lightened. The aurora borealis radiated before him shimmering slices of lavenders, yellows and oranges, quivering… a good omen, like for the three Wisemen.

The blustering wind hammered at his truck, shouting of more stinging cold, sharp as acid smoke. He felt toward Peabody like a child who returns to the arms of a parent who has just badly beaten him. The car lights shone on vacant snow, no tracks to help him stay on the road. He squinted to find delineation, but all he could make out were the trees on either side to guide him. He was forced to drive slowly so as not to get stuck but he was frantic.

He was amazed at how Peabody hurried. How excitedly her skinny sharp body moved. She followed him in her own truck. How quick and agile she was crossing the ice-bound river.

-Florence, - he called out. At the sight of Peabody she sat up in bed.

-Lie down.- Peabody whipped out her stethoscope. -Damn,- she said as she listened.

-What? What?- Edifice asked and threw his coat on the floor next to Peabody's.

-That kind of heartbeat.-

-What?-

-Real strong.-

-Is that good or bad?-

-Don't blabber questions at me. I'm busy. You go find me a pan for blood.-

-Blood.- Edifice choked out. She didn't answer, but he realized, having seen goats and cows born. He reassured himself and took down a hanging pot.

-The fire. I don't like to be cold.-

He threw in more wood, fixating on her words. *–I don't like to be cold.*- Not about Florence or the baby being cold, just her.

-A sheet to put under her. Step on it. She's about to have it.-

Florence knew she was out of control, not like drinking, not that kind, but from a force, as strong as a driving hurricane. Her body ruled, king of her thoughts and will. Her body gripped her lungs roaring out bestial grunts and gigantic earthquake gaspings with just enough time to take a breath.

Peabody was standing in between her legs and for a fleeting moment Florence pictured her between Gerty McHuron's legs, and Gerty groaning with pleasure and Peabody's rapacious passion.

Edifice wanted to lift Florence up and run away with her. He laid his face next to hers and his arms around her shoulders. He knelt by her.

-Get back,- Peabody yelled.

-No.-

-I'm in charge here.-

But he stayed stroking Florence's sweating head.

-Push like hell,- Peabody said calmly, -like you're pushing a truck up a hill.-

Her effort made nothing hurt anymore.

-Get that baby out. Now, push now. Breathe. Push.- Florence reached up and pulled Edifice's face down and he placed his lips on hers so the next time she bellowed her bellow filled his lungs.

-Look at that,- Peabody called out. -The head is coming right at me. Slippery little bastard.-

Florence could feel Peabody tugging. Then the baby wriggled out, slipping like a freshly caught fish, the feet tickling her as the baby arrived. The dog barked. Florence's breathing gradually slowed as if she'd reached the summit of a difficult mountain and at last could rest.

No sound came from the baby. Edifice looked up. Peabody had laid her on the table, not the bassinette and not watching her. The baby was not moving and was blue. Peabody had turned to her black bag organizing the contents.

Edifice grabbed up the baby, -What's the matter with her? She's not breathing. Do something.- The baby was limp. He held her up against his chest and patted. No sound. -Help me,- he shouted. He held her upside down. Faintly came a gurgle. Then a stronger baby cry into life. Peabody had not moved.

-Why didn't you help?- He shouted.

-I was only doing what I thought…what you should want.-

-You were going to let her die. –

Peabody did not answer. She snapped her black bag shut.

-Get out. You evil killer…get out..-

He gave the howling baby to Florence who drew her inside the covers.

-Disgraceful,- Peabody said. –Immoral. Should have left the bastard be.-

He picked up her coat and threw it at her. He shoved her out the door.

-I was only doing what was right.-

Florence fogging in and out could not fully take in the crisis or Edifice's stricken voice. She heard the door slam and then felt Edifice as he reached under the covers and tied the umbilical cord, and cut it with the scissors. Awkwardly he diapered the little girl and wrapped her in several baby blankets…the bloody quieting tiny creature, while Florence lay silent. He filled a bottle of formula and she drank with vigor.

Edifice laid beside Florence. The baby between them had stopped crying. Florence came to. They whispered to each other. She told him her plan and they fell into a fitful sleep.

CHAPTER **51**

*T*he next morning he remained asleep when she rose and dressed
and washed the baby. She stoked the fire and put on her boots.
Then she woke him.

He was already dressed, had risen in the early dawn to dress and
crawled back in bed. -Are you ready?- she asked.

-Yes.- he said, in a downcast voice.

The day was bright and warmer. Tanya, leaped into the truck ahead of
them. Edifice asked, -Florence, are you sure?-

-Yes, and you?-

-Yes.-

He drove. She was silent. She tried not to think of what they were
doing. She tried not to look too closely at the baby's sleeping face, to care.
The dog barked like a siren as they drove through the village.

Edifice parked as close as he could.

-You positive?- she asked him again.

-Yes,- he answered.

He was right behind her up the steps. She knocked. They heard movement inside.

The door opened. It was Noncie and when Papa saw he came to stand
beside her. The dog leaped inside.

Noncie gave a little cry when she realized what was in Florence's arms.
She rushed them in from the cold. Noncie looked with astonishment
down at the red round face with closed eyes sound asleep, her fat lips
puffing and sucking. They all four speechless, stared at the peaceful face.

Florence said, -Sister, you get to name her. –

-Name her?-

-Yes.-

All flustered, Noncie said to Papa, -You name her.-

-No,- Papa said, -you.-

The baby looked like Florence, round, pug nose, a whisper of hair. Noncie turned her head sideways to see more clearly. Florence handed the baby to Noncie. Noncie was tentative, held the bundle awkwardly and tightly as if she might slip away. She didn't dare move even to rock her. Never taking her eyes away she finally said, -How about Grace?-

Florence said, -Yes. I like that. Grace.-

-Good name,- Papa echoed.

Florence said, -She is yours. The baby is yours, Noncie.-

-What are you talking about?-

-She is yours. I mean that.-

-No. Not...-

-I'm giving her to you. Edifice and I are giving Grace to you.- She looked at Edifice to be sure. He nodded.

-I don't believe...- Noncie said.

-Grace is yours.-

-No.-

-Yes.-

-Grace,- was all Noncie could articulate as tears poured down her face.

Papa's head was squeezing with thoughts of... Goddamn, what a pickle. I'm stuck. I'm seventy something and I've got to raise another kid. I've got to stick around and help her learn to walk, talk, braid her hair, teach her to read, and play with her .. but defying his mind, grateful and joyful tears blubbered out. She had arrived like a catastrophic meteorite, stopping him in time.

-I have a box for the baby,- Edifice said. - I'll bring it in.- He wanted to leave the scene where his heart was overcome.

Noncie was in a trance, breathing hard, as if she had just come out of birthing herself. She collapsed on a kitchen chair. -You don't mean this. You're not giving me the baby.-

She lifted her head this way and that to try and see the small face. She ran her hands over her face, cheeks, forehead supple lips, her particularly curly ears, like Edifice's, and something about her, she didn't know what exactly, but imagined resembled her, like her own baby pictures.

Papa kissed Florence.

Noncie thought, hold tightly, not too tightly, and watch that her head doesn't bobble. Keep her warm. Sing to her. Papa had the better voice. He could sing to her. When she was able in the future she would say to Florence how her heart was overflowing with thankfulness and the irony of trying to rescue Florence had been reversed. Florence had rescued her.

*T*hree hours later Edifice and Florence climbed into the truck that Edifice had heated first. As they drove down the village hill Florence said, -I didn't want to.-

-Me neither,- he said. He glanced at her face. –We had to.-

She didn't cry. She was too numb. As they turned into their lane she asked, -Will they go back to Chicago?-

He didn't answer.

-Yes, they will,- she said and looked out at the snow beginning again.

-You don't know that. You don't know that at all.-

-They will want to raise her in civilization.-

They entered the silent cold cabin. Edifice rushed to build a fire and as she stood shivering he said, -I have a present that will warm you up. I made it especially for you, last spring before I could really believe that you loved me. And if that was still true by this summer I would open it-

She sat in the rocker.

He wrapped her in the quilt and pulled his chair opposite her and rubbed her feet.

–I've been thinking about something. They are hiring over at the Reedville wood factory. Maybe I can get a job.-

-That would be good. And I could make a big garden soon.-

-I will add a real living room, slowly add rooms. Another bedroom.-

-Maybe we can start over,- she said.

He knew what she meant. -Yes. We are still young.-

When the cabin was cozy he took down a jug from the shelf and two glasses and poured the wine. -This is the present.- He handed her a glass. -Dandelion wine. Maybe from now on we just only drink at certain celebrations.-

She nodded.

As they sipped they said nothing more. The bitter wine trickled down their sorrowing throats as they wrapped their arms around each other and let the liquor's warm and golden pleasure blot out what had been.

The End

FIC GOODMAN

Goodman, J. Carol.
The Logans in Flood
 Brook : a novel

01/03/18

CPSIA information can be obtained
at www.ICGtesting.com
Printed in the USA
LVOW03s1650061217
558856LV00003B/510/P